"Tell [me] where do you reside when not in London? Mrs. Parton has been foretelling your arrival for weeks,

Books by Louise M. Gouge

Love Inspired Historical

Love Thine Enemy
The Captain's Lady
At the Captain's Command
*A Proper Companion
*A Suitable Wife

*Ladies in Waiting

LOUISE M. GOUGE

has been married to her husband, David, for forty-seven years. They have four children and seven grandchildren. Louise always had an active imagination, thinking up stories for her friends, classmates and family, but seldom writing them down. At a friend's insistence, in 1984 she finally began to type up her latest idea. Before trying to find a publisher, Louise returned to college, earning a B.A. in English/creative writing and a master's degree in liberal studies. She reworked that first novel based on what she had learned and sold it to a major Christian publisher. Louise then worked in television marketing for a short time before becoming a college English/humanities instructor. She has had twelve novels published, several of which have earned multiple awards, including the 2006 Inspirational Reader's Choice Award. Please visit her website at http://blog.Louisemgouge.com.

LOUISE M. GOUGE

A Suitable Wife

Love Inspired

Recycling programs
for this product may
not exist in your area.

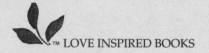 ™ LOVE INSPIRED BOOKS

ISBN-13: 978-0-373-82945-3

A SUITABLE WIFE

Copyright © 2012 by Louise M. Gouge

www.LoveInspiredBooks.com

Printed in U.S.A.

He that walketh with wise men shall be wise:
but a companion of fools shall be destroyed.
—*Proverbs* 13:20

This book is dedicated to my beloved husband,
David, who has stood by my side through
my entire writing career. I would also like to thank
Nancy Mayer and the Beau Monde Chapter of RWA
for helping with my research into the Regency era.

Chapter One

"Well, Mother, have you chosen a bride for me yet?" Lord Greystone surveyed the guests in the ballroom of his Hanover Square town house, already bored by the dull young misses who had been paraded before him by over-eager mothers.

"Greystone, it is simply appalling." Standing beside him, Mother waved her closed fan carelessly toward the throng of guests, many of whom were engaged in a lively country reel. "I cannot think of any of these silly *gels* becoming my daughter-in-law. If you married one of them, I should be forced to utterly forsake your company to avoid all that nonsensical chatter."

"If you fear you will be lonely, madam, perhaps you should consider hiring a new companion." He sent his parent a playful smirk, but failed to evoke even a hint of a smile from the poor dear. Although she would never admit it, Mother missed her former companion Miss Newfield since the young lady married Greystone's youngest brother.

"Nonsense." Mother inspected him up and down through

her quizzing glass, then brushed invisible lint from his blue satin sleeve. "I shall find you a bride who can fill the duties of a companion for me, someone who understands her responsibilities to family and Society."

"Hmm." Greystone resisted the notion of his future wife suffering under Mother's domination, as Miss New-field had. Perhaps after his marriage he should consider settling his parent in a dower residence. The house would be elegant and well staffed, of course, but at some distance from his other homes.

The thought stirred a strong measure of guilt in him. He and his two brothers owed everything to Mother. From the age of six, when his father's sudden death had vaulted him into the titular headship of the Greystone dynasty, he had followed her every teaching. She had made certain he and his brothers, especially Greystone, were well versed in their duties to king and country. Although they had often loathed her controlling hand, she had restored the family fortune Father had gambled away, making possible a future for each of them. A future she herself designed.

Tonight she had gone to great effort for his birthday, inviting numerous aristocratic families and their marriage-able daughters, ordering the best cuisine and hiring a fine orchestra. To match her scarlet gown, she wore the exqui-site ruby necklace that had been in his family for some two hundred years. It suited her so well, he decided she must have it even after he married, as a symbol of his gratitude for all she had done for the family.

Although he felt the utmost gratitude toward her, re-cently he had begun to chafe against her controls. All these years he had observed how she had ruled the fam-ily. But how did a husband and father manage his own house? His memories of Father offered no example, only horror and fear. What if he inherited the man's brutish ways? What if—

"Are you listening to me?" Mother's sharp elbow cut into his biceps. He stifled a wince and clamped down on a cross retort. "What do you think of Lady Grandly's eldest *gel?*" She waved her fan toward the comely Miss Waddington.

"Hmm." Miss Waddington certainly possessed the appropriate breeding and character, but she stirred no feeling in him at all. Now that he had seriously begun his obligatory marital search, a new longing had started to stir within him. He wanted to experience genuine love, a deep emotion toward his wife, such as both of his brothers felt for their brides. A feeling so strong that it made each of them willing to risk everything to have the woman he loved.

Yet those other, darker thoughts always accompanied that sentiment. What if he had inherited his father's propensity for cruelty? For evil? For profligate living? With no paternal example how could he truly become the good man he longed to be in the sight of God? Often after a burst of anger over some offense, real or imagined, he pondered whether he was even fit for marriage and fatherhood. Perhaps his brother Richard should continue as his heir. The newly ordained minister possessed an agreeable, temperate disposition and would never knowingly cause harm to anyone. But then such a passive course would mean that Greystone was neglecting his responsibility, something he would never do. He must choose a bride, must beget an heir. If he was fortunate enough to love the lady, then all the better.

Best get on with it.

"Do excuse me, madam. I should see to my guests." He bowed to Mother.

"Just so." She waved him toward the wall of young ladies without partners.

Instead Greystone strode toward the door, determined to play a few hands of whist with his brother Edmond. Greystone would seek the newlywed's advice about choosing a bride.

When had Edmond realized no lady would do for him but Anna Newfield? How had he been certain of his feelings, despite the vast chasm between their social ranks? How had he developed the courage to defy Mother's control? Perhaps as an officer over His Majesty's Dragoons in America.

Neither Edmond nor Richard remembered their father, so Greystone doubted they would ever emulate his wicked ways. On the other hand, Greystone's memories, forged from infancy, often found their way to the forefront of his mind, especially when his own temper threatened to explode like cannon fire. Then he prayed desperately that he might maintain control, unlike those few times in his youth when he had wreaked havoc on innocents. That must never happen again. He must never be like Father.

Pausing in the doorway, he surveyed the card room for the familiar head of dark brown hair. But his eyes stopped instead at the sight of golden curls framing the most exquisite female countenance he had ever gazed upon. Oddly his heart seemed to hiccup in his chest, and he had to remind himself to breathe. Even from a distance of some five and twenty feet, even in the flickering candlelight, he could see the sparkle of her blue eyes and her flawless ivory complexion. A pert little nose sat over full pink lips that were quirked to the side, as though she was concentrating on which card to play. From her sudden smile and decisive play he surmised the young lady could be

counted on to betray her hand, a charming trait that revealed a lack of cunning.

But who was she? As host he should have met every
guest at the ballroom door. Perhaps she was a latecomer.
He did not have to search far to find someone to present
him to her. Mother's good friend Mrs. Parton sat across
from the golden lady, and from their traded smiles, he assumed they were acquainted. If Mrs. Parton approved of
the young lady, that was good enough for him. He made
his way through the maze of populated tables toward his
goal. With each step closer to her his pulse quickened.

Four sets of feminine eyes turned in his direction, but
Mrs. Parton spoke first.

"Go away, Greystone. My partner and I are about to
win this hand, and I forbid you to interrupt, even if it is
your birthday."

Greystone laughed. "And a good evening to you, too,
dear lady." He stopped by her chair and placed a kiss upon
her plump cheek. Then he turned his attention to the other
ladies. "I do hope you are having a pleasant time, Lady
Blakemore, Miss Hart, and…?" He feigned innocent surprise, even as his pulse hammered wildly. "Forgive me,
miss. Mrs. Parton, will you present me to this lovely young
lady?"

"I will not." She waved him away. He gave her a charming grin as he had since boyhood, and she harrumphed.
"You never did mind well, Greystone." Exhaling dramatically, she folded her hand of cards and placed them
facedown. "Miss Gregory, may I present our host, Lord
Greystone. Greystone, this is my new companion, Miss
Gregory. She arrived in London just this afternoon."

"Charmed, Miss Gregory." To be sure, he was more
than charmed. He was enchanted by those calm sapphire
eyes. But while he kissed her hand, his mind scrambled

and his pulse slowed. So this was Mrs. Parton's long-awaited companion, and doubtless a penniless lady, if her unadorned, ill-fitting brown dress was any indication. If he chose a bride who was anything less than a baron's daughter, Mother would be devastated.

"Lord Greystone." The lady's bright pink blush charmed him all the more. Every unmarried young lady blushed, but somehow Miss Gregory's deportment bespoke something deeper than girlish nerves. Curiosity and interest quickly overrode his reservations regarding her status.

"Well, Greystone." Lady Blakemore stood, as did her companion. "Since you have interrupted our game, Miss Hart and I will take our leave and find the refreshments." Amid protests to the contrary, the two ladies disappeared from the room.

"Do forgive me. I have spoiled your game." Greystone did not regret it for a moment. "Did you lose much?" He glanced around for a pile of coins or tokens but found none. Miss Gregory stared at him as if he had three heads.

"Gracious, no." Mrs. Parton waved a silk fan before her ruddy cheeks. "You know I never gamble. Not even a button. Dreadful habit. Leads to ruin."

Miss Gregory's cheeks flamed even brighter, causing Greystone no little concern.

"Again, forgive me. I do not mean to be boorish." He sat in one of the empty chairs, knowing full well he was neglecting his other guests. But surely after spoiling their game, he could be excused while he set things to right with these two ladies. Or so he convinced himself. "Tell me, Miss Gregory, where do you reside when not in London? Mrs. Parton has been foretelling your arrival for weeks, but she told us nothing about you."

"My origins are of no consequence, I assure you, sir." The young lady lifted her chin. Her eyes glinted, and her lips thinned into a line. So she had a bit of spunk. He liked that. Few young ladies of the gentry spoke so boldly to a peer of his standing.

"Now, my dear." Mrs. Parton reached across the table and patted her hand. "Greystone is a treasured friend. He can be trusted with your secret."

The young lady shifted her eyes this way and that, as if she would escape this interview. Greystone began to regret quizzing her, even as his interest in her increased, along with his curiosity and an odd pinch of protectiveness. "If you are in some sort of difficulty, Miss…" He could not imagine a problem Mrs. Parton's vast wealth could not solve.

Again Miss Gregory lifted her chin, and wounded pride beamed from her elegant countenance. "I am not a mere miss. I am *Lady* Beatrice Gregory. My brother is Lord Melton. Perhaps you know him?" One perfect blond eyebrow quirked upward to accompany the question, as if she already knew the answer.

Greystone tried to inhale, but like last winter's nearly fatal illness, this revelation stole his breath.

"Ah. Yes. Of course. I know Melton. He was absent from the House of Lords today. I do hope he is not ill." He must get away. Must not let her charm him further.

Disappointment clouded Mrs. Parton's eyes. How well she knew him. How well she was reading him even now. But she of all people understood why he could not associate himself with the sister of a drunken, degenerate gambler.

"If you ladies will excuse me. My other guests—" He rose and offered a weak smile before turning to make his escape.

"Do forgive Lord Greystone." Mrs. Parton's round face creased with disappointment. "He truly must attend to his other guests. It *is* his birthday, you know."

"Yes, of course." Beatrice offered her employer a conciliatory smile, for her late mother had taught her well. *No matter what happens, no matter what feelings rage within her, a lady always maintains her dignity.* Mama had always exhibited graciousness despite Papa's neglect, and never had Beatrice felt the need to emulate her more than now. The instant she saw the horror on Lord Greystone's face—a rapid withdrawal of interest at the mention of her brother's name—her breeding held strong. With a practiced vise grip on her emotions, she maintained her posture and poise, even offering a smile to the gentleman's retreating back. But her disappointment was keen, her heart deeply cut. Would all of Society treat her this way?

Yet what could she expect from any gentleman, especially an eligible peer? Did not all noblemen spend their lives and fortunes as it suited them? Did they not all sit in church every Sunday, as duty demanded, and yet utterly neglect their duty to their families?

But daughters also had a duty—to marry well so that the family might benefit. Beatrice had always assumed her parents would find a husband for her, preferably someone wealthy and titled who could give Papa some sort of political advantage. Mama had promised Beatrice a grand London Season during which they would arrange the marriage. But Mama had died long before she could keep her promise, Papa had died before finding her a husband, and her brother had spent the past three years gambling away the fortune that came with his title. Beatrice loved her charming brother, but the new Lord Melton's wastrel ways had utterly destroyed her chance for marriage or even a Season when he squandered her dowry in hopes of recouping his losses. No gentleman wanted a penniless lady, no matter how old or formerly prestigious her family name. Still, her sense of injustice cried out that any man who did not see how different she was from Melton did not deserve her notice or her heart.

Still again, from the moment she had observed Lord Greystone's tall form and handsome face as he had threaded his way across the room toward her table, she had experienced a growing sense of admiration, at least for his outward appearance. Broad shoulders, thick, nearly black hair curled in the latest Caesar style, a lightly tanned complexion, high cheekbones and a slight cleft in his strong chin—features woven together to create an appealing presence. No doubt the gentleman knew his blue satin jacket reflected in those icy blue eyes, making him all the more attractive.

But no one could feign the kindness that shone from his countenance as he had spoken with Beatrice's employer. This was the gentleman of whom Mrs. Parton had spoken so highly in regard to his defense of the poor. This was a gentleman of godly faith, a worthy soul who shared Beatrice's concern for the downtrodden. But somehow his generous feelings did not extend to the sister of a wastrel.

"Shall we go to the ballroom?" Mrs. Parton stood and fussed with her gown, a deep purple silk creation with an orange print sash draped across one shoulder and fastened at the high waist with a golden broach. Her purple turban, which kept falling over her ruddy forehead, sported a blue-green peacock feather that bobbed when she moved. "I shall find you a partner for the quadrille, which should be the next dance, unless Lady Greystone has changed her usual order." When Beatrice remained seated, the lady tilted her head in question. "Well, come along, my dear. We'll not have any fun hiding here among the dowdy dowagers." She waved a chubby arm to take in the rest of the room and received a few cross looks for it.

As Beatrice rose, the bodice of her borrowed and over-large gown twisted to the side. She hurried to straighten it, but nothing could be done about the excess fabric. "I should not dance in this—" She wanted to say "rag," but that would be an insult to Mrs. Parton's daughter, for whom it had been made last year. But while the dark bronze gown might have complemented the young matron's auburn hair, Beatrice knew it washed out her own lighter features. "I fear I will trip."

"I'm sure you can manage, Miss Gregory." Although a twinkle lit Mrs. Parton's eyes, her tone and choice of address reminded Beatrice of her place.

Mortification brought a warm flush to her face. She was the daughter of an earl, the sister of his heir. She held precedence over Mrs. Parton, who was the daughter of a mere baron, the widow of a middle-class, albeit wealthy gentleman. But gratitude overcame shame, and Beatrice smiled at her benefactress. At one and twenty she was at last enjoying her first—and no doubt only—London Season. She must not expect to find a husband, even if Mrs. Parton should become agreeable to such a search. No, she was here to be the lady's companion and nothing more.

On the other hand this nonsense of calling her Miss Gregory instead of Lady Beatrice would be revealed for what it was: a fraud. Then no reputable person would have anything to do with her. But if only for one evening she could escape the pain caused by Melton's irresponsible behavior, she planned to make the most of it. A spirited quadrille might be just the cure she needed to heal her wounded pride.

The bright third-floor ballroom, though not terribly large, was exquisite, not unlike the ballroom at Melton Gardens in County Durham. Tall windows on the south side revealed the last dim glow of daylight over the rooftops on the opposite side of Hanover Square. But one would hardly know evening had arrived. The brilliant candlelight from numerous girandoles was magnified by their mirrors, while sparkling crystal chandeliers hung from a ceiling carved with a swirling leafy pattern. Beneath their feet, the polished oak floor had been dusted with chalk to keep dancers from slipping, and a sizeable orchestra sat on a dais at the east end. The scents of countless perfumes and pomades hung heavy in the air, making it difficult to breathe one moment and delightfully pleasant the next.

Beatrice stood next to her employer with growing hopes she would soon put to use the skills her dance master had praised in her youth. Several men were seeking partners, and one or two looked her way, then at Mrs. Parton, as if considering a request for an introduction. But against her will and all good reason, her eyes sought a certain tall viscount and soon found him.

Halfway across the room Lord Greystone stood beside a gray-haired matron of medium height wearing a scarlet gown and a glittering ruby necklace. From his close attention Beatrice guessed the lady was his mother, even though the severe expression on her thin face did not in the least resemble Lord Greystone's warmer countenance. Beatrice admired the solicitous way he leaned toward the lady, wishing she could be the recipient of such kind gazes. She released a quiet sigh and forced her attention back to the dancers forming groups for the quadrille.

Beside her Mrs. Parton suddenly gasped. "We must go." She gripped Beatrice's forearm and tugged her toward the door.

"But—"

"*Tst.* Come with me." Mrs. Parton jerked her head toward two gentlemen who were making their way through the crowd toward her.

Melton! Her prodigal brother. And he had the nerve to

give her their secret wave, running a hand over one ear, then touching his chest over his heart. As they were growing up, they often played with the village children and had devised several signals to win games. This one was a promise always to listen to each other, always to care for one another. But after he destroyed his own reputation and her possibilities for marriage, she had long ago decided he had forever shattered that promise. Now only horror filled her, and she willingly permitted herself to be led away.

Count on Melton to destroy her chances for even one night of happiness. Well, now he could count on her to refuse to acknowledge him in public.

Coward. Greystone had berated himself from the moment he had so boorishly left the two ladies at their table. Lady Beatrice had quickly hidden her mortification, but not before he had seen the hurt in her eyes. Lovely eyes, blue as sapphires. Golden hair, ivory complexion—but he must stop thinking about her. Brooding over an unacceptable lady would do no good at all. Instead he would ask Mother's opinion on whom he should approach for this next dance.

"Have you met Mrs. Parton's companion?" Not the question he had intended to ask.

"No. Is she here?" Mother glanced beyond him. "Humph. Pretty enough, if one cares for the pallid sort." She stared up at him, her eyes widening in alarm. "Now, Greystone, you must not give consequence to this *gel*. 'Twas bad enough for your brother to steal *my* companion. You must not steal Julia's. In any event, you are Lord Greystone, and none will suit for your bride but the daughter of a duke—or at least an earl."

"Ah, we've moved up the ladder with our expectations, have we?" Greystone stifled a laugh. Mother's ambitions were not unlike every Society parent's, each and all seeking some sort of advancement. He would tell her the truth about *Miss* Gregory, except that he was still trying very hard not to notice the young lady, much less give her any attention. Once again his eyes betrayed him just as his words had. But when he looked in her direction, he saw to his vexation that Mrs. Parton was dragging her from the room. Just as well. He could have no future with the young lady, but not for the reasons Mother stated.

In the corner of his eye he noticed two gentlemen following the ladies. What was Melton doing here? And that scoundrel Rumbold? Neither had been invited to this fete. Furthermore, Mrs. Parton seemed in a rush to elude them. Offering a quick apology to Mother, Greystone strode across the room to intercept the interlopers so the ladies might make their escape.

Lord Melton could hardly believe his eyes. Beatrice had looked directly at him, had seen him give her their secret wave and was actually giving him the cut. His own sister, the one whose presence had gained him access to this ball. He could only stand in shock.

"Come along, Melton." Frank Rumbold gripped Melton's arm in the same manner that Mrs. Parton had taken charge of Beatrice. "This will turn out even better if we catch them on the ground floor. Then we can walk them home."

"If you think that is best." Melton had permitted his older friend to guide him for three years, but they'd had a few setbacks socially. Actually more than a few. As if by some tacit agreement, members of the *ton* now refused to admit Rumbold into their drawing rooms. After Beatrice's debut in Society, he and Rumbold hoped to amend the situation. With wealthy Mrs. Parton as her sponsor, his sister would meet only the best of Society and could draw them into her growing circles. He often felt stabs of conscience that he lacked the funds to sponsor her debut, much less a dowry to bestow upon any gentleman fortunate enough to win her hand. But Rumbold had expressed interest in her. Now that he had seen her, it should take very little to complete the marriage agreement. That is, if he could manage to arrange the introduction.

"Good evening, Melton." Lord Greystone approached them, a tight smile on his arrogant face. "I fear there has been some mistake. This ball is only for invited guests." He waved a hand toward the door. "Perhaps you will permit me to escort you out." He nodded toward two footmen, one of them the fellow Rumbold had paid to let them into the affair, claiming Beatrice had their invitation. Now the man acted as if he had never seen them.

"We were just leaving." A sudden thirst struck Melton. He needed some brandy from that drink table in the corner. "But first may I introduce—"

"No." Not even looking at Rumbold, Greystone spoke politely, but there was a hint of anger in his tone. The two oversize servants who flanked him made his intentions clear as he again gestured toward the door. "If you please."

"Come along, Melton." Rumbold chuckled and clapped him on the shoulder as if it were all a fine joke. "We have four more invitations for the evening. Let's not waste time here."

They soon found themselves on the street amidst the carriages belonging to those attending the ball. To make matters worse, one or two of the awaiting drivers were imbibing freely, yet Melton had to endure his thirst.

"I am Lord Melton," he muttered to his companion. "An earl of the realm. How dare a mere viscount cast me out of his house?" He glanced down the street toward the town house next door, Mrs. Parton's abode. Somehow the old bat and his sister had already managed to disappear behind the massive front door.

Rumbold followed the direction of Melton's gaze. "That will change once Lady Beatrice and I—" The idea seemed to encourage him, for he once again clapped Melton on the shoulder. "But really, my boy, you will have to bring her under control. What kind of sister gives her titled brother the cut?"

Melton snorted out his agreement. "Indeed. What kind of sister?" But that nagging conscience once again jabbed at his mind. She had always been the best and sweetest of sisters. Somehow that Parton woman, with no title at all, had turned Beatrice against him. To forget their secret signal was not unlike forgetting the whole of their childhood friendship. It was all entirely too much. He would need more than one drink to get over the pain her cut had caused.

Chapter Two

"The very idea." Mother snapped the pages of the *Times* over her breakfast plate, barely missing her sausages. "It even made the papers. How dare Melton attend your ball uninvited?" She sniffed with indignation. "And bring a guest whom no decent member of Society will receive."

Greystone well understood she expected no response, and he was in no humor to give one. His mood was as gray as the London weather outside the tall, narrow windows of the town house's breakfast room. Since the early hours of last evening's ball, he had pondered the situation with the young earl and his beautiful sister. Mrs. Parton was of course above suspicion, but he could not be so certain "Miss Gregory" was innocent in the matter. His inner turmoil had kept him awake for hours.

Before sleep had at last claimed him, he'd come to the conclusion that Frank Rumbold had devised the whole plan. That culprit was nothing less than a sharper, an ill-born scoundrel who had ensnared more than one young aristocrat new to London's gaming dens. And a newly raised peer of two and twenty years, one with a known penchant for gambling, was a prime target for an older man intent upon forcing his way into Society. Rumbold was reputed to be a peer's illegitimate son with ambitions to advance to the nobility, an utter impossibility. Had he accepted his fate, he might have found some acceptance and a reasonable position in life. But because of the path he had chosen, misusing naive nobles and their heirs, he could scheme all he wanted, but the best he could hope for was to slink around the dark edges of Society. No one of significance would ever grant him consequence, unless forced to. Fortunately it had taken very little convincing to send the two men packing last evening.

"Did Melton not have a sister?" Mother's question cut into Greystone's thoughts, and his hand stilled with a bite of jam-covered bread halfway to his mouth. "I seem to recall the late Lord Melton had two children." She folded her paper and set it on the table. "Surely she is out by now. Poor *gel*. Surely no one of breeding will associate with her."

Just as Mother spoke, he made the mistake of taking the bite and was rewarded by almost choking on it. If only she knew.

"Really, Greystone, do chew your food."

"I beg your pardon." He gulped his entirely too-hot coffee, which brought forth another bout of coughing.

Mother stared at him, her eyebrows bent into a scolding frown. Even the footman behind her watched him with alarm.

"Never mind." He held up a hand to prevent the man from coming to his aid. "I am well."

Another sip of coffee ensured his physical recovery, but not his mental improvement. Now was the time for him to tell Mother about Lady Beatrice. *Now*.

No, not now. Maybe he would leave it up to Mrs. Parton. She was to blame, after all. Had she not brought the girl to London, had she not brought her to last night's ball,

Melton would never have had the nerve to seek entrance. Yet had she not brought the young lady, Greystone never would have been introduced to the most enchanting creature he had met this Season. Or during any of the previous six Seasons since he had taken his seat in the House of Lords.

As often before, the accusation resounded in his mind: *coward!* At eight and twenty years, why did he still try so hard to avoid stirring his mother's anger? This situation was not of his making, but rather, the result of her best friend's machinations. Let Mrs. Parton sort it out for her.

Yet shame, or some emotion he could not name, would not let him go. Last week he had waxed eloquent in Parliament in support of Wilberforce's proposal to abolish slavery in all British colonies. He was even now working with Lord Blakemore on a bill to grant pensions to soldiers and sailors wounded in the recent wars with France and America. Soon he would find his own cause to champion and had every confidence he would achieve success with it. Why, then, could he not speak up to his mother about a matter of minimal social significance?

"Her name is Lady Beatrice, but I do not know whether she is *out*." He bent over his plate, cutting into his sausage as if it were a beefsteak. "She is the mysterious companion Mrs. Parton has been raving about for weeks." Awaiting the explosion, he risked a glance at his parent.

Her lined but still lovely face paled, and her jaw dropped ever so slightly. "And exactly *when* did you plan to tell me this?" Now her eyes blazed. She stood so abruptly that her chair tipped, caught by the able footman. She slapped her serviette onto the white damask tablecloth and strode toward the door, muttering words he could not decipher.

Greystone forced away the familiar childish guilt and

anxiety that tried to claim him. He had done it. Had faced Mother's ire. And yet he survived.

But would Mother's friendship with her lifelong friend survive, as well?

"Now, now, my dear, you really must eat your breakfast." Mrs. Parton nibbled daintily at her own food, three gravy-covered Scotch eggs and a pretty French pastry filled with vanilla crème, the aromas of which failed to excite Beatrice's appetite. "You must maintain your health if you are to keep pace with me." Seated at the small round table in the brightly decorated breakfast room, she chuckled at her own wit, a habit which Beatrice had, until last evening, found agreeable.

One ball—that was all she had prayed for, a harmless enough request for an earl's daughter. She had resigned herself to Divine Will for the rest of her life, but could she not enjoy one evening worthy of someone of her station? Even wearing another lady's cast-off gown, which she'd not had time to alter, she had found herself eager to dance once she'd heard the music. But she had not even been able to so much as observe the elegant Lord Greystone gracing the ballroom floor, much less dance herself. And all because of Melton's horrid intrusion. While she did have some curiosity about the handsome older gentleman with her brother, he could in no way match up to the nonpareil Lord Greystone.

Beatrice sighed. The Lord had spoken. She must bear the burden of shame cast over every wastrel's family, as though their lack of restraint tainted all of their relatives. No one would ever give her a chance to prove her own character. No one would ever wish to attach himself to the sister of such a man. Still, she could never despise Melly. Had he not defended her from a pack of wandering dogs when they were but children? Had he not taught her to ride her pony? Had they not grieved together when Mama died? But such brotherly devotion would not recommend him to Lord Greystone, whose disapproval of her brother had been obvious when he cut off Melly's attempt to follow her from the ballroom. What had the viscount said to him? She found herself hoping it was a scathing setdown, for surely someone of Lord Greystone's character could turn her foolish brother from his imprudent ways.

"Eat, child." Mrs. Parton tapped her fork on the edge of Beatrice's plate. "You must have energy for our outing this morning."

"Outing?" Beatrice shook off her sullen musing, for sullen was the only proper name for her mood. She had never been one to pout, but these days she could hardly cease to do so.

"Why, yes." Mrs. Parton laughed in her merry way, and both her plump jowls and her rusty curls bounced. "If you are to accompany me out into Society, you must have proper clothing. We must shop on Bond Street before it is too late."

"Too late?" Beatrice's face heated. Her absurd questions made her sound like a ninny.

"Why, yes." More chuckles. "Ladies generally shop in the morning before the gentlemen and the lower classes take over the shopping district."

"Ah. I see. How interesting." In the village near Melton Gardens, Beatrice shopped whenever the mood struck her. Or rather, whenever she managed to set aside a few coins for her own needs. "But surely you know I am without resources."

"Why, my dear girl, you are my employee. Have you noticed my servants' fine purple livery? Do you think I brought you to London to follow me about wearing tatters?" She took a sip of tea and another bite of her French pastry. "Indeed not. I shall provide a wardrobe for you to suit every occasion."

Beatrice avoided looking down at her gown, a faded, much-mended orange chintz. Should Lord Greystone happen to see her dressed so meanly, she would never live down the shame. But why should she care what he thought when he clearly held her in no regard? Still, her eyes stung with unshed tears over her miserable situation. "I thank you, madam. You are too kind. But what of your children? Will they not resent your spending their inheritance on me?"

"Ha. They have more than enough." She leaned toward Beatrice and winked. "More than enough and to spare. Furthermore there is no entail on my property, so I can spend as I please. And this afternoon I shall show you one place where I am very pleased to spend it."

Beatrice's heart leaped. "St. Ann's?"

The lady beamed. "St. Ann's."

"Oh, how wonderful. I have longed for this day."

"More than for a ball?" Mrs. Parton's eyes twinkled with kindness.

"Well," Beatrice drawled, "at least as much as for a ball." Indeed she had always looked forward to being involved with St. Ann's, Mama's favorite charity. She would concentrate on that worthy cause, not on some unreasonable peer who happened to live in the town house next door. Besides, she had no doubt such a gentleman would prove as distant and neglectful a husband and father as Papa had been. Despite his obvious admiration last night, she could expect nothing more from him.

On the other hand, Mrs. Parton's promise of a new wardrobe was far more than Beatrice had expected. She was, after all, the lady's hired companion and now had no claim to pride or vanity of any sort. But in less than an hour she found herself in a pretty little dressmaker's shop on Bond Street, where the delicate scent of rosewater filled the air.

The modiste fluttered around Beatrice like a butterfly, not at all put off by her plain country clothing. "*Mais non,* mademoiselle. Ze orange is not for you." The brown-haired woman, perhaps in her mid-forties, cast a quick glance at Mrs. Parton. "For madam, of course, eet ees perfection. But mademoiselle must have ze blue, ze pink and perhaps even ze pale green to enhance her flawless complexion and beautiful eyes."

Beatrice did not care for Giselle's excessive flattery, but she did admire the woman's skill, which was exhibited in lovely gowns draped over molded female forms. Beatrice longed to try on one of the exquisite dresses. Not since before Mama died had she worn such beautiful clothes, for Papa had never given her wardrobe the slightest consideration.

"Do you not think so, Miss Gregory?" Mrs. Parton's question interrupted Beatrice's dark musings.

"What? Oh, yes, I am certain—" She had no idea to what she was agreeing. "Forgive me. I was admiring this lovely gown." She fingered the delicate lace edging on the low-cut green bodice of a dress on display. Without doubt, this style would demand a fichu. Her hand involuntarily went to her neckline. While her dress might be old and an unflattering color, at least it was modest.

"Then you must have one just like it, but in pink sprigged muslin. Giselle, write it down." Mrs. Parton wagged a finger toward the modiste's growing list. "But for now, for this afternoon, you must have something to wear. Giselle has this blue already made." She took a walking gown from the modiste's assistant and held it up in front of Beatrice. "What do you think?"

Beatrice embraced the Irish linen garment and stepped in front of the tall mirror. By its delicate finishing stitches she could see it had been skillfully completed, no doubt for another lady near her size, perhaps someone like her who in the end could not pay her bill. Or, more likely, some spoiled miss who thought the waistline too high for the latest style and had changed her mind, leaving Giselle with an expensive castoff no wellborn lady would have. If Mrs. Parton took Beatrice to all the promised events, she risked being seen by the lady who had ordered it. Perhaps this was a part of God's journey for her, this stripping away of all her pride. But never mind. The people she would meet this afternoon would not judge her by her clothes.

"It is lovely. I thank you, Mrs. Parton." After measurements were taken for her other gowns and fabrics chosen, Beatrice donned her hastily altered new dress and followed her employer out to the black phaeton.

Mrs. Parton insisted upon driving the small carriage herself, but at least a tiger and a footman sat behind them in the jump seat, which eased Beatrice's mind. Melly once overturned his smaller phaeton while racing, and thereafter Papa had forbidden his sole heir to use the sporty conveyance. She prayed her brother had not taken up racing again, but she would not seek him out to ask him.

They wended their way through the busy streets, and Beatrice soon understood why upper-class ladies shopped before the crowds descended upon the area. The lower classes, even the women, shouted in the most colorful language she had ever heard, generating frowns from Mrs. Parton and heat in Beatrice's cheeks. Even gentlemen in fine suits and top hats, riding excellent steeds, seemed to have left their proper manners at home, for they rode as if the streets belonged to them and berated anyone who stood in their way, again in language no one should hear, much less use.

"Well, my goodness." Mrs. Parton waved her whip toward a wide boulevard where the crowds had thinned. "There's Greystone. I suppose he is on his way to Parliament."

Beatrice located the viscount among the few carriages and carts filling the street. He was the very picture of grace upon his black gelding. Her heart jolted, but she forced down her emotions. "Hmm. How interesting." She managed to keep her tone calm as she sank back into her seat, wishing all the while the phaeton top were raised so she could hide from his view. To her horror, he spied them and turned his steed in their direction. They met at the edge of the street in front of Westminster Abbey.

"Good afternoon, ladies." His expression appeared guarded, but he did tip his hat. Here was one gentleman who remembered his manners in the midst of all the rudeness and hubbub. "Did you complete your shopping before the crush?"

Beatrice noticed his gaze briefly touched on her new gown, and a look of approval flitted across his face. Then he frowned and gave his head a little shake, as if to snuff out any admiration. But how foolish she was. Why should she hope for his good opinion when he seemed determined not to give it? Humph. That was a favor she could easily return.

"Yes, we have finished," Mrs. Parton said. "And now we are off to St. Ann's. Miss Gregory has a great interest in my work there."

"Indeed?" The viscount's gruff expression softened. "Very admirable, Lady Beatrice."

Beatrice's face warmed, something she was growing

tired of. At home at Melton Gardens, she had never felt so discomfited so often. Had never, ever blushed. "I thank you, sir." She gazed upward and beyond him toward one of the Abbey's two square spires, lest he see how his small approval pleased her. How quickly she had abandoned her resolve not to wish for his good opinion—and all against her will.

"Most young ladies I know never give a thought to orphans or any other needy soul."

"Indeed?" Even her eyes betrayed her, turning back as if of their own accord to view the handsome viscount so grandly mounted on his fine horse. "Why, how do they occupy their days if not in service to some worthy cause?"

He shrugged. "My lady, I cannot guess. Perhaps shopping, visiting, gossiping, planning parties and balls. You have my utmost respect for your generosity." No smile confirmed his compliment.

Once again an infuriating blush heated her face, and she waved her fan to cool it. "You are too kind, sir."

"Not at all." He stared at her, and for several seconds she could not move. Or breathe.

"Well, go on then, Greystone," Mrs. Parton said. "We shall not keep you." She waved him away. "You are excused to go solve all of Prinny's problems."

"Madam, if I could do that, the world would stop spinning upon its axis." At last he smiled, then tipped his hat again. "I bid you both good day." He reined his horse around and rode toward the Parliament building in the next block.

Beatrice still could not turn her eyes away from his departing figure. What a handsome gentleman, so refined, so considerate of his mother's friend. But admiring him or any gentleman would bring her only heartbreak and disappointment. She must concentrate on the work ahead rather than dream of having the friendship of a gentleman who clearly did not wish to befriend her.

How annoying to realize that no matter what she told herself, her heart raced at the sight of Lord Greystone.

Chapter Three

"Here we are." Mrs. Parton drove the phaeton through the gates of a large property into a wide front courtyard. "St. Ann's Orphan Asylum. But it has become much more than a refuge for foundling girls."

Eyeing the seven-foot wrought-iron fence as they passed through, Beatrice felt a shiver of dread that diminished her former anticipation. The gray brick of the three-story building added to the asylum's foreboding appearance. This seemed more like a fortress, even a prison, than a home for children, though she approved of the tidy grounds. Unlike the street beyond the fence, not a scrap of trash littered the grassy yard, and not a single pebble lay on the front walkway.

"I delight in these visits," Mrs. Parton said. "The children are so dear, and the matrons do such fine work in schooling them and teaching them useful skills. Most of my maids were reared and educated in this school."

"Mama was going to bring me here." Beatrice swallowed the lump that rose in her throat. Her mother had become ill before she could keep any of her promises.

"Lady Bennington founded the institution, and your

mother and I joined her some twenty years ago." Mrs. Parton waved to the two men on the jump seat.

The tiger took charge of the horse while the footman helped the ladies down.

"We will be here awhile," Mrs. Parton told them, "so you may go around to the kitchen for a bite to eat. Miss Gregory, shall we go in?"

Beatrice followed her employer up the concrete steps to the large front door. A black-clad woman of perhaps thirty years opened it. "Welcome, Mrs. Parton. Please come in." The matron's eyes exuded warmth and welcome.

In the front hall they were met by the smells of lye soap and a hint of lavender. The floor was well scrubbed, and not a speck of lint or dust lay upon the polished oak hall tree or the framed pictures that adorned the long, wide entryway.

The matron spoke quietly to the young girl beside her, and the child hastened up the staircase. Soon the soft rumble of running feet disturbed the silence as over a hundred girls of all sizes and descriptions descended the steps and formed lines. Each girl wore a gray serge uniform and a plain white pinafore bearing a number.

Once again Beatrice swallowed a wave of sentiment. Like these girls she had no parents, but how vastly different their circumstances were. How sad to be an orphan, a seemingly nameless child with only a number on one's clothing for identification. Beatrice steeled herself against further emotion, for tears would not help the children and might inspire them to self-pity, an exercise she knew to be fruitless.

A slender middle-aged matron in a matching uniform offered a deep curtsey to their guests, and the girls followed suit.

"Welcome, Mrs. Parton." Another matron, silver-haired

and in a black dress, stepped forward. Authority emanated from her pale, lined face.

"Mrs. Martin." Mrs. Parton's face glowed as she grasped the woman's hands. "How good to see you." Her gaze swept over the assembly. "Good afternoon, my dear, dear girls."

Mrs. Martin lifted one hand to direct the children in a chorus of "Good afternoon, Mrs. Parton."

"Children, this is my companion, Miss Gregory." Mrs. Parton brought Beatrice forward.

Again the girls curtseyed and called out a greeting.

"Now," Mrs. Parton said, "what have you to show us?" She and Beatrice sat in upholstered chairs the matron had ordered for them.

The girls' sweet faces beamed with affection for their patroness while they recited their lessons or showed her examples of penmanship, sewing and artwork. Mrs. Parton offered praise and dispensed many hugs as though each was her own dear daughter.

Beatrice followed her example in commending the children. Over the next hour she found herself drawn to one in particular. Sally was perhaps fourteen years old, and Beatrice observed how well she managed the younger children. How she wished she could offer the girl employment, perhaps even train her as a lady's maid if she was so minded. But alas Beatrice had no funds for such an undertaking.

As they left the building, Mrs. Parton told Beatrice that the true beneficence happened later when her steward ascertained the institution's needs and budgeted the funds to cover as many of them as possible.

"I take such pleasure in helping them," Mrs. Parton said on their way back to her Hanover Square town house. "Not unlike Lord Greystone."

"How so, madam?" Pleasantly exhausted from the afternoon's charitable exercise, Beatrice still felt a jolt in her heart at the mention of the viscount's name.

"Why, he is the patron of a boys' asylum in Shrewsbury, not far from his family seat."

Beatrice experienced no surprise at this revelation, for Mrs. Parton had already mentioned the viscount's generosity. Of course she could not expect that generosity to extend to the sister of a wastrel, lest his name be tainted. She knew very little of Society, but that one lesson had stood at the forefront of her thoughts ever since she had met him the night before. Perhaps she could glean from that experience a true indication of his character. He might perform charitable acts to be seen by others, yet neglect his duty to family, as Papa had. Thus, she must do her best to ignore her childish admiration for his physical appearance and social graces.

But somehow she could not resist a few moments of daydreaming about what it would be like to have the good opinion of such a fine gentleman.

Greystone longed to dig his heels into Gallant's sides and race madly down Pall Mall. Unfortunately traffic prevented such an exercise, so he would have to find another method of releasing his anger. In his six years in Parliament, this was the first time he had stormed out in protest over the way a vote had gone, but he had no doubt it would not be his last.

Never had he been more ashamed of his peers. Or, better said, the majority of them—those who today had rejected a measure providing a reasonable pension for wounded soldiers returning from the Continent. How did the lords expect these men to survive, much less provide for families who had often gone hungry while their husbands and fathers were fighting for England? Greystone's own brother Edmond had been seriously wounded in America, but had the good fortune to be an aristocrat, as well as their childless uncle's chosen heir. He now had an occupation and a home, not to mention a lovely bride. The rank-and-file soldiers had no such security or pleasures. What did Parliament expect these men to do? Become poachers? Pickpockets? Highwaymen?

Somehow Greystone and his like-minded peers must break through the thick skulls and hardened hearts of those who regarded the lower classes with such arrogance. Almost to a man they claimed to be Christians, yet they exhibited not a whit of Christ's charity. Then, of course, there were dullards like Melton, who sat in the House like lumps of unmolded clay, showing no interest in anything of importance, no doubt waiting until the session was over so he could return to his gambling. No matter how young he might be, how could the earl be so uncaring? And how different he was from his sister.

Greystone had not failed to notice that Lady Beatrice appeared eager to accompany Mrs. Parton to the orphan asylum. With a wastrel brother who should be seeing to her needs, the lady no doubt had limited funds, which made her charitable actions all the more remarkable. Still, she wore a new blue day dress, which complimented her fair complexion far more than the brown gown she had worn last night. Perhaps she was better situated than it seemed. But then, why would she be Mrs. Parton's companion, generally a paid position? Why was she introduced as *Miss* Gregory?

That last question was the easiest to answer. Were he related to Melton, he would not wish for Society to know it, either. Yet dissembling could do her no good and much harm if she hoped to make a match worthy of her station.

But then, it would be difficult to find a gentleman whose charitable nature matched her own who would accept such an intimate connection to Melton.

His useless musings were interrupted when a coach rumbled past, drawn by six lathered horses and churning up dust to fill the air...and Greystone's lungs. He fell into a bout of coughing almost as bad as those he had suffered in his nearly fatal illness last winter. For a moment he struggled to breathe as he had then, but at last his lungs cleared. Being deprived of air was a frightening matter. He coughed and inhaled several more times to recover. If he arrived home in this condition, Mother would fuss over him and send for a physician.

His early arrival meant that the lad who watched for his homecoming would not be at the front window to collect his horse and take it around to the mews. Thus when Greystone dismounted, he secured the reins to the post near the front door. Then he took the three front steps in one leap to prove to himself that his illness had not permanently threatened his health.

Inside, a commotion lured him to the drawing room. The furniture was covered with white linens, and Crawford the butler knelt over something on the floor. Near the hearth stood a scowling, soot-covered man in black holding a broom with circled bristles.

"Greystone." Mother rushed toward him waving her fan, first in front of her own face and then his. "You must leave this instant."

He tried to block her wild gesturing, to no avail. "What in the world?" Foolish question. Obviously the chimney sweep had come to ply his trade. But that did not answer for the two servants hovering over the object on the floor.

"That horrid man and his filthy helper have utterly destroyed my drawing room." She continued to flutter the fan. "There is soot everywhere. You must not breathe it."

Indeed, he did have to cough away a few particles, but the air was tolerable. "I am well, madam. But what is that?"

As soon as he asked the question, Crawford moved back to reveal a small boy lying on the floor. "'Tis the climbing-boy, my lord. He had a nasty fall inside the chimney." The old butler's face was lined with worry. "If I may say so, sir, you should do as Lady Greystone says. This soot flying about cannot be good for your health."

As if cued, the boy began to cough as violently as Greystone had just minutes ago on his trip home. A black cloud issued forth from the lad's mouth, or perhaps his clothing, and then he noisily dragged in a breath.

"Shh." The young serving girl kneeling beside him eyed Greystone with concern as she patted the boy's face with a damp cloth. "His lordship's in the house. Don't be so much trouble."

In answer the boy wheezed and gasped again, and his head rolled back and forth.

"Good heavens, he cannot breathe." Greystone rushed to move the girl aside as memories of his illness made his own chest ache. The poor child might be suffocating. Recalling how it had helped him to breathe when he sat up, he knelt and gently pulled the lad into a sitting position, amid loud protests from Mother and Crawford. "There you go, lad. This should help."

"Aw, gov'ner, leave him be." The master sweep peered down at the boy. "'E's a faker, that'n. Just trying to get out o' work."

Rage flooded Greystone's chest. "Silence, you oaf." The child's eyes opened, revealing yellow, bloodshot orbs…and fear. Greystone gulped back his anger, for it would not help anyone. "Give me the cloth." He grabbed it from the girl and swiped it down the boy's cheeks and under his nose.

Orders and reprimands flew around him, but the only words he could discern were those of a voice speaking within his soul: *help this boy.* All he could answer was, *Lord, I am Your servant.* Doubtless this was the mission God promised to assign to him one dark night last November when Greystone had cried out to him, certain he would soon take his last breath. *I still have work for you* had been His answer. The irony was not lost on him. How well he knew the terror of not being able to inhale life-giving air. Now this poor climbing-boy, this thin, frail bit of bones barely tied together in human form, struggled to breathe. Yes, this was Greystone's work, his cause. A strange excitement swept through him even as fear for the moppet welled up beside it.

The boy gave out another violent cough. "Sorry, gov. I'll get back to work." He tried to wiggle out of Greystone's hold, but cried out. "Ow, me arm, me arm."

"Shh, easy, lad." Greystone touched the boy's appendage, bringing forth more cries. No doubt it was broken, if its slight crookedness was any indication.

"Hush, boy." The master sweep bent over him. "Hush, or I'll gi' ya sumpin' to holler about." He punctuated his threat with a curse.

Mother gasped. "How dare you?"

"Watch your tongue, sirrah." Crawford stepped toward the taller, younger man as if he would seize and eject him.

Greystone lifted the boy in his arms and stood, noticing that the brave child clenched his jaw to keep from crying out again. "Crawford, prepare a room for my little friend and fetch a physician. His climbing days are over."

"Now, see 'ere, yer lordship." The master sweep had the gall to step in front of Greystone to block his exit.

"I bought that boy and 'is brother for a pretty penny. 'E owes me work."

Barely able to control his rage, Greystone gave the man an icy glare. "You will be paid. That is, after I have investigated your illegal use of this child. He cannot possibly be old enough to work as a climbing-boy."

"I say you pay me now." The wild-eyed man must be mad to challenge a peer this way.

Greystone longed to smash the man in his brazen face. But that would not help the boy. "You are fortunate my hands are occupied. Get out of my house."

"If ya please, sir." The child's eyes watered profusely, and his tears formed ragged streaks down his tiny blackened face. "I gotta go with 'im. I gotta take care o' me little brother."

Greystone's eyes burned, the oddest sensation, for he never wept. Perhaps it was all this soot. But he too had younger brothers and would never leave either of them defenseless. He glared at the master sweep. "Bring me the boy's brother within the hour. If you do not, I shall personally hunt you down, and you will regret it for the rest of your wretched life."

While Mother continued to protest, he marched toward the front entry. Neither she nor the sweep nor anyone else would keep him from obeying God's prompting in this matter.

Crawford scurried ahead of him. "The nursery? The footmen's corridor? A closet in the attic? Oh, dear, where shall we put him?"

Although Greystone knew the old fellow was talking to himself, he offered a hearty answer to set his mind at ease. "The nursery will do."

They reached the entryway just as a footman responded

to a knock on the door. When he opened it, Mrs. Parton bustled in, followed by Lady Beatrice.

"Do forgive us, Greystone. Where is your mama? I should like to take tea with her." She stopped and stared at his sooty bundle. "Good gracious, my boy, whatever do you have there?"

But it was Lady Beatrice who held his attention. The regard filling her lovely blue eyes nearly made him stumble, nearly made him drop the child. After a long day in Parliament he would not mind coming home every day to that sort of admiration.

No, he simply must not think such things, must get away from her as soon as possible. But how could he when he would prefer nothing more than to sit down to tea with her and stare into those lovely blue eyes?

Chapter Four

Beatrice could hardly contain her laughter at the sight of Lord Greystone holding a bundle of sooty rags. This was the same elegantly garbed viscount she had seen earlier in the afternoon on his way to Parliament. But now his handsome black suit was covered with gray dust, and his once-pristine white shirt and cravat bore black streaks, as did his nose and left cheek. Although she tried to keep her composure, a smile escaped her as she silently echoed Mrs. Parton's question. Why on earth was the viscount carting about grimy trash when he obviously had sufficient staff for such menial work?

"Good afternoon again, Mrs. Parton, Lady Beatrice." Standing at the base of the staircase, the gentleman spoke in a nonchalant tone at odds with his scruffy appearance. The aristocrats of Beatrice's acquaintance would be mortified if caught in such a state. "Do come in. I am certain Mother will be pleased to see you."

"Gracious, Julia." Lady Greystone appeared from the drawing room on the right. "What an inconvenient time for you to call." The lady glanced between her son and Mrs. Parton, and annoyance filled her countenance. "Never mind. You may as well come in. Perhaps you can help me dissuade Greystone from keeping this little gutter rat." She waved her fan toward the rags in the viscount's arms.

The rags moved, and a tiny, tear-streaked face turned toward the viscountess. Beatrice's heart leaped into her throat. It was a child, a filthy street urchin. She had never known another person of any rank who would willingly touch such a creature, much less carry him.

"Why, it is a child." Mrs. Parton bustled over to the viscount. "My dear Greystone, whatever are you doing?"

The gentleman started to speak, but his mother rushed to join them.

"You see, Greystone, even Julia agrees. The brat has no place in this house. Oh, do come to your senses—"

"Mother!" The viscount sent her a scolding glare, but quickly softened his expression. "Please, madam, permit me to do what I know to be right."

Once again Beatrice's heart skipped. Although she had no idea what drama was unfolding here, she could feel only admiration for the gentleman's extraordinary kindness to both his mother and the child.

"Nonsense." The viscountess returned a glare that did not soften. "You simply cannot give such notice to the lower classes. It teaches them to rebel against their God-given place. Have we not been through this before?" She glanced at Mrs. Parton as if for confirmation. "If you must rescue him from his dreadful owner, then send him to your orphanage in Shrewsbury."

The viscount sighed. "Yes, perhaps I will. But he is injured, and I will not rest until the physician has tended him. Will you ladies excuse me?" He nodded to Mrs. Parton and Beatrice, then started toward the staircase.

"Greystone!" Lady Greystone stepped to the banister and gripped it with a gloved hand. "I forbid you to take him upstairs and spread his filth all over my household."

He paused and slowly turned. Beatrice could not entirely read the expression in his eyes, but for the briefest instant, she thought she detected a silent reprimand spark from him toward his mother like a tiny bolt of lightning. But once again his countenance softened, and his smile brightened those brilliant blue eyes. "We will be careful, will we not, my boy?" Murmuring to the child as to an old friend, he climbed the stairs and disappeared from sight.

Quiet descended upon the spacious oak-paneled entryway. For several moments Lady Greystone stood like a marble statue and stared after her son. Beatrice could hear hushed voices and sounds of movement in the drawing room, but this chamber seemed silent as a tomb.

At last the viscountess turned toward Mrs. Parton, her face a mask. "Shall we go to the small parlor for tea?" Her gaze landed on Beatrice, and one dark gray eyebrow rose.

"Yes, of course." Mrs. Parton beckoned to Beatrice. "But first permit me to present Miss Gregory, my new companion."

"*Miss* Gregory, indeed." Lady Greystone emitted a mild, ladylike snort. "Nonsense. I know full well who she is." She fixed her eyes on Beatrice with a hint of accusation. "Lady Beatrice, do not permit Julia to further endanger your marriage prospects by adding a lie to your résumé. It is enough that Lord Melton has done all he possibly can to destroy your family name."

Her words pummeled Beatrice like a housemaid's blows to a dirty carpet. If she was to be received in this manner everywhere Mrs. Parton took her, she might as well return to Melton Gardens.

"Now, Frances." Mrs. Parton wagged a finger at her friend. "It is not her fault Melton fell in with a bad lot. You must help me repair the damage to her." She looped an arm in Lady Greystone's and ushered her toward a corridor, with Beatrice trailing behind. "She may be reduced to being only my companion but—" She leaned closer and whispered something to the viscountess.

Lady Greystone stopped abruptly and stared down at her shorter friend, then cast a suspicious glance at Beatrice. "Do not dare to think—"

"Humph." Mrs. Parton urged her down the corridor again. "There are many fish in the sea, my dear."

While Beatrice had no choice but to follow, her mind took another direction. She had never had a truly close female friend with whom to whisper secrets. But she could not imagine why jolly Mrs. Parton chose such a cold, unfeeling confidante like Lady Greystone.

Memories of Mama's poise and graciousness swept into her thoughts. She straightened her shoulders and followed the other ladies into a bright, pretty parlor at the back of the house. No matter what her brother had done, no matter what censure came her way, she would hold her head high and never again deny who she was. Even when a gentleman like Lord Greystone withheld his good opinion from her, yet carried a dirty street child as if he were a precious jewel.

A myriad of thoughts assailed Greystone as he followed Crawford toward the fourth-floor nursery. He tried to concentrate on the imp in his arms, but the flawless, smiling Lady Beatrice invaded his mind. Had he mistaken her expression? Was she laughing at him or approving of his actions, as he had first thought? And why did it matter? Last night he'd dismissed any notion of taking an interest in her, a decision solidified by her brother's association with that scoundrel Rumbold. As Mother had taught him from childhood, no good could come from ill-advised friendships, for a man could find himself too deeply involved to escape the evil influences such associations could bring.

At the thought of Mother a hint of shame struck him. As he often did, he recalled his debt to her. He owed her everything: his life, his faith, his moral standards, her restoration of the family fortune Father had gambled away. Yet since his illness last winter he found himself less and less amenable to her instructions. She had a harshness about her that had never bothered him before, but now he found it inconsistent with the improvements he wished to make in his own character. Furthermore he found he could no longer align himself with her every opinion. Now he wanted to learn about and follow the teachings of Christ. Still, he would never cease to honor her, as the Biblical commandment instructed.

The child moaned, then bit his lower lip and shuddered. "Sorry, gov'ner." Tears filled his eyes, and he swatted at them with his uninjured hand.

"Never mind, my good man." Greystone swallowed his own sentiments. He wanted to give the boy a reassuring squeeze, but that would doubtless cause him more pain. "We'll have you fixed up in no time." He eyed the footman posted on the landing. "Bring hot water and a tub to the nursery."

"Yes, milord." The man hurried downstairs.

"Ain't ya gonna have me whipped, sir?" Curiosity rather than fear filled the boy's expression.

Now Greystone's emotions—rage at the master sweep, pity for the boy—threatened to undo him, so he did not risk an answer.

They reached the nursery, and Crawford held the door open. "'Tis a bit musty in here, my lord."

"Of course." Greystone stepped inside and surveyed the long-unused chamber. Dusty holland covers were draped over the furniture, and threads of light peered around the heavy drapes, glinting off dust motes hanging in the air. "Get someone in here to clean it as quickly as possible. But first uncover the bed so I can set my little friend down."

"But my lord." Crawford's pale eyes widened. "He is not fit for a clean bed. He must have his bath first."

"Bath?" The boy squirmed, then cried out and grasped his injured arm with his good hand. At each of his movements, Greystone could feel the child's bony frame.

"Never mind the bedding. It will wash."

With a martyred sigh, Crawford folded away the holland cover and turned down the counterpane on the four-poster bed. Greystone gently laid the boy down, amazed at his resilience. Although the lad shuddered and bit his lip, he did not cry out again.

"There, my lad. The physician will be here shortly to see to your arm." Greystone turned to leave, but the boy grabbed his hand.

"Gov'ner, won't ya let me go to my brother? The master'll beat him if I'm not there to take it for him."

Greystone cleared his throat to cancel the emotion this revelation caused. "Do you not recall? I have ordered your master to bring your brother here to keep you company."

The child blinked and frowned, then glanced toward the door with a wild look in his eyes, as if planning to escape. Hoping to reassure him, Greystone sat on the edge of the bed and patted his shoulder. "You may trust me, lad. Now tell me, what is your name?"

The boy gulped. "Kit, gov'ner."

"Do not say governor, boy." Crawford stood on the other side of the bed, where he had just opened the drapes, letting in a stream of sunlight. "You must address Lord Greystone as 'my lord.'"

Kit eyed Greystone, and Greystone offered a wink of confirmation.

"Now, Kit, you must wait here, or you may miss your brother's arrival. I shall send up someone to keep you company. What do you say to that?"

Kit's forehead furrowed. "I don't know, gov...milord."

Crawford harrumphed. "Why, you say I thank you, of course."

Kit spared him a glance before fixing a serious stare on Greystone. "I thank ya, o'course."

Greystone coughed away a laugh. "You are welcome, Kit."

"Ah, here you are." Mrs. Parton bustled into the room with Lady Beatrice in her wake. "Greystone, your mother is quite beside herself over your unexpected guest. I have relieved her mind utterly, for I plan to take on this little fellow's care myself."

"I beg your pardon?" Greystone stood and gazed at the lady in puzzlement.

"The child, my boy." Mrs. Parton laughed in her inimitable way. "I plan to take him away from you and care for him myself. With Lady Beatrice's help, of course." She gave Kit a maternal smile. "We shall make him quite our little pet, shall we not, my dear?" She sent the young lady a glance before approaching the bed.

Lady Beatrice gave him an apologetic shrug. "Lady Greystone does seem unhappy about your project."

"But you see, dear ladies, it is just that—*my* project. I have already made friends with young Kit, and I have no intention of surrendering him to you."

Kit's eyes darted from Greystone to Mrs. Parton and back again. Greystone gave the boy another reassuring wink.

"Hmm. Just as I suspected." Without a hint of hesitation Mrs. Parton patted Kit's dirty cheek with her gloved hand. "But do you have any idea of what you are doing?"

Feeling a bit put upon, Greystone stepped between the older lady and his new ward. "I shall inquire of the physician."

"Humph." Mrs. Parton wagged a sooty finger at him. "And what do you suppose a physician knows about taking care of children?"

He opened his mouth to answer, but had no idea what to say.

"Just as I thought." The lady shook her head, and her red curls bounced merrily. "You must let me have him, Greystone."

Here was another lady who had nurtured him all his life and for whom he had the greatest respect. Unlike Mother she harbored no secret bitterness, but was merry and generous in every way. Still, he was done with letting these good women rule his life.

"Forgive me, madam, but I cannot do that. His brother will be here soon, and I plan to care for the both of them."

Mrs. Parton scowled at him, at least as much as her permanently merry face would permit. "Your mama will be greatly disappointed. As will Lady Beatrice. Won't you, my dear?"

The young lady blinked in obvious confusion. "I... Well...yes, of course. But Lord Greystone must do what he thinks is best."

"I thank you, madam." He gave her a nod. "At least someone thinks I can manage it." From the startled yet pleased expression on her lovely face, he wished he had not shown quite so much gratitude.

"Very well. Have it your way." Mrs. Parton looped an arm around Greystone's and moved him away from the bed. "But you will grant us visiting privileges."

"Yes, of course." The words came out before he had time to consider all the implications. Had he granted Lady Beatrice unlimited access to his house just when he had determined it was best to avoid her very appealing presence? How could he possibly retract his words without appearing ungentlemanly?

Chapter Five

Her emotions churning, Beatrice watched the battle of wills between her benefactress and the viscount. On the one hand she wanted to laugh at Lord Greystone's obvious struggle to overrule Mrs. Parton. She could see that rank was not held in high regard between these two friends. The observation sent a pang through her, for she longed to enjoy such friendships. She also wanted to comfort the distraught child, who held one hand over the other forearm and had lost his battle against weeping. Mrs. Parton had not held back from touching the boy, so Beatrice went to the bedside and brushed filthy black hair from his forehead, sending a cloud of soot over the white pillow. A smoky smell emanated from him, along with the scent of rancid perspiration. At her touch the child ceased his tears and stared up at her, eyes wide.

"Coo, miss, yer the prettiest lady I ever did see." He winced as he spoke.

She smiled at his artless compliment. "I thank you, sir. And you are a dandy young fellow." She glanced at Lord Greystone, whose bemused expression made her want to laugh. But the child might misunderstand, so she merely smiled. "May I look at your arm?"

The boy winced again. "Aw, miss, I ain't clean." He sniffed loudly and ran his good arm under his damp nose, making more of a mess of himself.

"Never mind that." Beatrice shoved away her feelings of revulsion. The poor child could not be faulted for the life to which he had been born. And he could be cleaned up just like the immaculate orphans she had seen only two hours ago. "Now let me see your arm." She touched his threadbare shirtsleeve, testing the frail arm beneath. "Have you broken it before?"

After a tiny gasp of pain, he said, "Aye, miss," on a whimper.

"Hmm." Beatrice swallowed the emotion his admission stirred within her. What a horrible life he must live. She glanced at Mrs. Parton, who gave her an inscrutable look, and decided to plunge ahead. "Of course the physician will know more than I, but I think the arm is not broken, merely sprained. Because of the old injury, it no doubt causes more pain."

"Indeed." Lord Greystone eyed her skeptically. "And upon what do you base your diagnosis?"

Bristling at his doubtful tone, she withheld a tart reply. After all, the viscount could not be aware of her experiences ministering to her brother's tenants. She turned her attention back to the child. "Can you wiggle your fingers?"

He raised his frail hand and complied. "It hurts."

"As it will for some time." She turned back to Lord Greystone. "Still, I believe a bath will not harm him if care is taken for the injury."

Her words set off another bout of tears. "No bath, miss, gov'ner. Please, no bath."

"Hush, boy." The aged butler, who had been scowling from the other side of the wide bed, shook a bony finger at the child. "You will do as you are told."

The little one cringed and trembled so fiercely, soot drifted up from his entire body.

"Shh." Beatrice caressed his cheek. "Have you ever had a bath?"

Wide-eyed, he shook his head, and more soot dislodged from his person. "'Tis sumpin' terrible, they tell me."

At that Lord Greystone and Mrs. Parton laughed, his baritone providing a perfect harmony to her soprano.

Beatrice continued to caress the boy's cheek.

"Not at all, Kit. A warm bath is just the thing to make a new man of you," said Greystone.

He moved closer to the bed and chucked the boy under his chin, absorbing another dose of the soot that seemed to have already drifted to every corner of the room. At the same time, the viscount's arm brushed against Beatrice's, and a pleasant shiver swept over her making her fully aware of his height and masculine presence. Gracious, what was the matter with her? She cleared her throat and returned her attention to the child.

"Lord Greystone speaks the truth. You may trust him." Her words earned her a warm smile and a conspiratorial wink from the gentleman, and another pleasant feeling swept through her. A bit breathlessly, she suggested, "Perhaps you can send for a footman to do the honors?"

"It has already been ordered, Lady Beatrice." Again his smile stirred a giddy feeling within her. "I do believe we think alike in this matter." A frown darted across his brow, but he shook it away and focused on the child. Then, as if to confirm his words, several footmen entered the bedchamber carrying a large brass tub and buckets of steaming water.

Kit squirmed and sniffed, his eyes wide with fear. Her heart breaking for his terror, Beatrice bent down as close as she dared and whispered, "If you are brave and let them bathe you, I shall ask Lord Greystone to bring you sweet-meats as a reward."

"Sweeties? For me?" Now his wide eyes filled with wonder. He held his arm, sat up and seemed to shake off his fright. "I'll do it fer you, miss." He offered her an impish grin. "And for the sweeties."

Again Lord Greystone and Mrs. Parton laughed in harmony. Beatrice joined them, filled with a sense of a companionship such as she had not experienced since Mama died.

Against his better judgment Greystone permitted himself to enjoy the moment. He could not deny that Lady Beatrice intrigued him. This was no spoiled lady who refused to let her clothes be soiled by the work at hand. In fact she seemed not to notice the soot on her pretty new frock and white kid gloves. How different was her willingness to be involved with this child from her brother's apathy to any charitable matter introduced in the House of Lords. How could a brother and sister be so dissimilar? Greystone tried to build an inner wall to block out the effects Lady Beatrice had on him, but her gentle, generous spirit breached all his defenses. With luck this would be a passing attraction, one that would mellow into kind regard. For now there was a child to deal with, and the lady was putting him to shame in comforting the lad.

"Ladies, perhaps you would wait outside while the servants tend to our new friend?"

"Yes, of course." Mrs. Parton, who had been uncharacteristically quiet for the past few minutes, beckoned to her companion. "Come along, Bea."

Lady Beatrice gaped briefly at her employer, then complied with her order. "Yes, of course."

"Don't leave me, miss." Kit reached out as if to grab her arm and almost fell out of the bed for his efforts.

Greystone caught and righted him. "Easy, lad."

"I shall come back when you are presentable, Kit." She looked at Greystone, and her blue eyes sparkled with amusement. "And when you are presentable as well, sir."

"What?" Greystone quizzed her with a look, then glanced in the mirror over the nearby bureau. Like Kit, he bore streaks of soot all over his face, hardly the visage a peer wished to display in front of ladies. Yet he could not object when it brought such amusement and, dare he say, a feeling of amity with the most charming, selfless young miss he had ever met.

"Come along, Bea." Mrs. Parton clasped Beatrice's hand and led her from the chamber. "We will have that cup of tea with Lady Greystone while we wait."

Beatrice did not resist her leading, but she did balk at the byname her employer used. "Mrs. Parton—"

Before she could voice her complaint, a plump young housemaid in mobcap and apron came charging up the corridor dragging a tiny boy who was as dirty as little Kit. The girl stopped in front of them and curtseyed.

"Begging your pardon, mum, but her ladyship sent me up with this one to join the other." The maid's upper lip curled with distaste, and she held the boy away from her.

The child's eyes were round, and his lower lip trembled. In fact, his entire body shook, sending soot into the air, but he did not speak.

"Well, now." Mrs. Parton bent down to give the boy a smile. "Won't Kit be delighted to see you, my boy?"

A flicker of hope lit his eyes, and he gave her a solemn nod.

Mrs. Parton waved a hand toward the door. "Then let us not waste a moment. Take him inside."

"Aye, mum." The girl knocked on the door, and a footman answered. After a brief exchange he took charge of the child and closed the door. She brushed her hands together. "La, mum, I haven't ever seen such dirt on a person in all my born days."

The maid's impertinence in engaging a guest of the viscount in conversation brought a rebuke to Beatrice's mind, but Mrs. Parton merely chuckled.

"I would not disagree." She glanced at her soiled gloves. "And how nice of the boys to share it with us."

The maid laughed all too familiarly for Beatrice's taste. Who had trained this girl? Why, instead of lowering her eyes, as custom dictated, she even stared Mrs. Parton full in the face.

"Now." Mrs. Parton seemed not to notice the impertinence. "Who are you? And how long have you been in service?"

"I'm Lucy Crawford, mum." At least the girl had the sense to curtsey. "My grandfather's been the butler here at Lord Greystone's ever so long, and he just got me hired."

"Ah, yes. Crawford is a fine fellow." From her friendly manner, one would think Mrs. Parton was talking to an equal, not a servant. "And what will your duties be?"

Lucy shrugged. "I'd hoped to be a lady's maid, but as there's only one lady in this house, and Mrs. Hudson takes care of her, I'm not sure what all I'll be doing." She gave Beatrice a shy smile. "Do you have a lady's maid, miss? I should ever so much like to do your pretty hair. I have a talent for it, if I do say so myself."

Beatrice withheld a gasp at the girl's effrontery, even as humiliation filled her. "No, I have no maid." Melton's wastefulness had required her to let the woman go two years ago. Beatrice had been forced to manage on her own at home, but now that she was in town and needed to look her best, she had to depend upon Mrs. Parton's lady's maid, Poole, to help her dress.

"But you are employed here, Lucy," Mrs. Parton said. "You are in training with your grandpapa, and I am certain he would not wish you to leave."

The girl chewed her lip and stared at the floor. "No, mum." Then she gave Beatrice a bright smile. "But if I could get away from time to time when my duties are done, could I work for you? I won't even ask a wage, just so I can get the experience."

Before Beatrice could respond, Mrs. Parton nodded with a measure of reserve. "Yes, that is a possibility. What do you think, Lady Beatrice?"

Beatrice could not help but think her employer's way of addressing her was for the girl's benefit. But Mrs. Parton's charity gave her pause, as well as a hint of self-rebuke. Helping Lucy learn a skill was not much different from working with the girls at the orphanage. And it would be grand to have her own maid again.

"I believe it is a possibility." Perhaps she could also give the girl some lessons in proper decorum, as well.

"Oh, miss, um, *my lady,* thank you." Lucy clapped her hands and bobbed another curtsey. "You won't be sorry."

Mrs. Parton chuckled, but also wagged a finger at the girl. "Now, if this works out, you must not shirk any duties here at Greystone Hall. I will not tolerate a shirker." Her words echoed Beatrice's own concerns. What would Lord Greystone think of her enticing away one of his servants?

"Aye, mum. I'll do it all."

Laughter within the bedchamber drew their attention, and they all watched the door expectantly.

"I cannot wait to see what those darling boys look like

under all that soot." Mrs. Parton voiced the very idea Beatrice was thinking.

As if in response to her curiosity, Crawford opened the door. "Lady Beatrice, Mrs. Parton, Lord Greystone requests your presence."

As they entered the chamber, the butler's bushy gray eyebrows arched at the sight of his granddaughter, but he said nothing to her as she followed them in.

Clustered around the two boys, who were wrapped in linen towels, Lord Greystone and the footmen were still laughing, despite all of them being drenched and dirty.

"Can you believe it, Mrs. Parton?" The viscount waved them closer. "The lads are blond. Why, I doubt their own master would recognize them now."

Indeed Beatrice thought the two mites bore no resemblance to their former selves, though they still had a gray cast to their skin and black lines embedded in various spots.

Mrs. Parton harrumphed in her good-natured way as she checked their ears and fingernails, taking care special care with Kit's injured arm. "It will take a number of baths to get rid of the last of the soil, but you have made a good beginning."

"As you say, madam." Lord Greystone bowed with an exaggerated flourish. "But I shall leave the next washing to these good men." His brow furrowed briefly. "Perhaps you can advise me…never mind. You have brought the solution with you." He beckoned to Lucy. "Crawford, we have discussed the direction of your granddaughter's training, and now I know exactly what she will do. The lads will require a nursemaid with youthful energy to keep up with them, and she is just the one to do it."

Lucy emitted a tiny squeak that sounded to Beatrice

like a protest, but Crawford's quick glare silenced her instantly.

"As you wish, sir." The butler gave her a furtive wave, and she curtseyed even as she bit her lower lip and stared at the floor.

Beatrice's heart went out to the girl, despite her failure to know her place. Chasing two small boys all day would leave her little time and energy to learn the duties of a lady's maid. But Beatrice would not interfere. After all, she could not pay Lucy. Perhaps this was the Lord's will for the girl, just as He willed for Beatrice to be humbled by the restrictions of her own situation. In this matter both of them must endure their disappointments.

To her shock, Lord Greystone approached her. "Did you enjoy your visit to St. Ann's?" Despite his friendly tone, he did not smile.

Still, her foolish heart skipped at this singular attention. "I did indeed. The girls are very sweet, and they adore Mrs. Parton." Looking up into his intense blue eyes, she found herself a bit breathless.

Now he grinned, but his smile was directed at the older lady. "As do I, and all who know her." True affection beamed from his eyes, and Beatrice could not help but long to receive that sort of approval. Before she could offer her own praise of her employer, he turned to Crawford with orders about the care of the boys.

Beatrice watched the viscount while admiration for his Christian beneficence replaced her personal longings. She could not imagine Papa in this setting. He had barely noticed his footmen, let alone bantered with them as Lord Greystone now did. Nor had Papa ever extended any kindnesses to the children in the village near Melton Gardens. He had left all charitable work to Mama, and she had relished those activities. Yet in this family it was the viscount who enjoyed helping the helpless. Perhaps she would have to revise her former opinion that all peers thought only of their own interests.

"Come along, Bea." Mrs. Parton once again pulled her from the room. "At last we can have our tea with Lady Greystone."

Cringing again at the nickname, Beatrice nevertheless followed. But if she had her choice between taking tea with the haughty Lady Greystone and tending orphans with the lady's suddenly amiable son, she had no trouble deciding which she would rather do.

Chapter Six

Greystone had never felt such satisfaction over a simple act of charity. Or perhaps this was not quite so simple. He still had to contend with Mother. But somehow the approval of Mrs. Parton—and, he must admit, Lady Beatrice, as well—reassured him that he was doing God's will. And to think that the young lady cared nothing about soiling her new gloves and gown. That was a wonder in itself.

For his part he found the soot on his own breeches and shirt something akin to a badge of honor. But a few marks on his clothing were nothing like the many bruises on the two little boys. Obviously they had been caned, for large welts covered their backs and legs. Greystone was sickened to think of anyone treating a child so cruelly. He had felt the whip when he was near Kit's age, and the sight of those injuries caused his own back to sting with the memories.

Gilly, Greystone's body servant since he had turned four years old, had washed away tears and tended wounds, but never spoken a word against Greystone's father, though he had inflicted countless physical and emotional wounds.

"My lord, the physician is here." Crawford motioned to the young, black-clad gentleman who had just entered the chamber.

"My lord, I came as quickly as I could." Dr. Horton gave Greystone a quick bow before turning his attention to the boys. At the sight of them he blinked, his brown eyebrows arched and his jaw dropped. "My lord—?"

"Yes, my good man." Greystone put on a serious face, although he wanted to laugh at the confusion on the man's countenance. "These are my new charges." As he made the declaration, the weight of his new responsibility bore down upon him. Did he have the right to assume the care of these lads? He must find out who they were and whether their parents had truly sold them to the master sweep, lest he be considered a kidnapper. Just the work for his brother Edmond, who was studying law. Or, in the event criminals were at work in this, perhaps a Bow Street Runner.

While the footmen cleaned up the mess caused by the thrashing boys in the bath, Greystone apprised Dr. Horton of the events of the past two hours. He ended with orders that he should not mind the embedded grime, for it would grow out eventually. At least he hoped so, for if not, it would mark the lads forever and limit their possibilities. And while he could have left the chamber and been done with the affair, he found himself unable to abandon the two round-eyed boys, one wincing in pain, the other quaking in fear.

"Easy now, Kit. What is your brother's name?" Greystone asked.

Kit had been cradling his injured arm in the other, but he let go and put the good one around the smaller lad. "This 'ere's Ben, sir." He whispered something in his brother's ear that seemed to comfort him, for his shaking grew less intense.

"I am pleased to meet you, Ben." Greystone gave him a slight bow, earning a gasp from Dr. Horton.

"Why, my lord, these are nothing but—"

"My charges, as I said." Greystone schooled the man with a sharp look. "You must treat them with all courtesy." He softened his expression. "Do tend to his arm straightaway. I shall not rest until we know its condition."

After an examination of said appendage, the doctor confirmed Lady Beatrice's astute diagnosis. "Not broken, but severely sprained. It seems a previous break healed incorrectly. The only remedy is to re-break it and set it properly."

Kit exploded with a howl of protest. "I like me arm as it is, gov'ner." At Crawford's scolding harrumph, he winced and added, "milord."

The distress on his face, mirrored on Ben's, cut into Greystone's heart. Poor terrified children. "There now, do not be frightened. We have no intention of causing you further pain."

"Most of the bruises will heal soon enough." Dr. Horton completed his examination of both boys and prescribed treatment for several ailments, both internal and external. "And of course they are dreadfully thin, as climbing-boys must be to do their work."

His comment brought Greystone up short. Of course sweeps must be small enough to crawl inside chimneys, and many were children. It was a nasty but necessary business, for London would burn to the ground without well-cleaned chimneys. But he could not countenance such young boys being pressed into that service. He must examine the laws to discover exactly how young a climbing-boy could be, and perhaps find some way to ease their lives. "Yes, well, Kit and Ben will soon be too fat for cleaning chimneys."

That earned a few sniffles until he knelt before them with a reassuring smile. "What do you say, lads? Would you like to learn a different trade?"

Each one gave him a solemn nod, although he doubted they knew what he meant.

"Well then, we'll get you some clothes and food while we decide exactly how to proceed." He beckoned to the housemaid, and she stepped forward, her face as blank as her grandfather's always was. "Lads, you must obey Lucy at all times, understand?"

More solemn nods. Kit leaned toward him and whispered, "Th'other lady promised sweeties."

Greystone chuckled. "Lucy, did you hear that? If they eat all their dinner, you must see that they have sweeties afterward. If you have any questions, I am certain Crawford can advise you." He ordered one footman to dash out and purchase clothing for the boys. Another was sent to the kitchen for food. The rest continued to clean the nursery and make it fit for habitation.

With all set in motion, Greystone at last quitted the room and descended to his second-floor chambers, content that his new venture would be a grand and enjoyable success.

Gilly emerged from his small bedchamber attached to the larger room, his eyes widening in horror as he took in Greystone's appearance. He cleared his throat, as if correcting himself, and schooled his expression into his usual placid smile. "Well, milord, what have we been up to today?" He removed the soiled jacket and cravat, staring at them as if wondering how to repair the damage.

Greystone laughed. "Quite a mess, am I not?" He quickly explained the situation, receiving Gilly's usual acceptance of anything he said. The least he could do was offer a way out of the work his valet would have to do to restore the garments. "Why not just toss them, old man? They're just clothes. Easily replaced. Unlike a human life, no matter how humble." He was surprised by the emotion on Gilly's face, a reddening of his eyes and a slight sniff, if Greystone was not mistaken.

"A fine thing you're doing, milord." Gilly kept his eyes on his work as he cleaned Greystone's face and hair. But then, as a servant, he rarely looked Greystone in the eye. In fact he had not done so for many years, not since Greystone had taken his seat in Parliament, as if that had signaled a parting of the ways for them. He missed that deeper connection with the man. Maybe now was the time to recapture it.

"I am pleased to have your approval."

Now Gilly directed his gaze to Greystone's eyes, and he blinked, then smiled. "Thank you, milord."

Greystone returned a grin, and warmth spread through his chest. With Gilly's endorsement he was once again struck with the certainty that he was doing the work of God. As his heart lightened in exultation, Lady Beatrice's approval came to mind. With Mrs. Parton he could count three people in his corner regarding the little boys. He wished the younger lady's approval did not please him quite so much. Wished he did not think of her quite so much.

Interesting how she had correctly diagnosed Kit's injury. No doubt she had ministered to her brother's tenants, just as Greystone's mother often visited the people of their Shropshire village, taking them food, clothing and medicine. Yet Mother always seemed to begrudge her duties, or at best tolerate them, while Lady Beatrice had clearly delighted in helping with the boys. He had no doubt that the young lady had been trained in managing a home and an estate. And no one could deny she was a singular beauty. Why must he search further? What more could a peer wish for in a wife?

Simple. He could wish and pray for a lady whose name was untarnished by a reprobate brother.

"Mrs. Parton, it is exquisite." Standing before the wardrobe mirror in her bedchamber, Beatrice turned this way and that to see every detail of her new pink evening dress. As dictated by this year's fashions, the waistline hung halfway down the midriff, which she found more comfortable than the higher, tighter bands. The sheer full-length sleeves hugged her arms, but did not bind. And the lace-lined neckline was high enough to protect her modesty. Would Lord Greystone view her with approval in this creation as he had the blue day dress? She dismissed the wayward turn of her thoughts and directed her attention to the lady beside her. "Giselle's seamstresses must have worked without rest to complete it in three days. How can I ever thank you?"

Her benefactress chuckled, then sobered. "'Tis no more than your dear mama would have done for you, my child." A tiny sniff escaped her. "I am pleased to provide a wardrobe appropriate for my companion."

Beatrice sighed. "Yes, madam." She was deeply grateful to Mrs. Parton, but must she always be reminded of her reduced status, even as she found a moment of enjoyment?

"But I have decided it would be wise to accept Lady Greystone's advice." Mrs. Parton reached up to adjust the silk scarf and strand of pearls her lady's maid had entwined in Beatrice's hair. "Hmm. I do believe this requires another pin or two." She set about searching the dressing table drawer.

In a mere five days of being in London, Beatrice had learned her employer often became distracted. "Lady Greystone's advice?" The viscountess had given counsel on many topics as the three of them had sipped their tea the other day. But the majority of her warnings had to do with avoiding chimney sweeps and other such members of the working classes.

"Yes, dear. Do try to keep up." Mrs. Parton clicked her tongue. "We must not present you as Miss Gregory, as I first planned. Such a scheme will be all too easily exposed, and you will suffer for it. Some members of the *ton* may even think you have tried to deceive me."

An odd tendril of hope threaded through Beatrice. Would she now be elevated to the position of ward rather than employee?

"No, we will introduce you by your rightful name, and no one need know you are in my employ."

So much for Beatrice's fondest wish. Why did she not leave London right now and return to Melton Gardens? At least there she would receive the highest respect of the tenants, who never blamed her for their master's failings.

Mrs. Parton's thoughtful frown was reflected in the wardrobe mirror. "And of course we must make it clear that you have nothing to do with your brother. I have given orders to the entire staff that he absolutely must not be permitted to enter this house."

Her proclamation cut like a knife into Beatrice. As much as she did not want to be seen with Melly in public, she refused to believe he was utterly lost to her. But she would comply with Mrs. Parton's orders in hopes that their refusal to receive him would shame him into reformation. And of course she would continue to pray day and night for her wayward brother.

This evening, however, she had the responsibility of being a good companion to her employer, which would bring her both joy and sorrow. Attending the Royal Olympic Theatre in Drury Lane with Mrs. Parton had been among Mama's favorite activities when she had accompanied Papa to London every spring. She had often promised to take Beatrice to plays and balls during her debut Season. Left at home in the schoolroom with her governess, Beatrice dreamed of the coming adventures, but Mama died of a fever before she could keep her promises. At one and twenty Beatrice was long past the proper age for a debut, and she doubted Mrs. Parton planned to introduce her at one of Her Majesty's Drawing Rooms. But for now she would try to enjoy this evening as though Mama were with them, scheming to find the perfect husband for her only daughter.

Alas, for the past several days Beatrice's thoughts of marriage were followed straightaway by thoughts of the viscount who lived next door. But despite Lord Greystone's playful winks and banter about their shared interest in the little chimney sweeps, *Lady* Greystone made it clear Beatrice was not completely welcome in her home and was received only because she was Mrs. Parton's companion. Even Lord Greystone had advanced his friendliness no further. Beatrice chafed at these unfair judgments against her because of Melly's reputation, but there was no remedy for it.

To carry them to the theatre, Mrs. Parton had ordered her new blue-and-white landau, drawn by her favorite team of four white horses. The two ladies sat side by side facing the front of the elegant carriage so they could best enjoy the scenery as they traveled. Emerging from Hanover Square, they observed many other stylish carriages conveying members of the *haute ton* to parties and routs and festivities to celebrate Napoleon's defeat.

At the thought of such gaiety Beatrice dismissed the pain of her own disappointments. After years of war perhaps England and all of Europe could breathe more easily. Beatrice decided the future looked brighter than it had since Mama died, at least for the moment.

The carriage clattered over the cobblestones, but the thick cushions covering the benches and the springs on the wheels protected the passengers from severe jarring, making conversation pleasant. The air was filled with various scents, spring roses and honeysuckle vying with the evidence of passing horses on the roadways. As the landau turned this way and that on the streets leading to Covent Gardens, the always jovial Mrs. Parton extolled the talents of the renowned actor who would soon entertain them.

"Mr. Robert Elliston is quite handsome, to be sure. He will no doubt thrill us as Richard III, although I cannot think he could surpass his performance as Hamlet. Have you seen any of Shakespeare's plays performed, my dear?"

Beatrice felt her own excitement growing. "No, madam, but I have read them all."

"Oh, gracious." Mrs. Parton eyed her with alarm. "Even *Titus Andronicus?*"

Beatrice gave her a sober nod. "And did not sleep for many a night afterward."

"I should think not." Mrs. Parton shuddered, as if to shake off her own memories of the bloody tale. "But tragically, real life is often mirrored in these dramas." After a moment her smile returned, accompanied by a twinkle in her eyes. "We are meeting Lord and Lady Blakemore at the theatre and will share their box, then go to their home near Grosvenor Square for a midnight supper. They have invited a few other friends, although Grace did not tell me whom."

"I should like that." Beatrice found herself hoping a certain viscount would be in attendance. In fact, Lord Greystone's handsome visage continued to dance across her mind as the landau stopped in front of an imposing building.

"Here we are. The Royal Olympic Theatre." Mrs. Parton waited while the footman opened the door and handed her down. "Come along, my dear."

Beatrice scooted across the velvet cushion and reached for the white-gloved hand extended to assist her, all the while fussing with her skirt to keep it modestly in place. But as she emerged from the carriage and looked up to thank John Footman, she gazed instead into the very face that moments before had filled her thoughts. Her pulse quickened with guilt, as when her governess once caught her stealing a sweetmeat before supper.

"Lord Greystone."

But to her chagrin, the gentleman did not return her smile.

Chapter Seven

Why did she have to look so beautiful? Exquisite, in fact. As members of their little party greeted each other, Greystone had no option but to believe that Mrs. Parton and Lady Blakemore, perhaps even Lord Blakemore, had conspired to arrange this evening. Otherwise why would the earl have taken the trouble of driving by White's to invite him to the theatre? Yes, Blakemore did have some information to impart regarding the laws about child chimney sweeps. Yes, his countess did have her own pretty companion who, Greystone suspected, would be put forward to him for a bride, should they fail to match him with Lady Beatrice. Schemers, the lot of them. He had a mind to have done with it and offer for the Duke of Devonshire's dull granddaughter, who owned no opinions of her own except those concerning expensive frocks.

But Lady Augusta could never hope to display a dress as Lady Beatrice graced this stylish new creation. No ill-fitting castoff, this, but a perfect fit over a perfect form. Its warm pink shade brought a rosy blush to her flawless ivory cheeks and heightened the blue of her intelligent eyes. Only the questioning frown upon her fair brow marred her beauty, and he was at fault for it.

"My lady." He offered a bow, then his arm to escort her into the theatre, but his attempt to smile was more of a grimace. He could feel it. Could see it reflected in the hurt that darted across her eyes, in her diminished smile that still succeeded more than his.

"I thank you, sir." She placed a gloved hand upon his forearm and permitted him to guide her in following their friends through the theatre's wide doors. "I did not expect to see you in our party this evening."

"Ah, well." He managed an honest smile at last, hoping to appease her. "We are at the mercy of our elders, are we not?"

"What a pity." Now those blue eyes snapped to his, and her tone held a hint of frost at odds with the warm evening air. "Tell me, sir, what would you prefer to be doing rather than attending a performance by the celebrated Robert Elliston?"

Warmth crept up his neck, and he felt—but denied— the urge to tug at his collar. She had all too easily read his reluctance to be in this company, playing this part. Oh, if only she could know the depth of his reasons, not one of them having to do with her, other than her brother. Now the heat in his chest fired up again over the injustice of it all. But he had made too many solemn vows, had too many missions to complete for the Almighty to ruin them all by evil associations. He must not permit himself to become attached to Lady Beatrice.

Beatrice urgently wished to remove her hand from Lord Greystone's arm, but she would surely get lost in the well-dressed throng entering the theatre. She located Mrs. Parton in the crush ahead of them only because of the white peacock feathers in her turban.

Still not responding to her question, which she had

intended as a challenge, Lord Greystone escorted her through the double doors and across the broad lobby, where they joined their party at the foot of an elegant red-carpeted staircase.

"Do let us go right up," Mrs. Parton said. "I want to see who is here. Of course Prinny will be late, if he comes at all, but surely there will be someone fascinating to see." With an impatient wave of her hand she began her ascent, with everyone else following after.

"Humph." Lord Greystone deigned to lean toward Beatrice as they followed the others. "As if we were not sufficiently fascinating to her." He offered her a grin, but Beatrice felt no pleasure in it.

She may have spent her entire life in County Durham, but numerous peers and their families had visited Melton Gardens over the years. She had learned from those aristocrats that overdone manners and silly humor often masked insincerity. Clearly Lord Greystone's attempt at wit was meant to mask his discomfort over being left to escort her. She should not let his deficiencies affect her, but they did. What should have been a thrilling experience for her, one she had anticipated since childhood, was now nothing less than an exercise for her in that same kind of insincere courtesy. How ironic. They had come to be entertained by actors, but they themselves were performing roles neither wished to play. But as the daughter of an earl, she deserved courtesy and would demand it. If she must perform, at least she could write her own lines.

"You did not answer my question, Lord Greystone. What would you rather be doing this evening?" She gave him a little smirk to show him she would persist until he answered.

A frown darted across his brow, but his smile quickly returned, and he stared directly into her eyes. "You mistake me, my lady. I am delighted to be in this company. No other place in the world would suit me."

Well played. But she also felt a measure of pride over not wilting under his gaze, even if her heart did flutter in the most annoying manner. Yet such a reaction was a waste of time, so she let the matter drop and renewed her determination to enjoy this evening.

The theatre looked just as Mama had described it. On the second floor of the playhouse, private doors and lavish draperies led to seating areas partitioned off on both sides from similar spaces around the balcony. Lord Blakemore's box was comfortably furnished with two rows of velvet-cushioned chairs. Below them was seating for the general audience, and above was the gallery where the lower classes could purchase seats for a penny or two.

The most lavish private box bore the crest of the Prince Regent, but His Royal Highness had not yet arrived, if he was coming at all. Beatrice was only mildly interested in seeing him, for the prince's well-known self-indulgent lifestyle did not garner her respect. With such a ruler as an example, no wonder Melly surrendered to every temptation London had to offer a naive young peer.

"Come along, my dears." Lady Blakemore directed the ladies to the front row of the box, while the two gentlemen sat behind them. At least four more people would fit in this space, and Beatrice hoped Lord Blakemore had invited others. Now that she had an appropriate wardrobe, she would be pleased to meet other members of Society, even other unattached gentlemen. Perhaps some of them would regard her more favorably than Lord Greystone. Despite her lack of a dowry and all marriage prospects, her foolish heart could not help but long to be courted, or at least admired, especially since this viscount refused to perform that office.

At the thought of him, and very much against her will, she glanced over her shoulder and saw him in quiet conversation with the earl. She heard a word or two, enough to learn that they were discussing the little chimney sweeps.

"My investigation turned up no parents," Lord Greystone said. "Apparently the master sweep bought them from an orphanage. I sent him compensation equal to his purchase price, though he actually deserves prison, in my way of thinking." He shook his head. "We simply must put an end to such wicked use of tiny children."

"Wilberforce is up for it," Lord Blakemore said. "After his success in abolishing the slave trade, he has come close to abolishing slavery itself within the Empire. I believe he has many friends in the House of Commons who will support anything he puts forth."

At his words a guileless and joyful smile lit Lord Greystone's entire face, reminding Beatrice of his generous nature toward the poor little sweeps. Her heart skipped, but she quickly tamped down her giddy feelings. It seemed that every five minutes she needed to remind herself that the viscount had no interest in her, and she must not permit herself to be wounded by his aloofness.

Further, she had come to see a play, her very first, if one did not count the annual Christmas plays presented by the children in the village church. With some effort she turned her attention to the large stage that extended across the opposite side of the theatre. A luxurious crimson curtain hid the actors and scenery. How delightful it would be to peek behind the red velvet to watch them donning costumes and perhaps practicing their lines.

"Why, there sits Mademoiselle St. Claire." Mrs. Parton held up her quizzing glass to view a young lady in a box on the other side of the large room. "One would think she'd have followed old Louis to Paris to snare a husband from among the restored French aristocracy."

"Perhaps she has her eye on an English peer." Lady Blakemore tilted her head toward Lord Greystone.

Interrupted midsentence, he gave her a questioning look. "Madam?"

"Never mind." Lady Blakemore chuckled, and Mrs. Parton laughed outright.

Lady Blakemore's companion, the pretty, stately Miss Hart, said nothing but seemed to deliberately keep her attention on the crowd below. Beatrice had no idea who the lady's family was, but her manners were impeccable. No doubt she was wellborn but also without a dowry, and thus had sought employment with the countess.

Beatrice surveyed the occupants of the large auditorium and found most of the audience engaged in conversation. No one seemed the slightest bit excited, as she was, about the upcoming entertainment. But with her comfortable chair in Lord Blakemore's box being the farthest from the stage, she could watch the other ladies and learn proper decorum for this setting.

One thing was certain: she would never giggle and flirt the way some ladies in the upper balcony did. Their behavior and gaudy dresses brought heat to her face. Had they no modesty? Yet they were surrounded by attentive gentlemen. Beatrice would gladly do without such attention rather than behave so outlandishly. Why, one showily dressed woman had an arm slung across the shoulders of a well-dressed gentleman, whose curly blond hair and broad forehead seemed familiar...

Melly! Beatrice cringed at the realization that her

brother was mingling with such company. She ducked behind the partition of Lord Blakemore's box and turned her attention back to the curtain, praying the play would begin soon.

Melton's heart felt as if it had been cut in two with a sword. Did Beatrice really think he had not seen her ducking out of sight so that once again she would not have to acknowledge him? There she sat, glittering like a fine jewel even in the midst of her well-dressed friends. He was so proud of his sister. No one in this vast theatre would have noticed if she had given him their secret sign. But what could he expect? She was spending her time with that horrid Greystone, who even now looked at her like a besotted fool. Melton wanted to smash the arrogant viscount right on his aristocratic nose.

No, that was not fair. Greystone had shown her only respect from the moment they had stepped into the box. But he was a rather dull fellow—not one word of scandal, either interesting or boring, was ever attached to his name. Still, Beatrice could do worse. Or better. Oh, bother. She must marry Rumbold, and that was that. It was the least Melton could do for the man after all he had done for him, paying his gambling debts and finding him a place to live after Melton had been forced to sell his town house. At that thought a nagging guilt stirred within him. Since seeing her at Greystone's ball, he had begun to realize all that his gambling had cost them both. He, not Mrs. Parton, should be taking care of his sister.

"Blimey, milord, what's the sulky face fer?" The gaudily dressed girl, probably no more than seventeen, ran a hand over Melton's cheek. "Yer no fun at all."

He shoved her hand away as gently as possible. This was not the kind of woman he wanted to keep company with. But decent ladies, even his own sister, would not welcome his friendship. What had he done to deserve that? He would have to ask Rumbold. Something would have to be done, and soon. He was an earl, for goodness's sake, a member of the ruling class. He sat in the House of Lords and helped to lead England.

But the pain in his heart ate at him, and the only thing that would soothe it away was another drink.

In the corner of his eye, Greystone saw Lady Beatrice shrink back in her chair, almost like a child playing hide-and-seek behind the box's red velvet panel. A quick glance to the upper gallery explained her actions. Lord Melton was consorting with a rather disreputable mob, and no doubt his sister wanted to avoid his notice.

Greystone sighed. Years ago his brother Edmond had chosen evil friends, and the entire family had suffered for it. But Edmond had been sent away to the military, where his life had changed drastically. Newly married to a vicar's daughter, he was now a model of decorum and had a promising future as a barrister. Perhaps Melton could change, too. Unfortunately he was a peer, and no one could consign him to the harsh discipline of the army, no matter how much his family suffered for his actions.

Empathy for the lady welled up inside Greystone, and he tried to think of something consoling to say to her. What lighthearted comment would turn her attention from her sorrows? Just as he leaned toward her, the massive curtains began to part, and Lady Beatrice's posture straightened. Even in profile he could see the excitement in her expression. A strange ache filled his chest. He would not mind introducing her to the many innocent charms of London: parks, fairs, leisurely voyages on the Thames. Earlier when she had challenged him regarding his poor

attitude, he had been a little annoyed, but admiration replaced his ill-humor. The lady had spirit, as he had seen the
night he had met her. But until Melton mended his ways,
Greystone dared not associate with her more intimately.

And in this moment, he resented that injustice.

The audience grew quieter, although not entirely silent.
Beatrice decided that many people had come to socialize
rather than observe the performance. But once the curtain opened to reveal a magnificent setting, her attention
settled on the lone figure limping from behind a stone col-
umn. Was this deformed hunchback the handsome Robert
Elliston she had heard so much about? Now the audience
hushed, and Beatrice held her breath.

"'Now is the winter of our discontent—'" he paused
dramatically, surveying the audience with a victorious
look "'—made glorious summer by this sun of York.'"

As his deep rich voice intoned the familiar line, a shiver
ran down Beatrice's spine. How well she had known her
own winter of discontent, yet no bright sun promised *her*
a glorious summer. But such thoughts would only ruin her
enjoyment of the play, so she dismissed them summarily
and permitted the players to draw her back in time some
three hundred years, when England had enjoyed another
significant victory like the recent one over Napoleon. So
well did the actors represent their characters, especially
Mr. Elliston, that Beatrice decided to join the fantasy and
pretend she was viewing history as it happened, just like
a mouse in the corner.

Greystone had never cared much for *Richard III*. His
stomach turned at the idea that a prince could murder his
own nephews so he could claim the Crown. Aware of the
arguments contrary to Shakespeare's premise, some who

insisted that Edward IV's younger brother Richard was blameless in the boys' deaths, Greystone nonetheless was convinced Richard had arranged the foul deed. In over three hundred years, no evidence had been found in the Tower or any written records to support the man's guilt or innocence. But a clever minion could cover any crime.

Yet as Greystone watched the performance, he could find no fault in the actors, especially the two youths—or were they young women?—who portrayed the princes. They reminded him of his little chimney sweeps, despite the disparity in their stations in life. Bearing the same names as their father and uncle, "Prince Edward" displayed the same protectiveness over little "Prince Richard" that Kit exhibited for little Ben—the same instinct to protect those under his care that Greystone had always felt for his own brothers. The younger boy, Richard, had the same spunk Ben possessed and seemed more prone to mild mischief than his brother. The idea that someone would have no qualms about harming two little boys, either by murder or misuse, transformed Greystone into a protective, avenging knight.

Or so he liked to think. There was still Mother to deal with in the matter. This afternoon he'd had to go to his club to escape her incessant disparaging remarks about his project to protect small climbing-boys. That is, he fled after he instructed Lucy to keep the boys in the nursery, whatever it took. Earlier in the day he had failed to find Bennington to discuss the matter.

Laughter broke into his thoughts as the audience no doubt responded to one of the few humorous moments in the play. Greystone glanced at Lady Beatrice, whose profile was as lovely as the front view of her face. She had covered her well-formed lips with a gloved hand, and her eyes were wide as if she were in shock, perhaps over the bawdy tone of the jests typical of Shakespeare. He should not have let his mind wander from the play. Perhaps he could have diverted her attention before the tasteless lines were spoken so she would not hear them. Someone had to shield the lady's sensibilities, since her brother had abandoned his duty to do so.

A glance toward the upper balcony confirmed his dislike for Melton, and a familiar anger burned in his chest. The foolish young earl was laughing with the rest of his disreputable crowd, people Greystone would not permit even to address Lady Beatrice. The thought brought him up short. When had he decided it was *his* duty to shield her?

No, he must not give place to such sentiments. The only conclusion to his unwelcome feelings for Lady Beatrice would be disaster, for just looking at her wicked brother made him want to slap some good sense into the imbecile. Just the way Greystone's father had done to him.

Chapter Eight

"Oh, do ride with us, Greystone." Mrs. Parton tugged on the viscount's sleeve as if he were an obstinate child, while the rest of the party leaving the theatre watched with amusement. "I shall feel much safer with a gentleman in the landau now that night has fallen."

Seeing the chagrin on that particular gentleman's face, Beatrice refused the blush that tried to fill her cheeks. After all, no one could claim she was responsible for this invitation. Her earlier clash, slight though it was, returned to her thoughts, and she did not wish for more unpleasantness with him. Still, she agreed with her employer that having a well-known peer in the carriage would likely discourage footpads who might not regard a driver, a tiger and a burly footman as sufficient protection for two ladies.

"Yes, yes, Greystone," Lord Blakemore said. "Do go with these dear ladies to protect them. We can discuss our scheme over supper."

"You most certainly will not." Lady Blakemore gave her husband a playful nudge, shocking Beatrice. She had never seen her parents tease or behave with anything but the utmost formality toward one another. "I forbid you to ruin my supper with political discussions."

"Of course, my dear." The earl eyed Lord Greystone and shook his head. "Ah, well, another time, then. We must permit the ladies to rule, must we not?"

Lord Greystone winced ever so slightly, a response Beatrice found odd until she recalled observing a silent battle of wills between the viscount and his mother regarding Kit. Although the viscount had displayed only respect for Lady Greystone, he had also refused her order not to carry the little chimney sweep upstairs. Then when Beatrice and Mrs. Parton had joined the viscountess for tea, the lady had complained about the soot all over *her* house. But of course her son owned it all, just as Melly owned Melton Gardens. Although Beatrice had managed everything for her brother since Papa's death, she had never claimed the property as her own. Indeed if Melly decided to marry—a frightening thought considering his current habits—Beatrice would gladly relinquish the management of it all to her new sister. She had no wish to rule anyone.

Perhaps Lady Greystone had been in control of her family for so long that she found it difficult to surrender the reins, despite Greystone's obvious competence. A new respect for the viscountess blossomed in Beatrice's mind. Raising three sons alone could not have been easy. And if the viscount's reaction to the earl's comment about ladies ruling was any indication, perhaps the battle for rule of Greystone Hall was not yet over.

Already in the landau with her back to the driver, Mrs. Parton instructed Lord Greystone to sit in the place of honor, the thickly upholstered bench facing front from whence he could see the passing scenery. But just as Beatrice started to take her place on the opposite seat, Mrs. Parton waved her to the spot beside the viscount.

"You will never learn your way around if you cannot see where you're going, my dear." She laughed at her own humor even as she waved over her shoulder to the driver. "To Lord Blakemore's residence, Harold." Satisfied that her orders would be obeyed, she turned back to the viscount, who appeared as uncomfortable as Beatrice felt. "Now, Greystone, you must tell us, what did you think of the play? Was it not completely enthralling? Was not Mr. Elliston exceptionally brilliant?"

He chuckled, a rich baritone laugh that sent a pleasant shiver down Beatrice's spine. She shoved away the feeling, refusing to let her heart become attached to a gentleman who clearly did not wish to be in her company.

"My dear Mrs. Parton, I shall not permit you to bait me."

"Why, how would I do that, dear boy?" Mrs. Parton reached across the wide space and tapped his knee with her folded fan. Even in the dim light of the carriage lanterns, Beatrice could see the twinkle in the lady's eyes. What was she up to?

"Oh, quite easily." He gave a careless wave of his hand. "Should I dare to proffer an opinion, perhaps Lady Beatrice will feel obliged to agree, as all young ladies are schooled to do." He sent Beatrice a sidelong glance. "Is that not right, Lady Beatrice?"

So the gentleman wished to take a turn at challenging her. Beatrice would gladly play along, for she missed the lighthearted teasing she and Melly used to share. She tilted her head in a playful way. "Why of course, Lord Greystone. A young lady is not considered well-bred if she is too strident in her opinions." She blinked her eyes several times to effect a naive expression such as she had observed in young ladies at his ball. "Therefore, I shall only be bold enough to say I agree with Mrs. Parton's opinion about the play *and* Mr. Elliston. That is—" another blink or two "—only if you think so, as well."

While Mrs. Parton laughed merrily, Lord Greystone took a turn at blinking. Then he seemed to comprehend the joke and laughed, too.

"You are an agreeable companion, Lady Beatrice." One of those tiny frowns darted across his forehead, but he quickly recovered his smile. "I am certain you are a constant source of comfort to Mrs. Parton."

What a clever way for him to distance himself from her. Disappointment crowded out the feelings of camaraderie that had tried to blossom within her heart. She had hoped he would give her a clever rejoinder, but he took the safe road and gave her a simple compliment. But what had she expected? She had begun to suspect that Mrs. Parton was pushing her toward the viscount, but with every push in his direction, Lord Greystone took a decisive step back.

Well, two could play that game. She had been hurt enough by her brother's destructive ways. She would not let Lord Greystone add to her pain, no matter how much she came to admire him for his charitable endeavors and his social graces…toward anyone but her.

What Greystone meant for a compliment had somehow offended Lady Beatrice, but he could not imagine why. Ah, well. He would be the first to admit he was not wise in the ways of young ladies, other than their simpering insincerity that Lady Beatrice had mocked so delightfully just now. After his first two Seasons in London, when most of the women he had spent time with were not ladies, he had at last heeded the advice of his godly brother Richard, studied the book of Proverbs and fled his youthful inclinations. Since that time, he treated every young lady as one might a sister lest any mistake his intentions.

Yet for all of the wisdom of Scripture about what not to do in regard to women, not a word in the Bible advised a young man as to how to court a lady. No doubt in biblical times wives were chosen by one's parents, just as Mother wanted to choose Greystone's bride. But the more he thought of spending his life with someone of her choosing, the more he wanted to unravel the mysteries of courting himself and find his own bride. And while he was ever mindful of the danger of becoming like his father, he had no choice but to marry, and soon.

For the present he could see his compliment to Lady Beatrice had not been well received, but why? Not that he was courting Lady Beatrice. Indeed he was not. Would not, in fact. Even without Mother's disapproval, even though the lady was kind and good and charitable, she nonetheless still had a brother with whom Greystone refused to be connected.

In the dim lantern light within the carriage he could see her uplifted chin, as if she were still displeased with him. A sheen over her eyes, not quite tears, seemed to denote some high feeling. He must appease her somehow, for he could not bear to see her unhappy.

"Goodness." Mrs. Parton huffed so hard, Greystone feared a reprimand was forthcoming. "I neglected to ask you, dear boy. What report do you have for us about our little chimney sweeps?"

Relief swept through him. He should know that this sweet lady would not berate him.

"They are well, madam, and have begun to look forward to their daily baths, as much to torment the footmen as for their own enjoyment of all the splashing about." He heard a muffled giggle beside him and decided Mrs. Parton's interruption was better than anything he might have planned to brighten Lady Beatrice's mood.

"Daily baths?" Mrs. Parton clicked her tongue in disapproval. "I knew they would need many washings, but daily? Surely that cannot be healthy."

"I had thought so, too, but Dr. Horton assures me they will not be harmed because the weather is warm, and they will be better served if all traces of soot are removed from them. The nursery, or more precisely, the playroom now, is also warm, so I suppose that helps to ensure their health."

Lady Beatrice tilted her head in that pretty way of hers. "But of course you open the windows to let in fresh air."

Greystone withheld a laugh. Although Lady Beatrice had been in London only a few days, she surely had noticed the bad air in the city. But how could he contradict her without offending…again? "Actually, I had not thought to do that."

She gazed at him with innocent intensity, and his heart took a leap to rival any his horse had made during a fox-hunt. "I have noticed at certain times, especially in the morning, that a pleasant breeze stirs the air. I have opened my window and been quite refreshed, though of course not as much as if I were in the country."

A wistful note accompanied her last words. Perhaps her Season in London was not measuring up to her hopes and dreams. Greystone found himself wanting to rectify that situation. He immediately quashed that impulse.

"I believe that fresh air will help the boys after their—" her voice faltered so slightly, he almost missed it "—unfortunate childhood." She straightened and blew out a breath of impatience, as if annoyed with herself, then stared at him with more of that charming intensity. "Lord Greystone, I have nothing but admiration for your charitable endeavors."

He gave her a crooked grin, feeling as he had when he was a student receiving praise from a professor at Oxford. "It is my duty, Lady Beatrice." Now he sounded like

Mother, who deflected all praise with claims of merely doing her duty. In tending to her obligations, his only parent excelled, but her heart never seemed to be engaged. When he married, he prayed his wife would have a true devotion to her charitable enterprises, just as Lady Beatrice exhibited.

He shifted in his seat and stared out the window of the landau, suddenly annoyed that thoughts of his marriage quest never left him when he was with Lady Beatrice.

Lord Greystone's sudden reserve plunged the carriage into silence, and Mrs. Parton seemed to have run out of things to say, as well. After the gentleman's earlier reaction to her teasing, Beatrice did not think it her place to entertain her companions, so she withheld any further comments. This time she had not been the cause of the viscount's withdrawal, at least not in any way she could discern. Copying his behavior, she stared out the opposite window to watch the passing scenery.

Lord Blakemore's home sat just beyond Grosvenor Square on a large plot of land with many trees, a small park and several ponds that reflected the light of the torches lining the circular drive to the house. The air smelled of roses and lilacs, but a tantalizing hint of roasting meat wafted into the carriage to remind Beatrice that it had been many hours since she last ate. She hoped Lady Blakemore's midnight supper would not be delayed by formalities.

Along with other arriving carriages the landau stopped in front of the mansion's columned portico, and footmen hurried from the house to assist the guests. The edifice possessed a stately grace that would surely impress even the Prince Regent. Beatrice imagined that the park and flower gardens would be a delight to visit in the daytime.

Once inside in the crush of guests, ladies handed their

light wraps to servants, while gentlemen surrendered hats of varying descriptions. Beatrice followed Mrs. Parton up the two flights of stairs toward the second-floor drawing room, with Lord Greystone close behind them. She wished she could look behind to see if he objected to his role as escort to the two of them, but decided such a move would be ill-advised on a staircase, lest she lose her balance and he be forced to catch her.

Instead she cast admiring glances at the marble statuary on the landings and tall paintings of Blakemore ancestors high on the walls along the way. To her surprise a sweet sense of anticipation began to warm her heart. All her life she had looked forward to a London Season filled with balls and soirees and midnight suppers. Even though her dreams had been delayed, even though she was a mere companion rather than a lady making her rightful debut in Society, she would not be constrained by her circumstances. After all, Mrs. Parton did not advertise either Beatrice's reduced circumstances or her own generosity in providing this opportunity, along with an elegant new wardrobe. Due to their decision not to hide Beatrice's identity, none but the closest of Mrs. Parton's friends knew she was being paid to be here. Thus she could abandon herself to the experience and enjoy it to the fullest.

Lord and Lady Blakemore had already arrived and awaited their guests at the door of the drawing room. When the butler announced each person's name, other guests eyed the newcomer with curiosity, interest or admiration. Beatrice noticed a few gentlemen looking her way and, not being acquainted with any of them, averted her eyes. But she could not stop the warmth creeping up to her cheeks because of all this attention.

Hours ago when she had left Mrs. Parton's town house, she had been satisfied with her appearance and especially her lovely pink gown. Others must have found her acceptable as well, for during the play's intermission, several gentlemen had rushed to Lord Blakemore's theatre box for an introduction. But at Mrs. Parton's instruction, Lord Blakemore fended them all off. "Not our sort," the lady had insisted, with the earl and countess adding their agreement. Indeed, from appearances alone, Beatrice had approved the decision without qualification and had even noticed Lord Greystone's confirmation. Still, it was not an easy matter to reject such obvious admiration, even though she had no doubt each and every man would retreat upon learning that she had no dowry.

With that reminder the joy that had filled her as she ascended the staircase vanished. Only an exceptional gentleman would overlook that undesirable situation. And if it were not enough to ruin her prospects, there was always Melly and his wastrel ways.

Her thoughts had become morose, so she decisively shook them off and looked to Mrs. Parton to guide her for whatever came next. The lady was in the process of dismissing Lord Greystone, voicing all due appreciation for his escort from the theatre. He bowed to them both, then strode away as if eager to get someplace else. Beatrice felt the loss of his presence, but buoyed her spirits by surveying her surroundings.

They moved deeper into the room, which was furnished with exquisite oak and mahogany furniture upholstered in blue-and-gold brocade. A mahogany hearth served as the centerpiece, and the requisite painting of the family seat in Hampshire hung above the mantel. Three groupings of wing chairs and settees were arranged about the chamber, while red and white roses arranged in tall, golden vases sat on occasional tables, filling the room with their heady fragrances.

But soon the aroma of the roasting meat Beatrice had noticed upon arrival crowded out the scent of flowers, making her mouth water and her stomach demand satisfaction. Surely the meal would be announced soon, or she would have to find a place to sit down for all her dizziness.

"Mrs. Parton." A pleasant-looking gentleman approached and bowed over the lady's hand. "How lovely you are this evening. One may always depend upon you to brighten any room." To his credit his gaze did not leave Mrs. Parton's face, although anyone could see Beatrice standing close beside her.

"Why, such flattery, Winston, but I thank you nonetheless." Mrs. Parton's smile held nothing but approval, which piqued Beatrice's interest. "How well you look, my boy. I take it you are finding your footing without difficulty in the House of Lords?"

So the gentleman bore a title. Beatrice found her curiosity, if not her interest, growing. As Mrs. Parton had said, he did look well. Quite handsome, in fact, upon further scrutiny. Above medium height, more than a head taller than Beatrice, with blond hair and gray-green eyes, he exuded both confidence and boyishness. His black suit and pristine white shirt and cravat gave him an air of gravity, although not too severe. All in all he appeared to be everything proper in a gentleman. Yet Beatrice felt no stir of emotions as when she had met Lord Greystone. Perhaps such feelings were more of a hindrance than a reason to hope that a gentleman might find her appealing.

"Yes, madam, I am growing comfortable there. I have a mentor in Lord Bennington, which helps more than you can imagine." Now he glanced at Beatrice, but so quickly she almost missed it.

"Ah, yes, I heartily approve of Bennington as someone who can guide you." Mrs. Parton chuckled in her merry way. "I see you have noticed my lovely companion." She turned to Beatrice. "Lady Beatrice, may I present Lord Winston, a distant relative of mine whose barony patent goes back to the days of Henry VIII. Winston, may I present my...*friend,* Lady Beatrice?" Mrs. Parton's kind reference warmed Beatrice's heart.

"It is an honor, Lady Beatrice." Lord Winston executed a perfect bow over her extended hand as she curtseyed.

"I am pleased to meet you, Lord Winston." Beatrice decided to make her connections known at once. She refused to have another gentleman invest time in making her acquaintance only to flee. "Perhaps you have met my brother, Lord Melton?"

"Melton?" His blond eyebrows arched, but not in a manner to suggest disapproval. "Yes, of course. Pleasant fellow. Witty, actually."

Again Beatrice's heart warmed. "Yes, he has a fine wit."

"Dinner is served," the butler intoned from the doorway, and guests began moving in that direction.

"If you have no objection," Lord Winston said, "I should be honored to escort you ladies to supper." He glanced at Beatrice, but addressed Mrs. Parton. "And if I may be so bold, would you object if I call upon you next week?"

Beatrice drew in a quick breath. He knew of her brother, yet he still did not object to furthering their acquaintance.

"Of course I do not object, my boy. Do come calling."

He offered an arm to each of them as they lined up with the other guests in order of precedence for the processional to the dining room. As they moved toward the door Beatrice found herself staring ahead at Lord Greystone whose severe frown seemed to shout disapproval. But perhaps she misread that dark look. After all, if Mrs. Parton approved of Lord Winston, he must be above reproach.

Chapter Nine

"How fortunate that Lady Blakemore arranged for you to be seated next to Lord Winston." Still in her purple satin dressing gown, Mrs. Parton munched a buttered roll while early afternoon sunlight streamed in through the open window beside her. "You made quite an impression on him, my dear."

Sitting across from her at the small table in the lady's bedchamber, Beatrice sipped tea while she considered a response. Mrs. Parton had been more than kind in hiring her. Would she object if Beatrice acted the part of eligible lady rather than a companion? And if not, was Lord Winston a gentleman whom Beatrice wished to accept as a suitor?

"His attention was very flattering." And all the while Lord Greystone had given them dark looks from the opposite side of the table. Beatrice could not think of any reason for his obvious displeasure, and whether it was aimed at her or the baron.

Mrs. Parton gave her a quizzical look. "Do you have some objection to his interest?"

Her question sent Beatrice into a mild confusion. Her employer's entire demeanor suggested she had no opposition to Beatrice accepting suitors. But while she could not keep from hoping it was true, she dared not depend upon it.

"As kind as Lord Winston was to me, I noticed in him an obvious hauteur toward Mr. Penry, who sat on my left." The handsome, well-dressed young gentleman apparently had ties to trade, but Beatrice had no chance to pursue the subject. The baron had commanded all of her attention.

"Ah, yes." Mrs. Parton clicked her tongue. "Dear Winston has taken on old Bennington's haughtiness in regard to those whom they find inferior, especially those in trade. It seems that years ago Bennington's only sister eloped to America with a sea captain. Not a heroic naval captain, mind you, but a common merchant captain. Even before then, the old earl was always strict about social order. That is sure to rub off on Lord Winston." She shrugged and added a bit of butter to her roll. "But they are associated with the best people in Parliament and can be trusted to lead England in the wisest path. And like the ladies of their families, I suppose they have their charitable works, as well."

Beatrice could not imagine Lord Winston carrying an injured little chimney sweep to his nursery or seeing to the child's health and future. Oh, why had she been a witness to Lord Greystone's remarkable act of charity? She feared no gentleman could compete with his kindness and generosity, traits she would demand in anyone who wished to court her.

"Mind you," Mrs. Parton went on, "as a the daughter of an earl, you are worthy to marry the most august peer, even a duke, though I do not know of many unattached dukes I would recommend these days. I believe Blakemore's daughter snared the last of the good ones." She gazed off toward the window as if trying to remember any other such gentleman.

"Marry?" Beatrice could no longer bear the uncertainty of her position. "Dear Mrs. Parton, I must confess that one day I do hope to have my own husband, my own home. But it is my understanding that you brought me to London to be your companion, not to seek a husband."

The lady's jolly laughter filled the bedchamber. "But my dear, I am a romantic clear to my bones. If you fall in love with a worthy gentleman, of course you must marry."

Happiness bubbled up inside Beatrice, even as tears coursed down her cheeks. "I knew it. I knew my mother's dear friend would rescue me." She reached across the table, almost spilling the white china creamer, and grasped Mrs. Parton's fingers with a trembling hand. "You are too kind, madam. Too kind."

"Not at all, my dear." Mrs. Parton returned a gentle squeeze, her eyes shining. "We were four merry girls together in boarding school—your mother, Grace, Frances and I, all dreaming of handsome peers to whisk us off to marital bliss." She straightened and dabbed her eyes with her serviette. "Three of us did make remarkable love matches. One of us was not so fortunate."

Beatrice quizzed her with a teary look. "Do you refer to my parents?"

"Not at all, my dear. They were happy in their own way. One cannot judge by one's own expectations." She leveled a meaningful gaze on Beatrice, but Beatrice could not grasp that meaning.

"But who, then?"

"Lady Greystone." Mrs. Parton leaned toward her. "You must not think this is gossip, my dear. I simply wish for you to understand the lady next door, the mother and only parent to three remarkable sons." She sniffed, more from indignation than to manage her tears. "Had their cruel, abusive father lived to rear them, I despair to think of how they might have turned out."

"Ah. I see." Beatrice sent up a silent prayer of gratitude that Papa had merely been neglectful, although some might consider neglect a form of cruelty. "I thank you for telling me." Now she began to comprehend Lady Greystone's severe demeanor. "Your words are safe with me."

"Now enough of this." Mrs. Parton inhaled a deep breath and peered out the window beside her. Her gaze seemed to focus on something beyond Beatrice's view, and one eyebrow arched while a wily look glinted in her eyes. She glanced at Beatrice's morning dress, then at her own purple dressing gown. "Ah, what a beautiful day. We must hurry and put on our new day dresses and bonnets and go out for a drive."

"Oh, I should like that." Beatrice downed the last of her tea and rose to leave. On the way to her room she realized she should have urged Mrs. Parton to take the landau and let the chauffeur drive. If her employer insisted upon driving the phaeton, Beatrice's enjoyment of the afternoon would be severely challenged.

"I have never seen a happier couple." Greystone sat opposite his brother Edmond and his new bride as his barouche wended its way through the streets toward Hyde Park. He sat with his back to the driver, having given his guests the place of honor so they could observe the oncoming scenery, but they seemed to want only to view each other. "If you were both not already handsome to a fault, your happiness would make you so." Greystone had never known Edmond to display a temper. But then, he had not known their father. Surely Anna would be safe from the cruelty Mother had endured. Their children would suffer no whip, as Greystone had.

His arm entwined with Anna's, Edmond gazed fondly at his bride, who returned a glowing smile. "Your approval means the world to us, brother," Edmond said.

Greystone grimaced. "I assume you refer to our mother's lack of the same."

"Oh, dear." Anna frowned. "I do hope Mother Greystone no longer harbors objections to our marriage." Her dark brown curls, pushed forward by her bonnet, formed the perfect frame for her fair countenance. "She could not have been more helpful with the wedding." Worry filled her eyes. "Is she terribly lonely? I mean—" She bit her lower lip.

"Do not concern yourself, sister." Greystone wished he had not mentioned his parent. Perhaps he should add some humor to the discussion. "Mother has always found ways to keep herself busy." He sat back, picturing the scene he had come upon the day before. "Yesterday Lucy lost track of the chimney sweeps, and when I came home Mother was in a high temper." He chuckled at the memory, feeling not the slightest bit of guilt. Mother always failed to see the humor in life's absurdities.

"Oh, dear." Anna's green eyes clouded. "Perhaps Lucy is not suited to the job."

"Ah, well," Greystone said, "she is young and still learning. Furthermore, I have no doubt that once the boys no longer bear the sooty signs of their former trade, Mother will make them her little pages."

Edmond barked out a disbelieving laugh. "You want to let her rear two boys, considering the way she reared her own three sons?"

Greystone shrugged and shook his head. With two liveried footmen riding on the back of the barouche and able to hear every word, he really should not make or encourage disparaging remarks about their parent, for it would only foster disrespect for her amongst the servants. "'Tis a fine day, is it not?"

Edmond signaled his understanding with a slight nod. "Indeed it is."

Greystone leaned back to enjoy it all. The breeze was not too brisk, the city odors not too pungent and the sun not too hot. He had left Parliament early after voicing support of Lord Blakemore's current project. Now he wanted to let his mind wander to less serious matters. Thus he had invited his brother and sister-in-law to join him for a drive. He owed his life to this lady, for she had nursed him through his illness last winter, and her gentle nature soothed not only him, but his whole household. Had Edmond not claimed her first, he might have developed stronger feelings for her than brotherly affection. But from the moment he had met her, he could see their mutual interest and had done all he could to encourage their love, despite Mother's attempts to destroy it.

The carriage driver pulled the horses to a stop at the entrance to Hyde Park. "Begging your pardon, milord, do you have a particular path you'd like to take?"

"Not at all, Porter." He looked over his shoulder at the stout, greying man. "Surprise me."

"Yes, milord." The driver touched the brim of his hat and turned back to urge the horses forward.

As they started down the road, a gust of wind carried the pastoral scents of mown grass and lilacs, just the thing to make the drive more pleasant. Greystone even detected the scent of meat pies, doubtless coming from a vendor's cart somewhere in the park.

"Perhaps we could find Mother Greystone another companion." Anna gazed off and tapped a gloved finger against her cheek, as if trying to think of just such a person.

"And have some poor girl suffer under her temper as you did, my darling?" Edmond winced as he realized his error. "By the by, Greystone, I noticed that the companion Mrs. Parton boasted about has arrived. From across the room at your birthday ball I could see that Lady Beatrice is quite a pretty girl." He glanced at Anna. "Though not quite the fairest of the fair." He turned a teasing smirk toward Greystone. "You could do worse than marry the sister of an earl. And she lives right next door to you. How convenient."

"Do keep your matchmaking plans to yourself, Edmond." An odd sensation filled Greystone, an unpleasant twisting of some sort in the vicinity of his stomach. "I refuse to be attached to Melton in any way." Now the unpleasant feeling rose into his throat. Why did his own careless words regarding Lady Beatrice seem so distasteful? "In any event she was quite taken with Lord Winston last night at Blakemore's supper. And, I might add, the fellow was quite taken with her."

"Lord Winston?" Edmond coughed away a laugh. "Poor fellow. I wish him well."

He leaned toward his Anna, and she gazed up at him so devotedly that Greystone's heart ached. How grand it must be to share that kind of love. And to think, Mother had tried to pair Anna with Lord Winston.

Forcing his thoughts in a more charitable direction, Greystone wished the young peacock well. The baron had done admirably to attach himself to Lord Bennington, unlike Melton, who had chosen Rumbold for a mentor. But Greystone did not care at all for Winston courting Lady Beatrice. She deserved—come to think of it, what did such a lovely, accomplished lady deserve? Certainly not a stuffy baron several ranks below her brother. In fact she also did not deserve a brother who prevented her from making a match worthy of her grace and beauty.

And what was he doing in regard to his own marriage search? All he could manage was a hopeful prayer that the Almighty would direct him to a lady who suited him as well as his brothers' wives suited them. And the sooner the better, before Mother tried to force someone of her choosing upon him. *Lord, Thou knowest whom I should marry. I pray Thee, do make haste and bring her across my path.*

To rein in the envy trying to seep into his soul as he watched the happy couple across from him, he stared out over the park. A flurry of activity near the entrance caught his attention. Horsemen, nurses with carriages, barking dogs and pedestrians were scattering in all directions, and he soon saw the reason. A black phaeton pulled by a lathered gray horse galloped across the roadway and onto the grass. As best he could see, the carriage was driven by a lady, with another lady clutching the side of the vehicle and back of the seat. When they drew nearer, he saw the lady's footman reach for his wig just as it flew from his head, while the tiger was grasping for his hat. Clearly the horse was out of control. Horror swept through Greystone as he recognized the driver.

"Great heavens, it's Mrs. Parton!" *And Lady Beatrice!* "Porter, stop. Edmond, we must stop them."

Before the barouche came to a stop, Greystone jumped out, beckoning his footmen with a snap of his fingers. They leaped from their perch, and the four men dashed across the meadow toward the oncoming horse.

"Whoa, whoa!" Edmond raced ahead, crossed the beast's path and lunged for the harness, while Greystone flung himself at the other side, securing a hold but failing to stop it. They were dragged across the grass, even when the footmen added their weight to the endeavor. At last

Edmond managed to employ his cavalry experience and leaped upon the creature to bring it to a stop with another resounding "Whoa!" The horse reared on its hind legs and whinnied in protest, but obeyed the order, then stood shuddering and huffing as if grateful to be under control.

"Oh, bother." Mrs. Parton, whose green peacock feathers hung half-broken from her slightly askew orange turban, looked at her rescuers with mild annoyance. "Why ever did you stop us, Greystone, Edmond? Did you not see I was giving my horse some much-needed exercise?"

"Mrs. Parton." Gripping the bridle, Greystone puffed out her name as he struggled to catch his breath. He had never scolded a lady, but he was having great difficulty not doing so now. Her companion's face was paler than ivory, her blue eyes widened, and she still grasped the side of the vehicle, yet she made no sound. Brave girl!

"Perhaps your grooms should take on that responsibility from now on." What possessed this dear lady to do such a thing? Was she losing her mind?

"Nonsense, my boy." Mrs. Parton's eyes crossed briefly as one broken feather waved in front of them and dropped into her lap. "Oh, bother. One of my favorites, too."

"Will you excuse me?" Eyes blazing, Edmond dismounted, gave the lady a curt bow and hurried back to his bride. Anna's face wore the same alarm they all felt, except for Mrs. Parton.

"Lady Beatrice." Greystone could not fail to be impressed by her straight, stoic posture. "Are you all right?"

"Yes." The single word came out on a high-pitched whisper, accompanied by a shudder so slight that, had he blinked, he would have missed it. "I thank you, Lord Greystone." She looked at Mrs. Parton, who was fussing with the reins as if impatient to continue her journey. "Madam, if you have no objection, may we walk about the park for a while? I should very much like to view the Serpentine."

Greystone did not miss the slight pleading tone in her breathless voice. "A splendid plan. Do allow me to escort both of you ladies to the river. We may even be able to purchase some meat pies and lemonade from that man over there with the food cart." By no means would he permit Mrs. Parton to drive away, with or without the young lady. "Please honor me with your presence, both of you. Edmond and his bride are—"

Mrs. Parton interrupted with a hearty sneeze. And another even stronger. "Oh, bother." She retrieved a lace-edged handkerchief from her reticule and sniffed into it. "They have just mown the grass, have they not? That always sets me to sneezing. *Tsk.* I should have sent someone to inquire before starting out." A sigh of resignation escaped her. "Just when I wanted to enjoy a day in the park." She emphasized her complaint with yet another sneeze. "Oh, do forgive me. We must return home." She tugged at her gloves, then gathered the reins.

"Perhaps my lady would consider—" The footman jumped down from his perch.

"I should check the horse—" The tiger grasped the bridle.

"Madam, surely after this adventure—" Greystone spoke at the same moment the other men so cleverly and respectfully voiced their protests. All stopped, and he took charge.

"Mrs. Parton, you have all my sympathy. I can see the elements are not favoring you today. Perhaps this good man—" he patted the tiger's shoulder "—could drive you. The phaeton has room only for two, so I shall take Lady Beatrice home. That is, after she has seen the Serpentine."

He felt certain the sudden tears and puffiness around

Mrs. Parton's eyes could not be feigned. This was not a part of some matchmaking scheme. The dear lady was truly suffering.

"Oh, bother." She sniffed into her handkerchief again, then sneezed. Through her tears, she looked at Lady Beatrice. "My dear, will you think I've deserted you?"

Lady Beatrice tilted her head in her pretty way and blinked at Mrs. Parton. How could a lady look so charming in the midst of her fright? "W-why, if it will not trouble Lord Greystone and his guests, I would not mind at all."

"Very good." Mrs. Parton eyed her footman. "Charles, you have lost your wig."

"Did I?" The young man patted his head. "Coo, mum, how careless of me." Greystone wanted to laugh at the lad's performance. A good servant never criticized his employer.

"Well, you look better without it. I really must reconsider the livery my servants wear. Now, shall we go?" Mrs. Parton waved to her tiger. "Home, Harry."

The footman returned to his post while the tiger took over the reins, and soon the phaeton was rumbling toward the park's entrance. Greystone could not be certain, but he thought he heard Mrs. Parton's inimitable laughter trailing after them. A tendril of suspicion crept into his mind, cut short when Lady Beatrice released a sigh so profound, he feared she was about to faint. Yet when he offered his arm, she gripped it firmly and gave him a steely look, as if she was determined not to succumb to her fright.

"To the Serpentine, Lord Greystone."

"Your servant, madam." He gave her a slight bow even as his heart lurched oddly. *Lord, please do not let me become attached to this charming, yet unsuitable young lady.* But the echo of the prayer for a wife he had lifted only seconds before the phaeton arrived at the park resounded within him.

No, Lord. Surely not.

Chapter Ten

The instant Beatrice took Lord Greystone's arm, a sense of security flooded her, as if she had gripped a rock. The feeling came from more than the strong forearm muscles so evident despite the thick fabric of his sleeve. Even if the viscount had not so heroically risked his life to stop the horse, his entire being exuded stability, safety, sanctuary, all the things she had longed for her entire life. All the things Papa and poor Melly lacked. Yet this gentleman confounded her. One moment he studied her with seeming admiration and concern. The next he turned away with a furrowed brow, as if refusing to grant her his good opinion.

For now she would simply be grateful for his intervention in Mrs. Parton's wild driving. While the other gentleman and the two liveried footmen had certainly done their part, especially the one who'd leaped upon the horse, it was Lord Greystone who had surprised her. One did not think of a prominent peer as someone willing to risk his life to stop a runaway horse. She had never seen Papa put himself out in the slightest way for anyone, much less risk his life. Lord Greystone truly was a remarkable gentleman.

While the two footmen hurried ahead, Beatrice and the viscount walked in silence toward a barouche that likewise was moving in their direction. The driver reined the four white horses to a stop, and one footman opened the door and folded down the step. A lady already in the conveyance moved from the front facing bench to the opposite one, and Lord Greystone directed Beatrice to the newly vacated place of honor. He settled on the white leather seat beside her, and the other gentleman took his place beside the lady.

"Lady Beatrice," the viscount said as the carriage moved forward, "may I present my brother and sister-in-law, Mr. and Mrs. Grenville?" He gave them a teasing smirk. "Do not expect much conversation from them. They have recently married and think they are the only two people in the world."

"May I offer my congratulations?" Beatrice smiled at the pretty bride. "Mrs. Grenville, your husband was beyond heroic in stopping the phaeton, as was Lord Greystone. Did you see them?" She still felt a bit breathless, and her words rushed out like a schoolgirl's.

"Indeed I did." The lady gazed at her new husband adoringly. "I was terrified for them and for you ladies, but I would not have expected any less from either of them."

"Edmond was a cavalry officer until recently." In spite of the careless way Lord Greystone brushed dust from his coat and breeches, his proud tone revealed an admirable fondness for his brother. "He has hung up his uniform for a barrister's wig."

"Both are commendable occupations, Mr. Grenville." Beatrice loved her brother, too, yet she could feel no pride in his actions of the past few years.

But she must not think of Melly in this pleasant company. Lord Greystone was the host, and she must look to him to direct the conversation. For the moment, he chose to be silent.

"Oh, look, Edmond." Mrs. Grenville sat up and pointed her ivory fan toward some object in the distance. "Remember the bench under that willow?"

Mr. Grenville nodded, but his gaze remained on his wife. "I came very near to declaring myself to you that day."

"And I to you," she said. "Ah, well. That came soon enough and in the Lord's time." They locked gazes, and both wore beatific smiles. Lord Greystone had been accurate in his description of their mutual devotion. Even as Beatrice admired them, she wondered if she would ever know such love. But whom could she trust to love her as this gentleman loved his bride?

"Ahem." Lord Greystone coughed artificially. "What did I tell you, Lady Beatrice?"

Dismissing her dismal thoughts, she laughed. "Come now, sir, have some understanding. One day you may fall in love. Then no doubt you will see the matter differently." From where had she summoned such a bold suggestion? She did not know the viscount well enough to tease him in this manner.

At first he blinked, and his jaw dropped slightly. Then he gave her a mischievous grin and rolled his eyes. "Heaven forefend. I shall never be as besotted as Edmond. Why, look at him. He does not even know you and I are in the carriage."

Relieved by his pleasant response, Beatrice nodded soberly. "Nor does she."

"What?" The gentleman in question turned their way. "Did you address us?" Now he gave his wife a sweet smile. "Anna, my darling, would you like to take a stroll and visit our special bench?"

"Why, Edmond, I cannot think of anything I would rather do."

With one lifted eyebrow Mr. Grenville questioned his brother, to whom he bore a remarkable resemblance.

"Yes, of course," Lord Greystone said. "I did promise Lady Beatrice a view of the Serpentine. Porter, take us over to yon willow tree."

"Yes, milord." The man directed the horses along the meadow road and drew them up on a patch of grass.

After the footmen assisted everyone from the carriage, Lord Greystone ordered them to fetch refreshments. Beatrice had eaten but a small breakfast, and after her ordeal, she looked forward to making up for her lack of food.

To her surprise, as they all walked toward the lush weeping willow, Mrs. Grenville forsook her husband's company and looped an arm around one of Beatrice's. "I have been looking forward to meeting you, Lady Beatrice. For weeks Mrs. Parton has been announcing your coming with great delight. Now that you are here, I know you will be a great comfort to her since her last child has married."

"I thank you, Mrs. Grenville." Although Beatrice was uncertain of the lady's rank, she permitted the familiarity. If she was learning nothing else from Mrs. Parton, it was that a person's worth and character could not be measured in titles or wealth. "However, I do hope I can persuade her to leave the driving to her servants."

"Oh, my, yes." Mrs. Grenville laughed. "I shall pray to that end. Ah, here we are."

Lord Greystone and his brother parted the tree's graceful branches like a curtain, revealing the promised stone bench, a shady refuge with a picturesque view of the river. The moment the two ladies sat, their arms still linked, Beatrice felt a kinship with her new acquaintance. Having no sister, she had always longed for an intimate female friend. Perhaps Mrs. Grenville was the answer to her prayers. Summoning courage, she decided to make her first attempt at forging a friendship.

"Mrs. Grenville, I understand you were Lady Greystone's companion." Beatrice would not be so rude as to ask how she bore the viscountess's haughty ways. "How did you come to that position?"

A shadow crossed the lady's face. "Mama died years ago, and then my father died last October. Papa was a poor country vicar, and though he thought he had left me a small inheritance, it could not be located. I was utterly destitute." She glanced toward her husband with a smile. "But our heavenly Father never forsakes us. He sent Major Grenville to me—he was bringing news of my brother, with whom he served in America. When the major learned of my situation, he took me straightaway to his mother, Lady Greystone, to be her companion." A soft laugh escaped her. "The lady was not entirely pleased, for she found that my coming overset her orderly world. But she grew to accept me—somewhat."

Beatrice stifled a laugh. So Lady Greystone disliked this sweet girl, too. "And it would appear that Major Grenville's world was a bit overset, as well. It is a testimony to his love for you that he gave up his army career."

"Indeed. But Edmond had always wanted to be a barrister. With Uncle Grenville's sponsorship and tutelage at the Inns of Courts, he will soon be able to accept his own clients." She cast another adoring glance at her husband before turning back to Beatrice. "Now it is your turn. Please tell me about yourself." Her fair cheeks turned a little pink. "That is, if I am not being impertinent to ask."

"Not at all." Beatrice gave her a reassuring smile. Everything about Mrs. Grenville invited confidence, and she seemed to want a friend, as well. As a vicar's daughter, surely she had heard her own share of confessions from her father's female parishioners. Confident of her discretion, Beatrice decided to trust her and dismissed a lifetime of reserve. "In truth, I am in much the same position that you were in before Mr. Grenville rescued you, although not quite as severe." She sighed as memories surged forth. "My parents are both gone, too, and my brother has held the title of Lord Melton for three years. In that time, he has fallen in with bad company and has wasted his entire fortune, including my dowry."

"Oh, my dear." Mrs. Grenville gripped Beatrice's hand, and her eyes reddened. "How you must grieve his fall."

Beatrice jolted slightly. This lady had unknowingly exposed her selfishness. She had meant to garner some commiseration regarding the loss of her wealth, especially her dowry, but Mrs. Grenville rightly pointed out what should be her greatest grief. "Yes, I do." It was not a lie.

"And of course that places you in a difficult position." Mrs. Grenville squeezed her hand. "Yet our heavenly Father did not leave you without resources either, for Mrs. Parton has taken you in." A twinkle lit her green eyes. "I think she must be a delightful lady to work for, wild driving notwithstanding."

Beatrice answered with a nod and a laugh.

"Well, then, we shall pray for Lord Melton to see the error of his ways and discover that true happiness can be found only in the Lord." Mrs. Grenville's fervent sentiments sent a warm flood of reassurance through Beatrice. What a good friend she had found! What a good example to follow. In spite of all the lady had suffered, she had never lost her faith in God. Beatrice prayed she could follow Mrs. Grenville's example and trust the Lord, even if she never found a trustworthy husband.

Seated together on the stone bench, the ladies made a pretty picture, and Greystone had a sudden urge to hire

their portraits painted this very day. But of course that
was nonsense and far too familiar a gesture toward a lady
he had no intention of knowing better. In any event Anna
had some skill at portraiture, so perhaps she would feel
inclined to paint her companion, should they become intimate friends. The thought of fostering that friendship
pleased him. Mentors such as Mrs. Parton were all well
and good, but nothing could be compared to having a
friend near one's own age. Mother, Mrs. Parton and Lady
Blakemore had each other, and Greystone valued his two
brothers as more precious than gold.

Now the ladies leaned together as closely as their wide-
brimmed bonnets would permit, and whispered just like
schoolgirls. From their smiles he expected them to break
forth in girlish giggles at any moment. He was more than
pleased to see Lady Beatrice enjoying herself, especially
with another lady. Last night she had been the epitome of
grace, yet he could see across the table that Lord Winston
was boring her beyond words.

Neither would Greystone have been pleased to see her
talk with Mr. Penry, who sat on her other side. He had
nothing against the man, except that he was in trade. How
curious that Blakemore invited several people of no promi-
nence to his supper. By giving them a minor bit of consequence, the earl seemed to say they could be considered
marriageable with members of the *ton*. And that would
not do at all.

No, in the matter of Lady Beatrice's prospects he must
look around for someone whose influence would not be
affected by her brother's wastrel ways. A duke, perhaps,
or someone from a reputable branch of the royal family
such as one of the distant cousins of the Prince Regent,
as long as the gentleman was of better moral character
than the prince. Even an earl could not be as tainted by

Melton as would a viscount, no matter how spotless that viscount's reputation.

But each thought of pairing the gentle lady with any man made his stomach twist as if he had indigestion. Nor should he continue to stare at her, even though he found her presence both soothing and disturbing. He strolled several yards away to escape the scent of her rose perfume, wondering idly why the footman was taking so long to purchase the meat pies.

Edmond followed and nudged him with his elbow. "Why the sour face? Our lovely companions will think you are displeased to be with them."

Greystone grunted. "Far from it. You know of my brotherly affection for your bride, but I find myself enjoying Lady Beatrice's company all too well."

Edmond chuckled. "And why is that a problem?"

Greystone glared at him briefly, but perhaps his crossness was ill-placed. "Her brother is under the influence of Frank Rumbold and has gambled away his father's fortune in three short years."

"Yes, I have heard that. But are you saying you reject the lady because of her brother's habits and associations?" Edmond shook his head in obvious disbelief. "I thank the Lord you did not abandon me when I fell under evil influences and lost my way in the gambling world. I shall ever be grateful to you for your constancy."

Greystone shrugged off his praise, even as fraternal affection warmed his heart. "You are a good man, Edmond. It was well worth the efforts to redeem you. Look what you've made of yourself."

"But Lady Beatrice requires no redeeming." Edmond glanced toward the ladies, who were still in deep conversation. "Yes, she is the sister of a misguided young peer, but she is also the daughter of an earl who left a solid if not remarkable legacy in Parliament."

"Ah, I see you have already started your law studies if you know what has happened in Parliament in recent years." Greystone began to regret bringing up the subject. He had expected Edmond's understanding and support.

"Do not change the subject." Edmond gripped Greystone's shoulder. "I am not suggesting that you pursue a lady you cannot love. I am merely saying you must not reject love because of something that is not her fault."

Greystone huffed out a sigh of annoyance. "Edmond, you know what Mother taught us. It is imperative that one's connections be above reproach if one is to accomplish anything. I am drawing up a bill to present in the House of Lords regarding the protection of climbing-boys. Those who oppose the measure will look for any reason to block my success."

Edmond nodded, but then shook his head. "A very commendable undertaking, to be sure. But Mother is not always right about everything."

"Here you are, milord." The footman approached with a large hamper. "When the pie man heard it was for you, he insisted upon preparing something special."

Grateful for the interruption, Greystone waved the footman toward the ladies. "Over by the bench, John."

The clever fellow retrieved a small table and two chairs that were kept tucked away in the boot of the carriage for just such occasions as this. Soon the party of four sat around the cloth-covered board enjoying simple meat pies, lemonade and strawberry tarts topped with clotted cream.

"What a lovely day." Lady Beatrice appeared freer of care than Greystone had ever seen her. "And to think they serve such delights in the park."

She took a bite of a tart, and a dot of cream remained

beside her lips. Which he decided in that moment were the most well-formed lips he had ever observed. Not that he was in the habit of studying lips. He had the urge to dab away the cream, but surely Anna would notice it and take care of the matter. No, of course she would not, for she was gazing, as always, at her new husband.

"Ah, well." Edmond gave Greystone a meaningful look and tilted his head toward her. "Wherever you find potential customers, you will find someone selling something."

"I suppose." Lady Beatrice took another bite and added more cream to her cheek. "Mmm. Delicious. I never imagined fresh cream was available in London. Why, one would think we were out in the country."

Greystone shot a cross look at Edmond before offering the lady a smile. "Madam, will you grant me the liberty of—" Using his serviette to clean away the spot, he tried not to touch her, but his finger brushed her soft cheek. For the briefest instant all strength left his arm.

In that same instant, she gasped. Then laughed. "Oh, my. Well, I suppose my manners are out in the country, as well."

While the others joined her in laughing, Greystone swallowed hard, forcing down the emotions trying so hard to overwhelm him. He must not fall in love with this lady. He *must* not.

Chapter Eleven

They finished their impromptu picnic, and Mr. Grenville suggested a walk along the Serpentine. "Forgive me, Lady Beatrice, I must steal my bride away from you. You do not object, do you?" Without waiting for an answer, and completely ignoring Lord Greystone's protests, the couple strolled away, lost once more in their own private world.

"Well." Beatrice stared after them, wondering how her mother would have repaired this awkward moment. Clearly the viscount did not wish to be alone with her.

"Well," Lord Greystone echoed. Hands fisted at his waist, he also stared after the retreating couple. Then he eyed Beatrice and offered his arm. "My lady, will you walk with me?" His teasing tone reminded her of Melly in his better days.

Returning a curtsey, she simpered, "Oh, my lord, I should be delighted." She looped her arm around his, then wondered if he had meant for her merely to set her hand on it. His placid expression gave her no clue or relief.

"'Tis a fine day." He waved his free hand to take in the sun, cloudless sky and the nearby bed of musky-scented marigolds where gardeners labored to remove weeds. "Would you not agree?"

Now she understood. He was recalling their few moments of levity in Mrs. Parton's landau last night as they drove to the play. Could she trust him to continue the jest, or would he back away again? "Oh, my lord, of course I would agree. Have I not told you? All young ladies are schooled to agree with gentlemen."

"As I have no sisters, I cannot answer yea or nay to their schooling." He furrowed his brow. "But I must confess that I enjoy a good argument, otherwise I would be dreadfully out of place in the House of Lords."

"Aha. Then I shall offer an argument." She smirked, but her heart was in her throat as she risked the joke. "To please you, of course."

He laughed in his musical baritone way. "Very good. What shall we argue about?"

"Why, since you postulated that the day is fine, offering evidence of the sun and a clear sky and those lovely blossoms—" she nodded toward the marigolds "—I must counter that the excessive heat causes a lady to wilt like an unwatered flower." To emphasize her claim, she brought up her fan and waved it vigorously.

"Humph. Well played." He thought for a moment. "Then I must counter that anyone can see that this heat is preferable to the bitter winter we have recently suffered."

"Humph, yourself." Beatrice scrambled for a response. "I cannot imagine that you experienced anything at all of the cold in Shropshire. In County Durham we felt the brunt of the North Sea wind all winter." She searched her mind for some of the witty remarks the villagers back home had made to buoy their spirits even as they'd suffered. "Why, it was so cold that the sheep were asking that we return the previous winter's wool because one coat was not sufficient to keep them warm." Oh, dear, that was rather clumsy. She must try harder.

But Lord Greystone seemed not to mind. He merely scratched his chin and scrunched his handsome face thoughtfully. "That was a mere trifle, dear lady. It was so cold in Shropshire that the foxes knocked at the door of the kennel to come in for warmth amongst our hounds."

"Humph." Beatrice pictured the absurd scene but would not grant him the favor of laughing. "I wore three woolen shawls every day. Sometimes four."

"We gentlemen shaved with a blade of ice."

"The smoke from all the chimneys froze in the air and did not melt until March." She emphasized her words with a shudder.

"Our suppers froze before the footmen could get them to the table."

"Our horses had to drink tea because all of the water troughs were frozen." She punctuated this with a smirk.

He chuckled, then laughed out loud. "My lady, I do believe you have bested me."

She shot him a smug look. "I have the advantage of having—" She stopped before blurting out that debating with Melly had honed her skills. That would entirely ruin this delightful afternoon. "Having a quick female mind not cluttered with weighty affairs of state."

He placed his palm against his forehead. "Terribly weighty, indeed. You cannot imagine."

Suddenly serious, she stopped and gazed up at him, her heart soaring with appreciation. "No, Lord Greystone, I cannot imagine."

He stared down at her, his gaze soft, and her pulse began to race. Was his opinion of her changing? Would he now regard her with kindness? If so, she would not ask for more.

As the elegant barouche rolled closer to Hanover Square, Beatrice wondered if she would ever again enjoy such a lovely afternoon as she had with her newfound friends. Lord Greystone's wit was delightful, and she had felt entirely free to jest with him. Although he continued to waver between amiability and sullenness, she decided his moodiness did not concern her. After all, he sat in Parliament and helped to rule England. Surely, even in his times of leisure, important thoughts invaded his mind that had nothing to do with his neighbor's companion.

She would not think his witty banter signified any further interest in her. Nor would she regard his removing the cream from her cheek as any more than a kind gesture intended to save her from embarrassment. She must forget the pleasant shivers that swept through her at his touch, must forget the way her heart leaped when he turned those blue eyes in her direction, whether accompanied by a smile or a frown.

To her surprise Lord Greystone ordered the driver to convey the Grenvilles home first, even though it meant she would be along for the ride all the way to St. James's Square, and then home to Hanover Square. It was a matter of convenience, she supposed, for taking her to Mrs. Parton's first would have been the cause of extra driving. But as it was still daylight and the carriage top was down, her being out with the viscount could not be considered improper.

Due to her uncertainty over whether she would ever see Mrs. Grenville again, Beatrice gave her an awkward but fond embrace before the lady disembarked from the carriage.

"Oh, we shall be friends, Lady Beatrice." Mrs. Grenville brushed a kiss on her cheek. "You may depend upon it."

"I hope so. Pray so." Beatrice already sensed the influence of the lady's faith upon her and did not wish to lose it.

Yet once they left the happy couple behind, Beatrice sat opposite Lord Greystone, feeling a bit bereft. And terribly awkward, for the gentleman seemed inclined to silence once again. But whereas she had thought his prior quietness her fault, she decided not to take the blame now. After all, he had freely invited her to stay in the park, had even offered an arm to take her for that short stroll beside the Serpentine after their tasty repast. Had bantered freely, even encouraged her in their jests. These were courtesies he might extend to any lady, but no rule of Society demanded it of him, and he certainly owed her nothing. Nor did she fault him for not speaking now. Perhaps they had exhausted every topic of interest for the day. With that settled in her mind, she sat back and enjoyed the passing scenery.

The carriage stopped in front of Mrs. Parton's town house, a four-story brick building with five bays across the front. Beatrice glanced up to a second-floor window just in time to see her employer wave, then disappear. What was she up to?

"I do hope Mrs. Parton has recovered from her affliction." Not waiting for the footman, Lord Greystone stepped down to the pavement and offered Beatrice his hand. "I should like to come in and find out so I can give my mother a report on her health."

"How very thoughtful." Once again the viscount surprised her with his kindness, something Beatrice had never observed in her father or brother. She accepted his assistance, and they both proceeded up the four front steps.

The butler had no doubt been watching, for he opened the door straightaway. "Lady Beatrice, Lord Greystone, Mrs. Parton is expecting you. Please wait in the drawing room."

Lord Greystone chuckled. "I believe that answers my question."

They did not have long to wait, for Mrs. Parton soon bustled into the room in her inimitable way and embraced them by turns.

"My darlings, I do hope you had a lovely time." She cast an expectant glance at Beatrice.

"Indeed I did. We had a delightful picnic, and Lord Greystone took me on that promised stroll beside the Serpentine." The enjoyment of the day bubbled over inside Beatrice, and she felt like a child reporting a happy event to her mother. "The river is beautiful, but I never realized it was man-made and more a lake than a river. Such lovely natural foliage grows all around it, and Lord Greystone pointed out the gardeners planting flower beds nearby." Oh, goodness, she really must quit babbling. The viscount would think her a ninny. If she could only reclaim her air of indifference toward him—but that was becoming more and more impossible.

"Ah, flower beds. That's just the thing to enhance the park's beauty." Mrs. Parton beamed her pleasure over the news. "I would imagine many gardens will be planted to celebrate Napoleon's defeat."

"But we are being neglectful, dear lady." Lord Greystone studied Mrs. Parton's face. "You look well, but have you recovered from your affliction?"

"Oh, pish tosh, of course I have." She sniffed nonetheless. "I simply must avoid new mown grass or hay and certain flowers—oh, dear, I hope they aren't planting marigolds."

Beatrice traded a look with Lord Greystone, but neither said a word. That silent understanding made her heart skip.

"But enough of that," Mrs. Parton said. "Now Greystone, your dear mama is out for the evening, so you must dine with us. That is, unless you have plans. Though I warn you, if you are going someplace interesting and proper, we will insist upon accompanying you. Will we not, Bea?" She squeezed Beatrice's hand and gave her a maternal smile, but a hint of slyness shone in her eyes.

Cringing as always at the byname Mrs. Parton insisted upon using for her, Beatrice did not dare confirm her assertion. She had been entirely too bold several times that afternoon. Instead she gave the lady a noncommittal smile.

"Mother is out?" Lord Greystone appeared a bit discomfited. "With whom?"

"Why, with Mr. Grenville, of course."

"My uncle?" His voice rose slightly, and his eyes widened, as if the idea shocked him, although Beatrice could not guess why.

"Why, of course." Mrs. Parton spoke with feigned impatience and even waggled a finger at him. "Now, see here Greystone, you know they have reconciled at last and are deeply fond of each other. While it is true that the Church and English rules of consanguinity and affinity forbid a lady to marry her late husband's brother, nothing prevents them from being good friends." She chuckled. "And just to silence the gossips, Mrs. Hudson is accompanying them. Can you imagine that? A chaperone at their ages?" She wagged her head from side to side, and her curls bounced their agreement with her humorous remark. "Now, do you have any plans for this evening?"

"No, no plans, but—"

"Good. That settles it." Mrs. Parton clapped her hands. "We shall dine at ten. In the meantime, go home and freshen up." She clutched his arm and led him toward the door. "I feel cheated over not having my time in the park today, and you two simply must provide me with some diversion."

"Of course, madam." Lord Greystone's smile was more of a grimace. "I am your servant."

As he bowed away from her and strode toward the door, Beatrice could not begin to guess why he would do Mrs. Parton's bidding when he clearly did not wish to.

If Greystone had any doubts that Mrs. Parton was trying to pair him with Lady Beatrice, this evening wiped them all away tidily. But he could not be certain the young lady was involved in her machinations. After all, as evident as her enjoyment of the afternoon had been, she had been quiet, almost dour in the carriage ride after they had left Edmond and Anna. He had not pressed her to talk. Indeed he had not been able to think of a single subject they'd not exhausted at the park, not to mention their delightful debate over the miseries of last winter. Now while Mrs. Parton, seated at the head of the table, prattled on about this and that, Lady Beatrice sat across from him, concentrating on her white soup as if determined not to look his way. Yet he could not keep his own gaze from her.

She wore a new frock, a pretty pink creation that brought a lovely natural blush to her ivory complexion. Her golden curls were expertly arranged to frame her perfect oval face. And her blue eyes caught the light from the candelabra in the center of the table and shone with some deep emotion he could not decipher. Was she distressed about some important matter? Was that the cause of her silence? Was he the cause?

"And then I said… Greystone!" Mrs. Parton tapped her spoon against her crystal goblet, and both Greystone and Lady Beatrice jumped. "Are you listening to me?"

"Forgive me, madam." In any other company he would have been embarrassed by his lapse. Should he worry that he felt so comfortable in Lady Beatrice's presence? "I will confess my mind is on other matters, a habit in which I would only indulge when I am with an understanding friend."

Mrs. Parton humphed her acceptance of his excuse, while Lady Beatrice tilted her head and focused her gaze upon him as if waiting for him to continue. But it was the older lady who spoke.

"Do go on." She waved to the footman to bring the next course. "Naturally, if it involves government secrets, we shall not press you to divulge them. Shall we, Bea?" She did not wait for an answer. "But if it involves our little chimney sweeps, well, then you must tell us everything."

He could hardly tell them he had been thinking of the lady seated across from him, but in truth, the boys were never far from his thoughts. "The boys' health improves daily, and Kit's arm is healing. When Parliament adjourns I plan to take them to my school in Shrewsbury, where they can enjoy the country air and learn a new occupation."

"Ah, very good." Mrs. Parton helped herself to the roast beef offered by the footman. "We are privileged, are we not, to be able to help the lower classes? I believe that is why God has given us so much. Our work at St. Ann's never ceases to be a blessing to me."

Lady Beatrice brightened. "Will we go again soon? I should so much like to see how Sally is faring."

While the ladies conferred over their plans for the orphan asylum, Greystone observed their enthusiasm with interest. Mrs. Parton had played a large part in his own charitable leanings, for her generosity came not from duty like Mother's but from a loving heart. Since his earliest days he had basked in her kindness and that of her late husband. Nor would he ever forget how the couple had saved Mother and him from his father. Would that he could depend upon Mr. Parton's godly example for his own character. But he could not forget his youthful outbursts, so much like his father's rages that had caused damage to the less fortunate. Perhaps this was another reason for his eagerness to dispense charity whenever possible, as if he could make up for his past ways.

"But I have been thinking," Lady Beatrice began. Once again Greystone had let his mind wander. "As much as I am enjoying London, Melly depends upon me to manage Melton Gardens. Perhaps I should go home for a while and make certain everything is all right."

Anger skittered through Greystone's chest. The fact that Melton left his sister to manage his estate displeased him beyond words. Was there no end to the gentleman's irresponsible ways? How Greystone would like to beat some sense into the earl's thick skull. But such thoughts always brought him back to the dangers of his own temper.

"But my dear, you cannot go." Mrs. Parton frowned. "Why, the celebrations have barely begun. You cannot miss the fireworks and balls. And I have learned from a reliable source that the Russian czar and his sister, the Grand Duchess, are coming soon to join the revelry over Napoleon's defeat. Do you not wish to see them and perhaps even be presented to them?"

"Well—"

"Oh, do help me convince her, Greystone. She simply must not leave."

Greystone took a bite of the too-salty roast to give himself time to consider a response. Of one thing he was certain: Lady Beatrice indeed must not leave London until her friends found her a worthy gentleman to marry. As for Melton Gardens, surely there was a steward to see to the tenants' needs. If not, and if perhaps matters there took a bad turn, Melton would be forced to accept his God-given responsibility and learn how to manage it all himself.

"Lady Beatrice, I believe that, should you go, Mrs. Parton will be bereft. Then what shall we do?" He offered them a playful smirk. "I cannot leave my duties to console her, so I fear that office remains yours."

She returned a serene smile that reached clear to her expressive eyes. "As your kind sister-in-law reminded me today, even when every man deserts us, God will be our consolation."

As she voiced that holy truth, peace flooded Greystone's soul. Apparently the two young ladies had bonded over more than bonnets and frocks. "Yes, Anna has a gift for reminding people about God's goodness." For some reason, he felt pressed to tell her of his own faith. "During my illness last winter, when I was all too aware of my own mortality, she led me to scriptures that assured me of my salvation in Christ."

Now tears shone in her eyes. "I am so happy for you, sir. Would that someone would lead my brother in that way."

A shard of guilt cut short Greystone's moment of joy. Never once had he tried to befriend Lord Melton or lead him away from Rumbold's influence, much less *to* a faith in Christ.

It is not too late.

The startling thought brought him no pleasure, just a heavy weight of conviction. But, he reasoned as he lay abed that night, dealing with a prideful young earl was hardly the same as helping poor little chimney sweeps. Whereas the boys were pliable and grateful, the earl might react with anger or devise some sort of retaliation that would hinder Greystone's charitable endeavors.

But his arguments to the Almighty sounded hollow no matter how he tried to word them.

Chapter Twelve

"And forgive us our trespasses, as we forgive them that trespass against us. And lead us not into temptation…" Concentrating on the holy words, Beatrice prayed along with the other congregants in Mayfair's St. George's parish church. As always during services, today she laid her own sins before the Lord and gratefully acknowledged His forgiveness. Then, feeling the nudging of the Holy Spirit, she also made the decision to forgive Melly for squandering her dowry and for all of his prodigal ways that brought shame to their family name. As if to confirm her thoughts, the minister presented a lesson about the Prodigal Son in his homily. Surely God had spoken to her this day, and she would endeavor to keep His words in the forefront of her mind.

The decision gave her a strong sense of peace that remained with her until the next afternoon. That is, until Mrs. Parton announced that she must visit an old pensioner and leave Beatrice at home. She also left a litany of instructions.

"I know Melton is your brother, Bea." The lady pulled on her driving gloves and adjusted her bonnet. "But while I am gone, you must not grant him admittance to my house.

These past days Palmer has made our excuses four times. But he must go with me today, and the young footman on duty may not wish to turn away an earl. If Melton comes, you must stay in your room and refuse to see him."

Beatrice's heart sank lower with every word. After speaking with Lord Greystone about her brother's soul two nights ago and receiving God's message yesterday, she had felt her own spirit craving just a few moments with Melly. If nothing else, they could recall their happy childhood days together. Melly must be experiencing that same longing, or he would not have come to call *four times*.

"I must visit Mrs. Dooley, and I must take Palmer. Without his superior height and air of authority, I would not dare to visit the tenement. And of course I would not take you to such a place." Mrs. Parton held Beatrice's gaze with a frowning stare. "Will you do as I say?"

Biting her lower lip, Beatrice nodded. "Yes, madam."

Mrs. Parton patted her cheek, then kissed it. "Oh, my dear, I know you love him. But I fear you will indulge his every whim. This is for your protection. Remember, you cannot trust him."

Again, Beatrice nodded. "Go on now. Enjoy your visit with Mrs. Dooley." The old woman's only son, once a young footman for Mrs. Parton's husband, had died in the war. Although nothing obligated Mrs. Parton to care for her, she did it freely and generously, as with all of her charities. Beatrice wished her employer could extend the same charity of heart to Melly.

The afternoon was overcast, with rain falling intermittently. Once Mrs. Parton left, Beatrice found herself at loose ends. Nothing to which she set her mind or hands seemed to satisfy her, so she decided to walk about the house for exercise. After a third trip up to her bedchamber and back, she descended the front staircase just as someone pounded on the door.

The nervous young footman by the door eyed her with concern. "Milady, should you wait in the drawing room?"

"Yes, of course, John. But do open the door. It is pouring outside." She walked across the parquet floor to make her escape. Behind her she heard the footman's wavering voice.

"Begging your pardon, your lordship, sir, but milady is out and—"

"Beatrice!"

She turned back in time to see Melly lunge against the footman's outstretched arm, but he could not get past the tall servant.

"Begging your pardon, milord, but—"

"Great day, man, can you not see the rain?" Melly stopped struggling and began to cough, but it sounded familiarly artificial to Beatrice, as when he had faked illness to avoid schoolwork as a boy. "I shall catch my death if you force me out there."

"But, sir—"

"Beebe, please."

At his childhood name for her, her heart plummeted, and she burst into tears. Racing across the wide entrance hall, she launched herself into Melly's arms, eager to forgive and forget all his trespasses. Throwing his wet cloak to the floor, he held her close, murmuring assurances and all the silly words they had made up as children.

"Oh, Melly, I shall be in such trouble with Mrs. Parton." She nonetheless grabbed his hand and led him toward the drawing room. "But I cannot bear to be separated from you any longer. Please tell me everything, *everything* you have been doing."

He laughed playfully, almost wickedly. "Well, I shan't

tell you *everything,* but I will tell you that in my third year in the House of Lords, I have begun to have some influence." He plopped down on a settee and stared around the room. "Nice place. I'm glad you have such a pleasant home away from home."

Beatrice's heart did another plummet, this time with guilt for the way she had neglected him. "Are you still living at the town house?"

"Um." He toyed with the tassels on a small pillow. "No. I, uh, I sold it."

"What—"

"Now, don't get in a mood. I did nothing wrong, and it was not entailed. And it did belong to me." He studied his fingernails and brushed them across the front of his coat. "You didn't leave anything there, did you?"

She gulped back her unreasoning anger. What he said was true. It all belonged to him. Once again she determined to forgive him. "No. I have never even seen it. You know this is my first time in London."

"Ah, yes. I'd forgotten."

How could he forget? Was he becoming just like their neglectful father? The thought stung as she paced across the Wilton carpet in front of the hearth. "And so, where are you living?"

"I have an apartment not far from St. James's Square." He looked rather pleased with himself.

The Grenvilles lived in St. James's Square, too. Perhaps…

He grasped her hand and pulled her down on the settee. "Now, Beebe, you must listen to me before the old bat returns home."

A chill went up her spine. "Mrs. Parton is not an old bat. She's loving and good and—"

"Humph. The way she keeps me from seeing you?" His

lower lip stuck out in a pout. "More like Cerberus guarding the gates of—"

"Stop that." Smacking his shoulder, Beatrice laughed, even as an odd foreboding crept into her thoughts. "I forbid you to compare her to a monster from Greek mythology. Listen, dear brother, she is Mama's old friend, and she's very much like a mother to me."

His eyes began to glaze over. He had not come to hear about her. Remembering her prayers for him, she set aside her own concerns. "Tell me more about your influence in Parliament." Brushing damp curls from his warm forehead, she thought he looked very much like a Botticelli cherub.

"John." She summoned the anxious footman who stood by the drawing room door. "Please send for tea and bring some towels."

Melly grasped her hand and pressed it to his round cheek, which was also warm. "See, you always take care of me."

Beatrice leaned over to kiss him, but drew back at the smell of whiskey. "You have been drinking."

He stared at her as if she, like Cerberus, had three heads. "Of course I have been drinking. Every gentleman drinks."

She had never noticed the scent of spirits on Lord Greystone. Perhaps he had a little port after dinner, but nothing to undo his senses, as drink always did to Melly. *Forgive him,* her inner voice said once again.

"Tell me more about your influence with the other lords."

He laughed, a rather giddy sound, not at all like the dear boy she had grown up with. "My good friend and, dare I say, my mentor, one Frank Rumbold, is guiding me in the right path, telling me what to say, whom to support—

something no one has ever done for me. Certainly not our *esteemed* father."

Beatrice sighed. To voice her agreement would not help. Papa may have been neglectful, but he had managed his estates with a wise, careful hand. She brushed a hand across Melly's sleeve, sending a sprinkle of water over her skirt. "I am glad you have a friend. But are you certain he is the best one to guide you?"

"Of course he is." He stopped when the footman brought the tea and towels.

While Melly used the towels to dry his coat, Beatrice set about pouring the tea. She took pride in remembering his preferences for two lumps of sugar and a generous splash of cream.

"I thank you, my dear." Melly took a sip. "I don't suppose we could add something to this to make it a little more interesting?"

She answered with a frown.

"Hmm. I didn't think so. Well, anyway, regarding our dear old father, you cannot imagine how many times he told me how disappointed he was in me. He said I should be more like you."

"What? Why, that's ridiculous. He never even noticed me, never gave me a compliment or—" This was wrong. To join him in condemning Papa would make it appear as if she were making excuses for Melly's wasteful ways. So she tried a merry chuckle that did not quite succeed. "If he thought I was so good, he simply failed to notice the mischief we both got into."

"Oh, we did have some larks, did we not?" Melly set his tea down and grabbed another towel, ruffling it over his hair and across his neck. Then, tossing it over the back of the settee, he grasped her hand. "But never mind that.

Beebe, you must permit me to present Mr. Rumbold to you. He is—"

"I must do no such thing." She tried to stand, but he held her firmly. His horrid desperation frightened her. Surely the whiskey was at fault. "Please release me."

He did, then patted her wrist. "Forgive me." Resting his head against the back of the settee, he placed a hand against his forehead. "You cannot imagine how much pressure I have to endure. Without Rumbold's guidance I would have made many mistakes. I owe him so very much. You simply cannot know. As it is, the best hostesses refuse to send me invitations to their balls and soirees."

Beatrice cringed at the thought of her brother—an earl, for goodness sake—being cut from the best social lists. So much political influence could be gained at those events. But he had brought it upon himself. Was this the time to confront him about his gambling and drinking? No, that would only bring forth more excuses.

He sat up and grasped her hands, but more gently this time. "You cannot imagine my mortification when Lord Greystone sent me away from his ball. Had Rumbold not consoled me, I should never have lived it down." He flung himself back against the settee. "And to think you are forced to live next door to that popinjay."

Never mind that it was his fault she was "forced" to live anywhere other than the town house Mama had loved so much when she came to London. She had promised to decorate a special apartment for Beatrice for her coming-out Season. With that memory she found it more and more difficult to maintain a forgiving spirit. At least she managed to refrain from reminding him of his failures. But when she opened her mouth to contradict his ill-fitting description of Lord Greystone, he sat up again.

"You must listen, Beebe. Even in the short time we were

there, Rumbold came to admire, no, *adore* you. You were the only lady at the ball he would have considered dancing with—that is, had we not been thrown out."

"What?" Beatrice recalled her curiosity about Melly's handsome, older companion that evening. But how could a gentleman form an attachment with a lady whom he had never met and had seen only briefly across a room? Surely her brother was exaggerating. Still, if he had done so much for Melly, perhaps she was wrong in refusing to meet him, even though Mrs. Parton held the man in contempt.

Melly stood and marched toward the hearth, then swung around to face her with a triumphant grin. "I have no doubt that once he meets you, Rumbold will make an offer to me for your hand."

"What?" Horror swept through her.

"Yes. Isn't that beyond generous? And you with no dowry."

Her stomach twisted. "No, of course I have no dowry. You have gambled it away." Beatrice could not stop herself, even though she sounded like a petulant child. Where was the forgiveness she had thought to offer him?

Her accusation rolled off of him just as the rainwater had. "Humph. What do you know? It was all mine, anyway. I am merely trying to take care of you."

She would not point out that Papa had expected Melly to set aside at least twenty thousand pounds for her, and more if the estate tenants continued to produce abundant crops.

"Do you owe him money?" She tried to keep an accusing tone from her voice.

He shrugged. "A little."

The sick feeling in her stomach increased. How much was a little? Had this man taken Melly's entire fortune? Or had he saved Melly from further loss? What did Melly mean about the man guiding him in the right path? Was

Mr. Rumbold a good man who had been excluded from Society because he lacked an acceptable social rank?

"Will you receive him?" Melly's earnest gaze, even accompanied by that slightly wild look, cut into her. Their childhood friendship claimed a large part of her heart. He'd once saved her life. She had no idea what pressures he endured in Parliament. Did he have projects as dear to him as Lord Greystone's little chimney sweeps were to him, projects he could not sponsor because he had gambled away his money? Oh, she truly must forgive him, whatever it took on her part.

"Yes." She could barely speak the word, but she had no other choice.

Melton should have felt a sense of victory, but oddly, he was disappointed that Beebe agreed to meet Rumbold. Yes, he'd cajoled her into seeing things his way, as he often had in childhood. But she had always been the strong one, the wise one, while he had never felt anything but unsure of himself. Well, he was sure of one thing now: if he did not arrange this marriage, Rumbold would ruin him.

Out in the rain again Melton tried to raise the umbrella the footman had given him, but the ridiculous thing broke. He turned back to the town house to get another one, but the door was closed. He could not face that obstinate servant again, so he hurried down the street to hail a hackney just leaving a residence across the square.

The driver stopped none too soon. "Where to, sir? Oh, Lord Melton." The ruddy-faced man eyed him skeptically. "Payment in advance, milord." He held out his hand.

The rain made it impossible for Melton to feign the slightest bit of dignity. He'd faced this situation often enough in recent weeks. He pretended to search for a coin in his waistcoat pocket, but knew he had none. "My good man, I shall pay you upon arrival at my apartment." He started to climb into the hackney.

The driver's long whip barred his way. "Sorry, milord. I don't go to Seven Dials. Now, if you'll excuse me." He reined his horse away.

Speechless, Melton stared after the conveyance until he felt the cold rain seeping through his coat clear to his skin. After a violent shudder he began his trek across London. He did not wish to go to that wretched neighborhood, either. But what choice did he have?

Only one. Beebe must marry Rumbold. And the sooner, the better.

Chapter Thirteen

Greystone arrived home in the rain just in time to see Melton push his way into Mrs. Parton's town house. As much as he wanted to march next door and find out what the earl was up to, he had his own responsibilities at home. He consigned the matter to God's protecting hands and Mrs. Parton's good sense. The dear lady would not be intimidated by Melton's title.

Once inside his house he had not even removed his cape or shaken the water from his footwear before Mother accosted him in the front hall.

"Those brats." She crossed her arms and impatiently tapped the toe of one shoe on the marble floor. "You simply must send them away, Greystone. I will not have them tearing about my house like wild dogs."

While he weighed possible answers, Greystone made a ceremony out of surrendering his coat and half boots to Crawford and donning the dry ones Gilly brought. He would never disrespect his mother with a rebuke or a reminder that the house belonged to him, especially not in front of the servants. But neither would he abandon the two small boys whom he had promised a better future.

With practiced patience, he smiled as if she had just announced her intention to adopt the children.

"I would imagine they are filled with boyish energy.
You remember how Richard, Edmond and I carried on."
He took her arm and led her toward the drawing room.
"Let us call for tea so I can get warm." With a nod, he or-
dered Crawford to see to it.

"Oh, my, Greystone, are you chilled?" She felt his forehead. "No, but you are a little flushed. Perhaps you should
take to your bed."

"Nonsense." He used her favorite word. "I am well. Let
us settle once and for all the matter of the little climbing-
boys."

"At last." She dropped into her favorite chair and waved
him to sit in the adjacent one. "I am pleased to hear you
have come to your senses. We shall send them straightaway to your school in Shrewsbury, where they will be
happy amongst all of those other brats...boys."

Her self-correction encouraged him. Was she soften-
ing? But perhaps that came only from her thinking she
would soon be rid of them. His best course was to act as
if she had not said anything.

"I will speak to Lucy and explain the importance of
keeping them in the nursery."

"Speak directly to Lucy?" Mother opened the gold silk
fan hanging from her wrist and fluttered it in front of her
face. "Gracious, Greystone, what is this world coming to?
You must speak to Crawford and have him relay the order."

She had schooled Greystone well in the proper chain
of command within the household, but he wanted to manage the boys' care himself. Instead of responding, he continued. "They could use some fresh air, of course, but I
am not yet prepared to let them go to the park. Their former master may attempt to snatch them again." He chuck-

led. "Although they are already becoming too plump for their former profession. I suppose they will make excellent tradesmen of some sort."

"Greystone!"

Surprised at his own calm, his own sense of certainty, he leveled a firm yet smiling look at her. "Mother, darling, I will keep the boys. I pray you, let us hear no more about them."

Her eyes reddened, something he rarely saw, and her fan moved rapidly before her.

"Did you have a pleasant evening with Uncle Grenville last week? We have not had a chance to share our news of that night."

She looked away briefly. "Pleasant enough." The chill in her tone said more than her words. It was none of his business. "And you. Did you enjoy your supper with Julia and that *gel?*"

He clenched his jaw to contain his sudden annoyance. But why did her cross reference to Lady Beatrice anger him? The answer was simple. Against his determination not to form an attachment to the young lady, that was exactly what he was doing. But of course he could not say so to Mother. "Pleasant enough. But you must help poor Mrs. Parton find another French chef. Her latest cook has an excessive fondness for salt."

Now she chuckled, a genuine laugh such as he rarely heard from her. "I shall do that." She rose from her chair. "And on that subject, will you dine in tonight?"

"I believe so." He had planned to go to his club, but a drive to White's on such a rainy evening held no appeal. "Why not invite Mrs. Parton and her companion in for whist?"

She stiffened. "Really, Greystone, is it not enough that I have lost Julia's company because of her 'companion'?

Must I endure Melton's sister in my own home?" She strode toward the door, clearly expecting no answer.

He should be used to her determination to be unhappy, yet a weight settled upon his chest. Perhaps it would be better to forego an evening of whist. He had dealt her a blow about the sweeps. The least he could do was not force her to endure the company of a lady of whom she clearly did not approve.

A lady to whom Greystone's heart insisted upon attaching itself.

"So your brother would sell you to this Rumbold person to pay off his debts." Mrs. Parton did not appear angry, only disappointed when Beatrice confessed to seeing Melly. And perhaps a bit indignant over Melly's behavior.

"Sell me?" Beatrice nearly choked on a bite of salty chicken. "But are not financial considerations a part of every marriage arrangement?"

Mrs. Parton set down her fork and shoved away her still-full plate. "My dear, Melton did not tell you everything about this man. Frank Rumbold is a desperately ambitious man. Marriage to you would tie him forever to your old aristocratic family and elevate him into Society. But he has made his fortune off of foolish young peers like Melton and other aristocrats addicted to gambling. He leads them as lambs to the slaughter." She stared off in silence. "I have failed to protect you, and now I know of no remedy for the situation."

Beatrice also shoved away her plate, but not for want of hunger. Mrs. Parton's cook used a heavy hand with salt and grease. "I—I could refuse to receive him."

"Hmm." Mrs. Parton gave her a sympathetic smile. "You promised that before, and you see how it worked out." She heaved out a deep sigh. "Furthermore if you refuse after saying you would receive him, Mr. Rumbold may find a way to…oh, there is no other way to say it. He may take revenge, either against Melton or you. I have seen him do it."

Beatrice stared at her in astonishment. "Revenge? But why? How?"

"As I said, my dear, he has great wealth, however ill-gotten it is. With a bribe here and a bribe there, he can accomplish whatever evil thing he wishes."

The few bites Beatrice had managed to eat threatened to return on her. "How could Melly become entangled with someone so evil? Perhaps I was wrong to forgive him, for it only made him think he could use me."

"He is merely following Rumbold's example. Men like that have a way of ingratiating themselves to young gentlemen. Melton has always had a bent toward gambling, so it was easy for Rumbold to ensnare him with flattery and friendship." She clicked her tongue and shook her head. "Gambling is an evil addiction. More than one young gentleman, and even some ladies, have been ruined by it."

Beatrice studied her hands and forced herself not to wring them together. "If only Melly had found a worthy mentor when he was elevated to the peerage, someone who would guide his feet on a wiser path."

"Humph." Mrs. Parton snatched back her plate and cut into her chicken as if she would butcher it all over again. "Blakemore tried to befriend him, but Melton would have none of it. Got rather insulting, in fact. Not like Lord Greystone, who was drawn only to the most upright Christian gentlemen. Oh, he had a year or two of foolishness, but not to his ruin. When his brother Richard and Lord Blakemore confronted him, he quickly mended his ways."

At the mention of the viscount's name, Beatrice's heart lurched. While she could not say she loved him, she did admire him exceedingly. Here at last was a trustworthy gentleman. But how could she hope for anything more than his friendship? She could never expect someone of his character to court her, lest he be drawn into an association with Melly, and thus Mr. Rumbold. And if she was forced into a marriage to Rumbold, no doubt she would lose every friend she had, including Mrs. Parton, Lord Greystone and Mr. and Mrs. Grenville.

She blew out a cross breath. "I shall refuse to receive Mr. Rumbold. I cannot, will not, be forced into marriage to such a person."

"I am so pleased to hear you say that." Mrs. Parton's round face beamed her delight. "Do permit me to advise you, my dear, that it will be best to postpone the meeting rather than cancel it. That way he cannot take too much offense. Then we will devise other ways to avoid him." Her expression turned maternal. "My dear girl, you said you have forgiven Melton. That is a good thing for your sake. Our forgiveness should be endless. But that does not mean we can give others license to destroy us. For your dear brother's sake, you must also require that he be responsible, even if that means avoiding him at all cost."

"Yes, I can see what you mean." Beatrice's stomach settled at last, and she retrieved her own plate and speared a bite of potato with her fork. "Oh, Mrs. Parton, I thank the Lord you are my friend." Joy bubbled up inside her. "And you may be certain that I will indeed let you advise me. In fact I shall never again do anything without your counsel."

A kind but wily look stole over Mrs. Parton's plump face, deepening the laugh lines around her eyes. "Knowing how easily Melton can change your mind, perhaps I should lock you in your room when I go out."

Rather than annoy Beatrice, the idea made her feel protected, as when her governess had forbidden her to play near the rapidly flowing High Force Falls on the River Tees that ran by Melton Gardens, lest she fall in and drown. Now Mrs. Parton was her protector, yet she could not help but wish a certain viscount would fill that office.

Chapter Fourteen

❧

"Oh, no, my dear." Mrs. Parton bustled into Beatrice's bedchamber. "Not the brown bonnet. You must wear the blue."

Seated in front of her dressing-table mirror, Beatrice considered the change. "But my gown is green."

"Green?" Mrs. Parton blinked as if seeing the elegant walking dress for the first time. "Oh, my goodness, no. You must wear the blue."

Beatrice started to protest that she always wore either blue or pink and would welcome a different color. But only three nights ago she had vowed to accept Mrs. Parton's guidance, and she would certainly not argue about such a small thing as her choice of clothing.

"As you wish, madam." She hurried to make the change with help from Poole, Mrs. Parton's lady's maid.

"Hmm." Her employer watched their every move with a critical expression.

"Are you displeased, madam?" Poole's gray eyebrows dipped into a worried frown.

"No, no, everything is fine." Mrs. Parton paced back and forth across the carpet. "This is simply taking too long. Bea, we must find a lady's maid for you."

Beatrice's heart skipped. "That would be splendid." Until this moment she had forgotten Lucy's request to learn the duties of that position. But no doubt the girl was busy with the little sweeps. Perhaps Sally at the orphanage would do.

Poole set the blue silk bonnet on Beatrice's head, then fluffed the curls around her face and stepped back for Mrs. Parton to inspect her work.

"There." Mrs. Parton gripped Beatrice's chin and studied her appearance from every angle. "Perfect. Blue is your best color. Brightens your eyes." Her approving smile stirred sweet memories of Mama.

"What will we be doing today?" With all this attention to her appearance, perhaps they were going to meet some august person.

"Why, visiting Lady Greystone, of course." Mrs. Parton peered in the dressing-table mirror and adjusted the pink peacock feather in her purple paisley turban. "It is her day to be at home."

All of Beatrice's eagerness evaporated. "Oh."

"Now, now, my dear, she is not an ogre." Mrs. Parton shooed Poole out with a wave of her hand. Once the woman left, she looped an arm around Beatrice's and led her out of the room. "Do not forget what I told you about her unhappy marriage and having to rear her three sons alone. Be generous in your opinion of Lady Greystone. After all, those boys have turned out quite well, so she cannot be such a tyrant."

"Yes, madam." One "boy" in particular came to mind, but Beatrice did not expect to see him. He would be in Parliament this afternoon.

As the two ladies swept out the front door and down the street to the next town house, Beatrice endeavored to settle her emotions. Whatever insult Lady Greystone hurled her way, she was determined not to respond in kind or in a way that would embarrass Mrs. Parton. But to Beatrice's surprise the viscountess received them graciously… somewhat.

"My dear Julia." She kissed Mrs. Parton's cheek. "You have been neglecting me." She received Beatrice's curtsey with a regal nod. "Lady Beatrice."

As they made their way to the drawing room, the two older ladies chatted like the schoolgirls they used to be. Here was a side of the viscountess Beatrice had not seen. Her pleasant manner toward her friend of a lower social standing was enough to erase any personal offense Beatrice might take. In fact, after observing their conversation for several moments, she wished once again for a friend of her own. How grand it would be if the viscountess's daughter-in-law visited today while Beatrice was here. She had not seen Mrs. Grenville in five days, and despite their brief acquaintance, she longed to spend more time with her.

"Good afternoon, Mother. I see we have guests." Lord Greystone strode into the room. His dark, windswept curls formed an appealing frame around his handsome face, and his blue eyes sparkled in the late-afternoon sunlight streaming in through the window.

Beatrice's heart did a dozen somersaults before she could grip her emotions. What an unexpected—she could think of no other word—*delight.*

"Mrs. Parton." The viscount bowed over the lady's hand and regarded her with a warm look before stepping over to take Beatrice's hand. "Lady Beatrice." His now guarded gaze did not quite meet hers.

Disappointment replaced delight. How could he be so cool toward her after their pleasant afternoon in the park, their lovely supper with Mrs. Parton? Containing her giddy emotions was no longer difficult. When he raised his eyes to hers, she was fully able to return a cool but polite nod, much like the one his mother had given her.

"Good afternoon, Lord Greystone." She would say no more. Truly she would not. "Has Parliament adjourned for the day?" Why, oh, why did her mouth betray her?

"Not at all." He settled into a chair adjacent to his mother and accepted a cup of tea. Beatrice made note of the single lump of sugar and dash of cream the lady put in for him, although she would never need that information. "The ramblings of the opposition went on a bit too long for my taste, so I decided to come home." He shook his head in disgust. "If they could just see reason—"

"No politics, Greystone." The viscountess stirred her own tea and spoke as one would to a child.

A frown darted across his face, but his smile was all acquiescence. "Of course. Forgive me."

"Oh, Frances," Mrs. Parton said, "do let me ask him about today's debate." Without waiting for a reply, she addressed the viscount. "You must tell us about the pension for the wounded soldiers. Has it been utterly defeated?"

"I fear so, dear lady. The hearts of many peers are like granite."

"More's the pity." Mrs. Parton's eyes reddened. "Well, we shall simply have to do what we can ourselves." She sniffed and dabbed her nose with a handkerchief. "Now, what about our little chimney sweeps?"

The viscount's expression brightened, while his mother's clouded. Beatrice had difficulty not laughing at the contrast. Then she sobered, remembering Mrs. Parton's appeal for a more generous opinion of Lady Greystone. Beatrice knew she must forgive the lady for her lack of warmth toward her, due of course to Melly's reputation. Yet one would think that after rearing three sons, she would have an abundance of patience and understanding toward little boys, whatever their station in life.

"They were fit and fine before I left this morning." He chuckled. "Although Lucy already looked a bit harried."

Mrs. Parton laughed. "But perhaps the girl is not strong enough to tend them."

"Humph." Lady Greystone scowled at her friend. "All the more reason to send them to Shrewsbury."

"Mother." The viscount spoke softly, but there was a hint of command in his tone.

The lady turned her scowl on him. "Humph."

Beatrice watched with interest. In the short time she had known these two people, she had observed a constant power struggle. Perhaps the viscount was slowly shifting into the place of true leadership in his own home. Beatrice could feel only admiration for his diplomatic dealings with his difficult mother. With such tact the gentleman would make an excellent husband one day. Though she could not imagine why she should think of him in those terms. That matter had been settled once and for all, for he clearly found no pleasure in her company. Yet after her disappointment over Melly, she felt encouraged to know at least one trustworthy gentleman.

"Now, Greystone, about Lucy." Mrs. Parton took a biscuit from the tea tray and waved it over her teacup, as if trying to decide whether or not to dunk it. "When the boys are napping or perhaps under the care of a footman, do you suppose the girl could come over and work with my Mrs. Poole? With the right training I believe she would make an excellent lady's maid."

A thread of excitement wound through Beatrice and lifted her spirits. Mrs. Parton's kindnesses never ceased.

"Now, Julia, do you not think that is a question for

me?" Lady Greystone's eyes blazed, and her smile seemed forced.

"Oh." Mrs. Parton looked from one to the other. "Why, I have no idea. Whom should I ask?"

Beatrice ducked her head and involved herself with her nearly empty teacup. So she was not the only one to observe the struggle between mother and son.

"I shall speak to Crawford," the viscount said as if he had not heard the question. Or perhaps, had heard it and was simply showing Mrs. Parton the answer instead of telling her. "Lucy is, after all, his granddaughter. As such, perhaps she is more suited to be an upper servant rather than a housemaid."

Lady Greystone's countenance seemed carved of the same granite that formed the hearts of the uncharitable peers. "As you wish."

Silence settled over the large, elegant drawing room. Beatrice tried without success to think of an appropriate subject to introduce. But, after all, it was not her place. Mrs. Parton consumed her biscuit as if it were a feast. Lady Greystone stared toward the windows as if inspecting them for smudges. Lord Greystone gave his mother a gentle, sympathetic smile, but the lady did not look his way. Nonetheless Beatrice was pleased to see his kindness. Should she have a son someday, she would wish him to be as good as Lord Greystone. But again, she should not think of the viscount and having a family of her own in the same moment.

To her surprise he turned his kind smile her way, and her traitorous heart skipped a beat. "Lady Beatrice, what will our Mrs. Parton have you doing next?" From the quick lift of one eyebrow, she could see he was teasing.

Her first thought was to say, "*Not* a ride in her phaeton." But she would not hurt her benefactress's feelings.

"I am certain it will be a grand adventure, which I await with bated breath."

Both he and Mrs. Parton laughed.

"Of that, I have no doubt, madam."

Greystone found Lady Beatrice's wit and honesty to be nothing short of delightful. From the moment he had seen her across the card room at his birthday ball, he had admired her expressiveness, her inability to hide her feelings. Today her brilliant eyes reflected the color of her elegant blue walking dress and bonnet, enhancing her beauty and threatening to steal his breath away. Mild alarm had shot across her lovely face when he had asked his question. Was she remembering her wild ride in the phaeton? If so, she had refrained from criticizing Mrs. Parton. Such kindness deserved a reward, and he knew just what to give her.

"Well, then, Mother, Mrs. Parton, if you ladies have no other plans in mind, may I suggest that we all go to the theatre this evening?" He heard Mother gasp softly beside him, but he would not be deterred. "I understand Elliston is performing Hamlet, and the Prince Regent is coming."

"That was the report last time," Mrs. Parton huffed, "but he did not appear."

"Ah, but this time he cannot change his mind. The Russian czar and his sister, the Grand Duchess, will accompany him, and he must not disappoint them." Greystone patted Mother's hand to command her attention. "Will you go with us, madam? I should be pleased beyond words to have your company." If she agreed, he would send an invitation straightaway to Uncle Grenville to join their party. He longed to foster their friendship, for Mother seemed a different, happier person in his uncle's presence.

"You know I do not care for the theatre." Her hard look

did not soften. "But by all means, go. I would not deprive you of Elliston's Hamlet."

At her harsh tone, Greystone winced, but did not respond. Nothing he did these days pleased her. What did the poor dear want from him? From anyone?

After several moments of silence, Mrs. Parton coughed softly. "Do you have a box?"

He forced away the dark clouds trying to spoil his mood. "Indeed I do. Blakemore has offered his, and we should try to fill it."

"What a grand idea." Mrs. Parton clapped her hands. "You must invite dear Edmond and Anna."

From the joyful look on Lady Beatrice's beautiful countenance, he could see that scheme brought her great delight. And in that moment, pleasing her—if only for one evening—became his singular goal.

Beatrice tried to school her face into an indifferent expression, but she could not manage it. She could think of nothing more enjoyable than another evening at the theatre, especially in Lord Greystone's company. Had she been wrong about his opinion of her? Before she could comment, however, the viscount's butler announced more guests.

"Lady Grandly, Miss Waddington and Miss Amelia Waddington."

"Oh, my." Mrs. Parton set down her teacup. "We have overstayed our time. Frances, we must leave so the baroness and her daughters will have you all to themselves. Come along, Bea. We must prepare for our evening."

"Yes, madam." Beatrice had noticed the mild alarm on Lord Greystone's face when the newcomers were announced.

While Mrs. Parton rose and brushed a kiss across Lady

Greystone's cheek, receiving no response, the viscount stood, as well.

"Mrs. Parton, would you like to see how our little sweeps are faring?" The sudden tightness in his voice added to Beatrice's guess that he did not wish to entertain the new guests.

"Oh, that would be grand." Mrs. Parton waved to Beatrice to follow.

They encountered the newcomers at the drawing-room door. Lord Greystone made introductions, and greetings and pleasantries were exchanged all around. The younger ladies stared at him with open admiration and seemed particularly disappointed when he bowed away, explaining he had a matter to discuss with Mrs. Parton. Beatrice understood their dismay. Both girls were reasonably attractive and no doubt seeking husbands. Lord Greystone would make a fine catch for any lady. Somehow that thought caused a stirring of jealousy, which Beatrice quickly dismissed. After all, she had no claim on the gentleman.

In the fourth-floor nursery the little sweeps were squirming in their chairs while Lucy worked on a sampler by the window. When the adults entered, the boys raced to Lord Greystone like eager puppies, coming just short of jumping on him.

"'ello, gov'ner," Kit chirped.

"'ello, gov'ner," Ben echoed.

Both boys were remarkably clean, and in fact bore little resemblance to the children Beatrice had met just over two weeks ago. Those daily baths would soon remove the last bits of gray around their necks and fingernails. They had also begun to plump up a bit, which added to their healthy appearance.

"Now see here, you little brats—" Lucy hurried after them, stopping just short of snatching them away from the viscount. "I've told you never to address Lord Greystone until he speaks to you. And it's *my lord,* not governor." The girl's manners and speech also needed improving, but Beatrice felt certain she could help her.

"There now, Lucy." Lord Greystone knelt and gathered the boys into his arms, such a kind gesture from an important gentleman. The tender look in his eyes reminded Beatrice of the Bible story in which Jesus said, *"'Suffer little children, and forbid them not, to come unto me.'"* The viscount was clearly demonstrating the faith he had spoken of several nights ago. The children were lapping up the affection, for they wrapped tiny arms around his neck.

What a contrast to all that Beatrice had ever known. Her own father had never so much as held her hand or brushed a kiss across her cheek. Yet Lord Greystone heaped kindness and generosity upon these little orphans. Her admiration for him swelled within her, and she approached and set a hand on the older boy's shoulder. "Hello, Kit. Do you remember me?"

He blinked, then grinned. "Coo, miss, 'ow could I forget such a pretty lady?"

"Why, thank you, sir." Patting his cheek, she glanced over his head to see Lord Greystone's approving smile. "Tell me what you have been doing."

Ben bit his lip, but Kit shrugged. "Not much, miss. That'n—" He aimed a thumb over his shoulder at Lucy, who had worn a scowl the whole time. "She don't like us doin' nothin' but sittin'."

"Hmm." Lord Greystone stood. "Hardly good for two energetic boys. Perhaps we should devise some activities to keep you busy."

Kit gave him a shaky grin. "We could clean the chimneys, gov. We want to earn our keep. That'n, Miss Lucy I mean, says we're just the same as stealin' 'cause we don't earn our keep."

Beatrice's eyes stung, and Lord Greystone cleared his throat. Did he share her belief that children this young should not be forced to work for a living?

"Lucy means well, my lads, and she certainly does earn *her* keep." He sent the girl a sympathetic glance, but she was looking toward the window with a scowl. "But right now you are my guests, so you do not have to do that. One day soon I shall take you to my school in Shrewsbury, where you can learn a trade to which you are well suited."

"Coo, gov'ner, that's kindness itself," Kit said.

"Kindness itself," echoed Ben.

Lord Greystone found a chair and once again gathered the boys in his arms, asking what trade they might find interesting. As they talked, Mrs. Parton questioned Beatrice with one lifted eyebrow. Beatrice nodded. They had put this off far too long.

"Now, Greystone, it is clear Lucy needs a rest from her duties," Mrs. Parton said. "I should like to borrow her later this afternoon to begin her training with my Poole."

"Ah, yes." Lord Greystone's smooth forehead creased as he considered the matter. "But as I said, I should first ask Crawford what he thinks. He wanted to guide his grand-daughter as she trains for service."

During this exchange Beatrice watched Lucy's scowl turn into a bright, open smile. "Oh, milord, I should be ever so pleased to be a lady's maid. Do say I may do it."

Beatrice could not fault the girl's enthusiasm, despite her lack of decorum. She looked forward to taking her in hand. Like Lord Greystone with the boys, Beatrice had no doubt she could teach Lucy everything required for the position she desired.

She would begin by teaching the girl a little respect for those whom she served.

Chapter Fifteen

"Oh, miss," Lucy chirped. "I'm ever so pleased to be your lady's maid, even if it's just now and then."

Seated at her dressing table, Beatrice studied the girl in the mirror. Lucy had cast off her mobcap to reveal brown curls cascading down her back, as if she would advertise her considerable hairdressing skills. Her plain brown dress and shapeless white apron had been exchanged for a black muslin gown with a form-fitting, embroidered bodice, perhaps borrowed from Hudson, the viscountess's lady's maid.

"Now, miss, you must tell me whatever you want me to do, and I'll do it spit spot." She fussed with Beatrice's hair. "Oh, this is grand, just as I thought. Nice and thick and so easy to work with." She gripped Beatrice's upper arms and squeezed, ducking down to catch her gaze in the mirror. "We shall have such a grand time, won't we, miss?"

"If you please, Crawford." Beatrice stood and moved out of the girl's grasp. She might understand her enthusiasm, but it was none too soon to begin teaching her proper behavior for her station. While Beatrice could forgive her slips, a future employer could take great offense at her familiarity and dismiss her on the spot. "You will address me as 'my lady.'"

Not at all embarrassed, Lucy tilted her head to the side and blinked as if Beatrice had just announced herself to be a goose. "My lady?"

"Yes. And, as lady's maids are customarily addressed by their last name, I shall call you Crawford." She tried to keep the annoyance from her voice, but Lucy seemed utterly unabashed.

"Lud, miss, my grandfather is Crawford." She seemed to realize her error. "I mean, my lady."

"Hmm." Beatrice sat down again. "That is a consideration." She thought for a moment. "Very well. When you are here, you will be Crawford. When I see you at Lord Greystone's, I shall call you Lucy."

"Oh, miss—" A hand flew up to cover her lips. "I mean, my lady, you are ever so kind. May I begin now?"

At Beatrice's nod, she began to brush and comb and curl and pin. She had already examined Beatrice's wardrobe and brought out a lavender gown for tonight's excursion to Drury Lane. "Mrs. Poole gave me this purple ribbon and a string of pink silk flowers. Shall I use them?"

Beatrice gave her another nod and settled back to watch in the mirror as the girl worked. Indeed she had great skill, at least with hair. It remained to be seen how she performed the many other duties of a lady's maid. The girl chattered on and on about too many subjects to keep track of, so Beatrice let her mind wander to this evening's adventure.

She and Mrs. Parton would ride with Lord Greystone, and she looked forward to seeing him again. This afternoon he had seemed cool to her at first. But by the time she and her mentor had left after visiting the boys, he had warmed considerably, especially in their agreement over

Lucy's training. Beatrice had done nothing to effect such a change, but still it pleased her. A gentleman would not invite guests whom he disliked to share a theatre box with him. And with the possibility of Mr. and Mrs. Grenville attending as well, Beatrice had no doubt this would be her most enjoyable evening since she'd come to London.

"And they're just like two little mice, miss, uh, my lady, scurrying about all over the place kind of sneakylike—"

"What?" Beatrice had not heard a word Lucy had said, but she did like the abundance of Grecian curls framing her face and crowning her head, with the purple ribbon and pink flowers woven throughout.

"The boys, miss. The dirty little chimney sweeps." Her upper lip curled in distaste. "I do wish you'd hire me straight out so I don't have to look after them no more."

Beatrice stared at her in the mirror. How could so much self-importance dwell in the granddaughter of a humble butler like Crawford? Who did she think she was? At the thought Beatrice felt a pinch of shame. Her own circumstances were not at all ideal and would not be until Melly assumed his responsibilities in providing a dowry. *Lord, please forgive me for my arrogance. If it is Your will, I shall endeavor to set an example of humility for this girl.* But Beatrice would do her no favor by treating her as an equal. England's social system simply did not work that way. Best that she learn her place in it, or she would never find a lasting position. Why, even the little boys seemed to understand that simple fact.

"You did a fine job on my hair, Crawford." She reached up to lightly touch a curl and smiled at Lucy in the mirror. "Now, shall we see about my gown?"

When Greystone saw Lady Beatrice descend Mrs. Parton's front steps, he had to remind himself to breathe. Her beauty stunned him and left him speechless, for she was the very image of an exquisite Grecian statue. Her flowing lavender gown reflected in her blue eyes, turning them a matching color. Her thick golden curls had never before been so artfully coiffed, and her cheeks shone with a natural rosy blush no rouge could ever match. He would not permit his gaze to linger on her full lips, lest his thoughts lead him astray. But when she stepped near to take his hand for assistance into his landau, the fragrance of her lavender perfume nearly proved his undoing.

Had she worn a haughty countenance or accepted his help into the carriage as if it was her due—which it was, and more—he would not have been impressed. Many a young lady donned aloofness as surely as she put on a new gown. But Lady Beatrice was all humility and kindness, always putting others before herself. This was what he longed for in a life companion.

The thought startled him. He must not think this way. Must remember her brother's waywardness and the harm he could do to any acquaintance. Why had he proposed this outing? Why had he let himself be drawn in by Lady Beatrice's beauty and graciousness? But he had, and now, if for only one evening, he must grant her every courtesy. And then perhaps he should abandon all association with her.

He handed her into the carriage and, as she took her seat, only a split second of awareness reminded him of the other good lady who required his assistance. He executed a smooth turn back to face her.

"Mrs. Parton, you are a vision." He handed her into the landau and climbed in to sit across from the two ladies. From here he could feast his eyes on the beauty of one elegant lady and delight in the merry wit of the other. As usual Mrs. Parton's turban—orange this time—hosted two

tall peacock feathers of the blue-and-green variety, which
made him glad the carriage top was down, lest they be broken. Her gown, a predominantly orange paisley creation,
nonetheless complimented her red hair and presented an
overall pleasing effect. But try though he might to give
them equal attention on the half-hour drive to Drury Lane,
his gaze strayed to Lady Beatrice more often than to the
older lady. Mrs. Parton did not seem to object in the least,
if her several winks at him were any indication.

"'To be, or not to be, that is the question.'" Elliston
intoned the famous lines with just the right amount of
haunted pathos for a tortured Renaissance gentleman.

*To continue this friendship, or not to continue it, that
is the question.* Greystone could not seem to concentrate
on the performance, although *Hamlet* was his favorite of
Shakespeare's plays. At this moment he understood the
Danish prince's anguish all too well. While Hamlet considered whether or not to take his own life, Greystone
considered whether or not to spend more time with Lady
Beatrice, a sure death to some of his influence among
his peers.

And then there was Mother to contend with. She was
quite displeased over his plans to escort Mrs. Parton and
Lady Beatrice to the theatre. But, then, Mother never
seemed pleased with anything. Did she never want anyone
to enjoy life simply because she chose to wed the wrong
brother all those years ago? But unlike the Danish queen
in this play, she could not marry her late husband's brother,
for the Church forbade it. Even though Uncle Grenville
had always been the very soul of kindness and goodness,
Father had been a monster, like Hamlet's murderous, un-
repentant uncle.

Without Mr. and Mrs. Parton's intervention, Father might

well have murdered Mother, perhaps even Greystone, his own heir. Mercifully he had not yet set his whip upon four-year-old Richard or two-year-old Edmond by the time he died. And neither brother was aware of their father's cruelty. But why tell them? To excuse Mother's bitter nature? She'd had over two and twenty years and many good things in her life to aid her in putting it all behind her. Yet she had not managed to.

"'Whether 'tis nobler in the mind to suffer the slings and arrows of outrageous fortune, or to take arms against a sea of troubles and by opposing end them.'" Elliston's Hamlet continued his desperate monologue.

Whether 'tis nobler to let Mother dictate the affairs of my life or to fight her at every turn. It would have been so easy to let her continue making decisions for him, but after his nearly fatal illness last winter, he felt God's urging that he must make his own decisions. He did not like to displease her, but he would not be dissuaded from his course regarding the little chimney sweeps.

With a sigh he tried again to put aside personal affairs and enjoy the play and his companions. At least Lady Beatrice approved of his taking care of the boys.

She sat at an angle to him, her intense gaze focused on the stage, her face alive with interest in the action. If she enjoyed attending plays to this degree, he must purchase his own box so they could attend upon a whim and not have to depend upon friends. *They?* No, he must not think this way. He and Lady Beatrice had no future together. In that, he did agree with Mother.

How many times must he remind himself? Yes, he must marry and produce an heir. But better to marry someone strong and indifferent, like Mother, than a gentle, sweet girl like Lady Beatrice. He could not bear to think of hurting her, especially if, or *when*, he became like his father.

* * *

Beatrice sensed that Lord Greystone was watching her, and she had difficulty not turning his way or reaching up to see if a curl had come loose. When she had emerged from the town house, he had stared at her with obvious approval, causing her no end of chagrin. In all her life she had never blushed, even when other gentlemen had expressed their admiration of her. But a simple look from this gentleman, whether accompanied by a smile, a frown or indifference, brought unwelcome warmth to her face.

Yes, she did find him utterly appealing. In fact he seemed to be everything she had always longed for in a husband. Yet Lady Greystone had made her dislike and disdain abundantly clear. Despite the struggle Beatrice had observed between them, Lord Greystone would likely not go against her in a matter as important as marriage, even if his admiration grew into something deeper. Beatrice would do well to face the fact that she had no future with him, and she must not encourage him, must somehow feign disinterest to save them both from grief. Besides, for all his outward actions and kindnesses toward the little boys, she still had no assurance that he would not become as distant and neglectful as Papa. His frequent shifts from smiles to frowns seemed to portend that very kind of behavior.

With some effort she forced her attention back to the play, refusing to look at the viscount. After all, she must have something to say about the performance during the ride home.

Queen Gertrude made her entrance, admirably portraying elegant grief. "'One woe doth tread upon another's heel, so fast they follow. Your sister's drown'd, Laertes.'"

Beatrice wept softly as the queen announced Ophelia's death, yet a new understanding and even empathy blossomed within her. Each time Beatrice had read *Hamlet,* she had mentally scolded Ophelia for committing suicide after the man she loved so cruelly rejected her. Should this aristocratic lady not have been made of sterner stuff? And yet, like Ophelia, Beatrice must drown her own dreams of finding a loving, constant husband.

As the landau rumbled over the cobblestones, Greystone felt a strong measure of satisfaction, even pleasure. When he had finally set aside personal concerns, he'd enjoyed the play immensely. Lady Beatrice seemed not to share his sanguine mood, but no doubt she was still affected by the tragedy. Perhaps he should open a discussion about the drama so he could point out that Shakespeare never failed to write a life-affirming finale. Whether a comedy, tragedy or history, the Bard always ended his plays by having some worthy prince restore the shattered social order and establish his own authority.

In this case Fortinbras was the sane and sensible foil to Hamlet, who let his emotions overrule his better logic. Indeed Greystone preferred to follow the example of Fortinbras rather than the tragic prince of Denmark. He would proceed in an orderly, logical way regarding all things in his life, whether it be presenting a bill in Parliament or choosing a wife.

His gaze strayed to the quiet young lady seated across from him. All too often thoughts of marriage brought her to mind. But that could never be. He must continue to look for some august peer to marry her, someone whose position would undo the damage Melton had done to his family. Perhaps someone older, wiser. But that thought soured his stomach.

"Well." Mrs. Parton broke the silence. "Prinny has let us down once again. I had hoped Bea could see him."

"Ah, well." The lady in question gave a charming shrug. "I was enjoying myself so much that I failed to notice."

Greystone knew he should ask the source of her enjoyment, the play or the company she was in, but he dared not. They continued their drive to Hanover Square and stopped in front of Mrs. Parton's town house.

"Will you come in, Greystone?" Mrs. Parton asked as he handed her down. "I have just hired a new French cook, and he has prepared a fine supper."

"I thank you, madam, but I must rise early tomorrow. Perhaps another time." He turned to offer a hand to Lady Beatrice, but she had already reached the pavement. In her lovely blue eyes he read obvious disappointment over his declining the invitation. "Well, then. I bid you ladies good-night. Porter, I shall walk home." He waved away his driver.

With all proper compliments spoken, he turned to walk the hundred feet to his own front door. Behind him he heard Mrs. Parton's overloud voice echoing along the silent street. "By the by, Bea, you recall that I gave Lord Winston permission to come calling day after tomorrow."

No, Lord. Not that dullard for our lovely Lady Beatrice.

But she was not his Lady Beatrice, and thus he had no say in the matter.

Chapter Sixteen

"Still awake, Mother?" Greystone surrendered his hat and gloves to Crawford and walked across the front entry hall to his parent. But when he tried to kiss her cheek, she stepped back, arms crossed. "What is it?" No doubt the little climbing-boys had broken a vase or swung on a chandelier.

"Your little pets have shown their true nature." Her eyes blazed, and her cheeks were pinched. "They have stolen my ruby necklace and refuse to return it. In fact the clever little thieves have added to their crime by denying they know anything about it."

Somehow her accusation rang hollow. Was this the first challenge to his resolve to take charge of his household? *Lord, give me the wisdom of Solomon.* "Where are they?"

"Locked in the nursery, of course." She glared at him as if he were the thief. "With two of our strongest footmen on duty to keep them there."

"Good." He ran a hand through his hair, ruining Gilly's careful work. "No doubt the boys are asleep, so we will address this in the morning." He gave her a slight bow. "Good night, Mother." Suddenly tired, he made his way toward the staircase. The day had been long, and many issues remained unresolved.

"You will not retire until this is dealt with."

He paused with one hand on the bannister, but did not turn back.

"Greystone!" Her voice echoed throughout the chamber. "I demand that you call a constable to take them away *now*."

After a silent prayer for help, he slowly turned to her. "Madam." He injected as much kindness as possible into his tone. "We are never at our best when we are weary. I will speak with you in the morning and will deal with the matter then."

Despite her angry huff and a sad bit of bluster, he continued his ascent. In his room he found Gilly asleep in a chair. The old man jumped to his feet and rubbed his eyes.

"Begging your pardon, milord. I didn't expect you for some time. Thought you might go out for supper after the play."

Greystone grunted at his own folly. Now he had three reasons to regret declining Mrs. Parton's invitation: Lady Beatrice's disappointment, Lord Winston's imminent visit and Mother.

"Gilly, what can you tell me about my little charges?" If anyone would know the truth, it would be his valet.

"My lord, I fear it's a muddle. One person saying one thing, another something else." He clicked his tongue. "That Lucy—" His eyes widened briefly. "Not meaning any disrespect to Mr. Crawford, you understand. But Lucy, well, the girl needs a bit more experience before she can handle two wee lads so full of energy." He helped Greystone remove his jacket and tie.

"Hmm." Greystone had not considered that when he assigned the job to her. From the look of Lady Beatrice's hair this evening, the girl might well be a better lady's maid than a nursemaid. "I shall deal with it all in the morning. In the meantime, please inform Crawford that the boys are not to be removed from this house, no matter what Lady Greystone says."

"Yes, milord." An odd smile lifted one corner of Gilly's lips.

"What do you find so amusing?" Greystone tried to sound severe, but failed. Gilly had been his body servant for four and twenty years. He was more like a favorite uncle than a servant, although he never crossed the lines of propriety.

"I'm just glad it's Crawford relaying your orders to Lady Greystone, milord." He grimaced. "Meaning no disrespect, of course."

"Of course." Greystone mirrored his grimace, but guilt followed.

Lord, please help me work through these problems and somehow honor Mother all at the same time.

"Should you not be at Lord Greystone's, Crawford?" Beatrice had permitted the girl to remove her gown and stays, then put on her dressing gown. Now she sat while Lucy removed pins and ribbons from her hair and brushed out the curls. "Who is watching over the boys?"

For once Lucy would not meet her gaze in the mirror. "I put them to bed, my lady." Some indecipherable expression crossed her face, and her hands shook as she wound the ribbon back on its spool. "But I wanted you to see I can help with the undressing, too, not just the getting ready."

Beatrice nodded. Something was wrong, but she must be careful how she questioned the girl. "Is everything all right next door?" She kept her tone light, as if asking about the weather.

Lucy still would not meet her gaze. "No, miss, uh, my lady." She dug the brush deep into Beatrice's hair, massaging the scalp as she swept it downward.

Despite the pleasant feeling of having her hair brushed, which always helped to relax her, Beatrice resisted the urge to let her guard down. "What happened?"

"Well, um, it seems the boys got into a bit of trouble while I wasn't looking." She blinked. "Mind you, I keep up with them as best I can. But sometimes when they dash away, I have to rest a bit before giving chase."

Beatrice hid a smile. Surely Lucy was not to blame for their mischief. "And what happened today?"

Lucy dropped the brush, but snatched it up with trembling hands. "They got into Lady Greystone's bedchamber and stole a necklace." Her voice wavered.

"Oh, my goodness." Beatrice swung around and grasped Lucy's hands, but still the girl would not meet her gaze. "You are not to blame for their mischief." Crime, actually. Children had been hanged for less, an abhorrent punishment, but the law of the land nonetheless.

Lucy chewed her lip for a moment. "So you don't think his lordship will dismiss me?"

"Why no, Lucy, not at all." Despite her words Beatrice was not certain she should console the girl. Something still was not right. But what did Beatrice know of such things? She had never confronted a thief in her home. The servants at Melton Gardens were honest Christians who took pride in their flawless service. "Lord Greystone is the kindest gentleman one could ever know. And I am certain he realizes your talents are better suited to being a lady's maid."

Now the girl brightened, and she brushed away tears. "Oh, do you think so, my lady?"

Even as she nodded to confirm her words, Beatrice felt a nudge of uncertainty. Once again she thought, *something is not right about this.*

"What do you mean 'gone'?" Greystone studied the two footmen who had been charged with confining Kit and Ben. As if to set the stage for a tragedy, a fog lay over the streets of London, and no morning sunlight brightened the nursery. "If the door was locked, how did they get out?" His stomach ached with worry over the two little scamps. Just yesterday Crawford had reported that their former master had been seen in the neighborhood but without the tools of his trade. Had he kidnapped them?

"Oh, they be sly ones, milord." The younger footman's wig and livery were askew, as if he had been sleeping, yet his eyes seemed alert enough. "Picked the lock, they did." Warren nudged the older man. "Ain't that right, Rob?"

Robert was a longtime employee, and Greystone knew him to be utterly trustworthy. "I don't know, my lord. They were sound asleep when I went down to fetch breakfast for them—" he nodded toward a tray of porridge and tea "—and I made sure the door was locked behind me. When I returned, the door was wide open, and they were gone." He shot a cross look at his companion.

"And you were sleeping, too?" Greystone did not care for Warren's attitude. Although he was a new employee, his failure to understand his duty could not be excused.

He shrugged, adding to the offense. "I worked all day yesterday, milord. A man's gotta sleep sometime."

"That is beyond enough." Crawford entered the room and stood by Greystone, his face aflame, his eyes blazing. "You are dismissed."

"One moment." Greystone lifted a hand to stop his tirade. "Crawford, I do not like to override your orders, but I want these men to join the search for the boys."

Robert appeared relieved, but Warren heaved out a great sigh. "Yes, milord," they chorused.

"In addition, Crawford, I want the entire staff to search the premises from the basement to the attic to see if anything else is missing." He put out a hand to stop the older footman. "One moment, Robert."

"Yes, my lord."

"Fetch me a Bow Street Runner. I shall give you a note."

"Yes, my lord." Relief shone in the servant's eyes. Here was a dependable man. But Greystone could not be certain about the other one.

"Oh, Frances, we came as soon as we could." Mrs. Parton bustled into the town house's front entry with Beatrice on her heels.

"You heard?" Lady Greystone's face was pinched with anger, but she submitted to Mrs. Parton's embrace. "Julia, you must support me in this. Greystone has the entire staff searching for the brats, but I am beside myself to think he will permit them to stay here if they are found."

Lord Greystone hurried down the front staircase, a footman close behind him. He stopped short when he saw Mrs. Parton, and his eyes flared briefly when he glanced at Beatrice. In spite of the distractions of the moment, Beatrice's heart skipped.

"Ladies, I fear you have come at an inconvenient time—"

"Not at all, Greystone." Mrs. Parton gripped Lady Greystone's hand. "We insist upon helping you, do we not, Bea?"

"Yes, of course." She hesitated to tell them of her unease

about Lucy's story. After thinking about it further, she'd decided that the girl had been nervous last night simply because of the situation, not because she bore any fault for the children's actions.

"Excuse me, ladies." Lord Greystone brushed past them on his way to the door and handed the footman a letter. "Make haste, Robert. The longer the boys are missing, the less likely it is that we will find them." Once the man hurried out, the viscount faced his mother. "Madam, please be at ease. I shall not rest until we have solved this problem."

"Problem?" Her voice shook. "It is a *crime,* Greystone. They have stolen a valuable heirloom necklace and have no doubt already sold it." The pathos in her tone rivaled Queen Gertrude's in last night's performance. Unfortunately the viscountess was not acting.

Lord Greystone swiped a hand over his eyes. "We will find out soon enough. Every honest jewelry dealer will be alerted to watch for it."

Beatrice's heart went out to him and his mother. "Lady Greystone, you have my sympathy for your loss. I recall seeing you wear the necklace at Lord Greystone's birthday ball." Never mind that she had not even been presented to the viscountess that evening. "It is an exquisite creation and looked so becoming with your scarlet gown." She rushed on before the viscountess could respond. "I will pray that it is restored to you very soon."

The lady stared in her direction, not seeming to see her. At last her eyes focused. "I thank you, Lady Beatrice."

As if everyone were stunned by her uncharacteristically gracious answer, silence ruled the front entryway for several moments. Beatrice made haste to keep her promise, lifting up a petition that all would soon be solved, that God would be merciful to the boys and to

Lord Greystone. And to poor Lady Greystone, whose anger for once seemed justified.

Lord, I cannot believe You brought Kit and Ben to me only to have them rob us. Did I mistake Your voice in my mind that day? Did the innocence in Kit's eyes mask his true character? And why am I more concerned about their disappearance than I am about the necklace?

Greystone knelt beside his bed, something he had not done in many years. But the full impact of the theft had brought him to his knees with self-doubt and a longing for God's wisdom. After all of his talk about wanting to help children who were forced to work as climbing-boys, he began to question every aspect of the project. He would not abandon it outright, but he had certainly lost his enthusiasm. Yet perhaps his peers whom he had regarded as hard-hearted were right. Perhaps the lower classes did not deserve help, for they would take advantage of any perceived weakness on the part of their betters who tried to raise their expectations.

And what of poor Mother? I intended to show her that she must stand aside and permit me to rule my own house from now on. But how can I inflict that pain upon her just when she has lost one of the few material objects she has ever valued?

He leaned his forehead against the mattress, longing for God's voice to answer him out of the darkness. Instead a vision of Lady Beatrice danced in his mind. This morning the concern in her eyes, her compassion toward Mother, had caused a shift in his determination not to further their acquaintance. Oddly, Mother had received her words of sympathy without a rude response. If any good could come of this situation, perhaps it would be a friendship between them.

Somehow that thought pleased him mightily. If Mother befriended Lady Beatrice, all of Society would have no choice but to do the same. If all of Society accepted her, he would no longer be required to fight his attraction to her. He had never before considered that possibility. But was this not just one more situation in which Mother was making his choices and Society was dictating his happiness? All of his objections seemed to lose their power over him, and a sense of excitement filled him over the prospect of following his heart.

For now, though, another situation loomed larger and more immediate. Every corner of the house had been searched for the boys, every chamber examined for signs of other missing items. Only the ruby necklace was gone. Poor Mrs. Hudson was bereft, as though the jewels were her own. She had been Mother's lady's maid for some twenty years and had never lost or misplaced so much as a well-used ribbon. When the usually calm woman had discovered someone had picked the lock on the jewel case and stolen its most valuable object, she had dissolved into hysterics. Greystone had had a difficult time reassuring her of his faith in her loyalty. Mother had even consoled her and insisted she was not at fault—another surprising act on the part of his parent.

Jeremy Slate, the Bow Street Runner, had been apprised of the situation and had viewed the scene of the crime, along with all possible evidence, of which there was little. The boys' old clothes had been burned days ago, and no one knew where they had lived before coming to Greystone Hall that fateful day. But if anyone could find the children and discover what they'd done with the necklace, or if they'd even stolen it in the first place, Mr. Slate was the man.

As he drifted off to sleep, something nagged at the back

of Greystone's mind. Kit and Ben had been quite proud of their new leather shoes and always resisted surrendering them at bedtime. Yet those shoes had been left beside their bed, both pairs lined up perfectly as when they had been taken off the night before. Why would they leave behind their most prized possessions?

Simply put, they would not. At the thought, he jolted awake, eager for tomorrow's arrival so he could investigate the matter in depth.

Chapter Seventeen

While Lucy fussed with Beatrice's hair, Beatrice fidgeted like a schoolgirl. No, like Kit and Ben had the day before yesterday while Lucy had ignored them. That thought settled her down. At each reminder of the children, her heart ached anew. They were innocent. She believed it, felt it, desperately wished it to be so.

"Oh, my lady, your first *at home*." Lucy expertly wound a curl and pinned it with a paste jewel pin. "Won't you be the talk of London when all the gents see what a beauty you are?"

Beatrice shifted again. "Crawford, you do not need to flatter me."

"No, of course not, miss." Her face reflected in the mirror showed no discomfiture at the rebuke. "I'm just saying what I see." She put the finishing touches on the coiffure and stood back to admire her work. "Do you like the pink or the blue today, miss?"

"Remember, Lucy, the correct address is 'my lady.'" Beatrice tempered her tone, but offered no smile. "If you do not use the proper address, you will never find employment, no matter how skilled your hands may be."

"But, my lady—" the girl gave her a saucy grin "—I

was hoping to work for you forever, like Mrs. Hudson for Lady Greystone." She rolled her eyes. "Though I wouldn't want to work for that old harpy. Lud, she can bite."

"Crawford!" Beatrice stood and spun around, gripping the girl by her shoulders. "You must not say such things. Surely your grandfather has given you some training in how to respect those for whom you work."

"Yes he did, my lady." Lucy's lower lip stuck out in a pout. "But you saw how his lordship treats them dirty little climbing-boys like they were his own born children."

"Do not change the subject." Beatrice huffed out a sigh and resumed her seat in front of the mirror. "In any event, you need not worry about Kit and Ben anymore." Saying their names renewed her grief and disappointment. She prayed Lord Greystone would not abandon his efforts to help other sweeps because those two had betrayed his trust. No, she corrected herself, *if* they had betrayed his trust.

"That's the truth." Lucy snickered and went about finishing her work. "But oh, could I tell you stories."

At the touch of her hands a raw shiver ran down Beatrice's back. Why had she not followed her better instincts and told Lord Greystone about Lucy's attitude? That alone was enough to send her back to her grandfather's tutelage. Why had Beatrice thought it would be easy to train her?

"We will not discuss the boys any further, Crawford." Beatrice swallowed her self-recriminations. She must present a pleasant face to Mrs. Parton's guests this afternoon, whoever they might be. But she would do it on her own terms. "Bring me the green gown."

If anyone found it less flattering than the pink or blue, so be it.

"I knew your father, Lady Beatrice." The Marchioness of Drayton, an ancient lady with pale blue eyes and lavender hair, beamed at Beatrice from her chair across the small grouping of furniture. "He was diligent in his duties and well thought of by his peers."

"I thank you, Lady Drayton." Beatrice could well imagine that Papa had always done his duty, to king and country, if not his family.

"And you my dear, how is your search for a husband proceeding?" Fluttering a blue lace fan before her plump, laugh-lined face, Lady Drayton did not wait for an answer. "I will be having a ball in two weeks, so of course you must come. Many of London's unattached gentlemen will be hastening to choose their brides before Wellington comes home, bringing in his wake war heroes who will want to flaunt their new titles and spoils of war."

"Of course we shall attend, Lady Drayton." Mrs. Parton laughed in her jolly way. "But there is hardly a dearth of young ladies for all of those gentlemen."

"No, not at all. The young people of your time were quite fruitful in producing sufficient offspring to go around, as were mine in the previous generation."

The two ladies laughed at their own wit, and Beatrice smiled at their merry ways, even as she considered the improbability that she could marry without a dowry. God had blessed her with Mrs. Parton's friendship, but she could not expect the lady to provide her with that essential part of any marriage agreement.

"Lord Winston, my lady," the butler announced from the doorway.

"Send him right in," Lady Drayton said, although Mrs. Parton was the hostess. Beatrice guessed a marchioness could do as she wished, and Mrs. Parton did not seem to mind.

Lord Winston entered the large room and, locating the ladies, strode across the space and bowed over Lady Drayton's hand. "My lady, I did not know you were here. Shall I postpone my visit?" He shot a glance at Mrs. Parton, who was blissfully busy with her tea.

"If you mean to dismiss me, Winston, you will have no luck. I shall not give way, so do not think to ask me." Lady Drayton winked at him, no doubt another privilege of her rank.

The baron gave her a little smile, clearly not offended. Beatrice wondered if she had misjudged him. Or was he cheerful only with his fellow aristocrats? He made his way over to Mrs. Parton, and the two exchanged the usual pleasantries. Then he settled his gaze on her. "Lady Beatrice, you look like a spring day."

"Oh, he is a poet!" Lady Drayton laughed, with Mrs. Parton echoing her. "Let us warn Byron that his place in the sun has been usurped."

Beatrice could not stop her own laughter, and she hoped Lord Winston would not misunderstand. "I thank you, Lord Winston. You honor me."

"Not at all." He took the chair beside her and accepted a cup of tea from Mrs. Parton. "I have thought often and agreeably of our last meeting and hoped to see you again."

"Again, I thank you, sir." She could not honestly return the compliment, for another gentleman had filled her thoughts of late.

"Mrs. Parton." Lady Drayton set down her teacup and rose. "Do show me that divine sculpture over there." She pointed her fan at a statue of a horse and rider set near a side door.

Mrs. Parton gave Beatrice a knowing smile. "Of course, Lady Drayton."

As the two women crossed the room, they whispered back and forth. Beatrice hoped Mrs. Parton would confide in her later about their intense conversation. Did she now regard Lord Winston, her own relative, as her favorite suitor for Beatrice's hand? The thought mildly dismayed her, for her heart had settled on another, even though she had no hope that he felt the same way.

"Lady Beatrice," Lord Winston said, "I have been spending some time with Melton since you and I last met."

Every thought fled. Unable to speak, she stared at the baron, aware of tears stinging her eyes. The tender sympathy in his usually haughty expression changed every opinion she had held against him.

"I thank you, sir." Remembering Mama's teaching, she managed to reclaim her dignity by clearing her throat and dismissing her tears. "Did you find my brother well?" And sober?

He moved his hand closer to hers but did not breach propriety by grasping it. "As I told you at Lord Blakemore's supper, I find him witty. But what I took for light-heartedness appears to be a mask for some deep—" He looked away briefly. "Forgive me. I can think of no other word but *despair*."

Her heart sank, and she struggled to maintain control. "How kind of you to be concerned." She would say no more on the subject. She had no doubt the baron knew of her brother's debts. Determined to change the tone of the conversation, she offered a bright smile. "Someday I must visit the House of Lords and watch the proceedings. I should like to hear him address his peers."

"I have yet to see him do so. Of course, you understand, not every peer addresses every issue." He glanced toward the other ladies, then leaned closer to Beatrice in a confiding manner. "I did not mean to distress you. In fact, I mentioned it only as a preface to asking if I may be of service to you in his regard." He drew back and frowned. "Forgive me if I am overstepping."

His generosity astounded her. "Not at all. I do believe Melly needs a good friend, someone of character who can lead him away from evil influences." Although she would prefer that a certain other nobleman would assume that office.

"Lord Greystone," Palmer announced from the doorway.

Beatrice's heart did its usual hiccup upon hearing his name, but she tried to keep from reacting to the viscount's timely entrance, lest Lord Winston misunderstand.

"Oh, my." Mrs. Parton bustled across the room to where Beatrice and the baron sat, with Lady Drayton close behind. The marchioness laughed the whole distance, while Mrs. Parton chuckled in her merry way. "We certainly do have an abundance of guests, do we not, Lady Beatrice?"

How kind of Mrs. Parton to address her formally in this company. Beatrice had yet to find the courage to correct her use of "Bea."

Lord Greystone strode into the room but stopped halfway to where they were gathered. "Ah, Mrs. Parton." His frowning stare settled on Lord Winston as he spoke. "Have I come at an inconvenient time?"

"Not at all, my boy." Lady Drayton once again projected her rank. "I was just leaving." She sailed up behind Beatrice's chair and patted her shoulder. "Walk me to the door, my dear. I should like to know you better."

Beatrice shot a quick glance at Mrs. Parton, who nodded. "Of course, Lady Drayton." She rose and walked around the chair.

The marchioness captured Beatrice's arm and ushered her out to the front entry. "Now listen to me, my dear. If neither of those two young imbeciles glaring at each other in the drawing room makes an offer for you, I have a grandson who has made a name for himself serving with

Wellington. He is a younger son of our youngest son, so he bears no hereditary title, but he has a large inheritance from his mother. Lord Drayton means to see to it that the Prince Regent grants him an earldom." She frowned, an expression at odds with her deeply embedded smile lines. "Of course we cannot guarantee that he has not taken up Wellington's…habits with the ladies. But a spirited girl like you can take him in hand with no trouble."

That revelation sealed a death warrant on any possible interest Beatrice might develop for the gentleman. Putting Mama's graciousness firmly into place, she gave the marchioness a warm smile. "You have paid me the highest compliment, Lady Drayton. Please be assured that I will consider it. But of course the young man will have his own preferences."

"Just so." Lady Drayton patted Beatrice's cheek. "But do keep him in mind." She gave her a wily smile. "You could do worse than marrying into the Marquess of Drayton's family."

But she could not do worse than marrying an inconstant gentleman. No, she would rather live her life as a companion, or even as a governess, than to marry someone with all the wealth in the world, but not a whit of character.

Chapter Eighteen

After a restless night with little sleep, Greystone had longed for nothing more than the consolation of the two people who would understand his concerns regarding Kit and Ben. He should have remembered this was Mrs. Parton's afternoon at home, should have recalled her remark about inviting Winston to visit her. But events of the past two days had obscured those memories, so he offered the requisite bows and greetings and sat for the obligatory cup of tea.

Once she returned from her conference with Lady Drayton, Lady Beatrice poured, adding one lump of sugar and a splash of cream before handing him the cup. Clever, thoughtful girl. She had noticed his preferences. His heart warmed at the thought. Everything she did drew him closer to the decision that he must pursue her. Despite his fears of being like Father, he felt the Almighty's nudging him toward this beautiful lady, and he had little power to resist.

"A fine day." Winston spoke to no one in particular.

"Indeed," Greystone said. "A fine day."

"Fine if one does not mind the fog." Mrs. Parton fingered the biscuit balanced on the edge of her saucer. "Even now one can hardly see across the square."

"Very true, madam." Clearly not listening to their hostess, Winston tapped a foot on the carpet and stared at Greystone.

Was that a challenge in his eyes? Greystone would gladly accept. He would not leave before he spoke to the ladies, and he would not speak to them while his rival was here.

Rival? Yes, exactly so. A thread of jealousy wove into his chest. While he could not yet declare his growing attachment for Lady Beatrice, he did not welcome the complication of Winston's competing for her affection.

"More tea, Lord Winston?" Lady Beatrice was the picture of grace and composure, and Greystone could detect no favoritism for the baron in her countenance.

"Why, yes." The baron held out his cup and saucer. She must have remembered his preferences as well, for he retrieved the well-sugared beverage with a self-satisfied grin. "I thank you, Lady Beatrice." He stirred and sipped while Greystone stewed. How long had he been here? A gentleman never stayed beyond fifteen minutes, twenty at most, so his hostess could see other guests. Was it not past time for Winston to leave?

"I must thank you again for your kind words about—" Lady Beatrice paused and looked around the group. "I mean…"

"Say no more, madam." Winston gave her a syrupy smile as sweet as the four lumps of sugar in his tea. "I flatter myself that my efforts to befriend Melton have not been without success, and I shall not cease until our goals are accomplished."

Our goals? Greystone almost spit out his beverage. But conviction forced him to swallow hard. Perhaps Winston was a good choice for Lady Beatrice after all. Now he recalled seeing him outside of Westminster clapping the young earl on his shoulder as if they were old friends. Melton had resembled a pleased puppy, not a peer who had been in Parliament for two years longer than Winston. But Greystone had been so determined to keep his hands clean, his reputation spotless for the sake of his charities, that he had not so much as offered Melton a handshake. Nor even a nod.

You, Greystone, are a pompous Pharisee.

And look what had happened to his so-called good works. Mother's necklace stolen. Two little boys lost. Shame ate away at him. Perhaps he should be the one to leave.

"Lord Greystone," Lady Beatrice said. "Did you bring us any news?"

Her gentle smile chased away his dejection as surely as morning sun dispersed fog. A strange new assurance gripped his heart. He did indeed care deeply for Lady Beatrice, and he would not stand aside and let Winston win her unopposed. And he would depart only when she sent him away.

"No, madam. No news." He brushed a hand over the brocade chair arm and stared up at the ornate rococo molding above the pink floral wallpaper. If need be, he would wait to speak to her until spiders spun their webs from corner to corner and across the sparkling chandeliers— something that would never happen in this immaculately kept house.

"Oh, Greystone." Mrs. Parton clapped her hands, startling everyone. "I just recalled that other matter we need to discuss. Can you wait?" She blinked her eyes innocently.

"Other matter?" Greystone questioned her with a look,

then realized her ploy. "Ah, yes indeed. I do have that information you wanted."

Winston frowned and set down his teacup. "Well, I can see I am delaying some important business."

"Not at all, my dear kinsman." Mrs. Parton stood, requiring everyone else to follow. "Do come back anytime."

The speed with which she graciously dispatched the baron impressed Greystone so much that he could hardly recall why he had come.

For the first time since her brother ascended to the peerage, Beatrice had a measure of confidence that he could be redeemed from his foolish ways. How grateful she was to Lord Winston for befriending him. Still, when Mrs. Parton accompanied the baron from the room, Beatrice found herself alone with Lord Greystone, and her heart skipped. A quick glance at the footman just inside the door reassured her that all was proper. "Lady Beatrice." Lord Greystone reclaimed his seat next to her. "May I speak with you?"

Worry threaded through her. "Is this about Melly?"

"Partly. Lord Winston has put me to shame, and I have no excuse for it."

"Sir?" She forced herself to breathe.

"Madam, I have been a Pharisee." Sorrow filled his expression. "I should have reached out to your brother three years ago when he first came to London, but his brashness...no, I will offer no excuse. I should have been more persistent in offering friendship." He seemed to struggle for words. "Now a better gentleman has set an example for me, and I shall endeavor to influence Melton to reform his ways."

"Oh, sir, you give me hope." She could barely keep from grasping his hands. "Perhaps you and Lord Winston can work together. The fourth chapter of Ecclesiastes tells us that two are better than one when trying to accomplish any worthy thing."

An almost comical grimace passed over his face, though she could not guess what it meant. "Yes, of course. I shall address the matter with the baron." He cleared his throat. "But I must tell you something else."

Again, worry teased at the corners of her mind. "Very well."

"You have occupied my thoughts since the moment I met you." He said the words simply, as if stating that the sky was blue. Again her heart skipped. "Yes, that is but a short time, yet long enough for me to know where my mind is leading me." A tender look filled his eyes. This was the admiration she had longed for since she had left the schoolroom, and she desired it from no other gentleman than the one seated beside her.

"Sir—"

He held up one hand. "Please permit me to finish. Then if you wish to cast me out, my fate will be well deserved."

She pressed her lips together. Casting him out was the last thing on her mind.

"Lady Beatrice, I pray it will not be offensive to you for me to say I have developed a great attachment for you."

She sniffed back tears. "It most certainly is *not* offensive."

He chuckled. "That gives me great encouragement. However, there are impediments to our deepening this attachment."

Yes, of course. Her brother. His mother. Yet the gentleness in Lord Greystone's voice made her heart ache with hope. "I understand."

"Then I shall speak plainly." He glanced away, frowning. "A peer is expected to marry and produce an heir, yet I cannot take on the responsibilities of a husband and father until I am certain I will not be the man my father was."

Beatrice drew back. This was not what she had expected. Yet his candor moved her. How easy it would be to protest that he would make an excellent husband, even though she had no assurance that he would. Nor did she have any idea what his father's failings had been. All she could offer back to him were her own doubts about marriage.

"I will not ask you to explain further," she said, "but I will confess my fear of marrying an ardent suitor only to find him as neglectful as my father was to my mother. To all of us."

Understanding lit those remarkable blue eyes. "Ah. That explains—"

"My brother's...desperate ways." And her own deep longing to be admired by a constant husband.

He exhaled another long sigh, obviously relieved by these confessions. For her part, Beatrice felt more than relief. She felt as if their friendship had embarked upon a journey that would ultimately lead to their mutual happiness.

"I realize you are of age and may do as you wish. But I believe that we honor God when we bow to conventions and do things properly. Therefore, if you have no objections, when I extend the hand of friendship to Melton, I will also tell him of our mutual feelings and ask his permission to continue our...acquaintance."

Once again, this was not what she expected, yet she could only admire his caution. He would forge ahead in spite of Melly's reputation, yet would not declare himself if her brother refused his friendship. As much as that hurt her, she managed to say, "That would please me very much." But another troubling thought must be spoken. "You must know that he can provide no dowry for me."

"I am not at all surprised." He brushed away her words like a bothersome fly. "But first things first. I cannot think he will lightly agree to accept me as a friend after I cast him out of my house the night of my ball. Thus I must go to him in all humility and first beg his pardon."

"Must you?" She recalled how Melly had used her gentleness to his advantage. "I would not like to see you humble yourself to him."

"Yes, I must." He took her hand and leaned close, resting his forehead against hers, an endearing gesture that portended a meeting of their minds. "And you must trust me in this."

In this closeness she detected the delicate scent of his cologne, an orange-blossom fragrance that made her delightfully dizzy. With some effort she sighed as she said the words, "I will trust you in this and in everything." Indeed, her trust in him had been growing since the moment she had seen him holding a dirty little chimney sweep in his arms.

He echoed her sigh. "Then we have an agreement?"

"We have an agreement," she whispered. Now if God would soften Melly's heart, there would no longer be any impediments to their happiness.

Unless, of course, one considered Lady Greystone.

Chapter Nineteen

Beatrice had never cared to linger over her toilette or study her face in the mirror for any length of time. But today she could see a difference in her reflection, a cheerful hope borne of knowing that Lord Greystone would do all in his power to befriend and help Melly.

Lucy, on the other hand, was strangely quiet, and her face appeared wan, as though she had been weeping. Her hands shook as she combed through Beatrice's hair, and she seemed to have lost her skill for making a proper curl.

Beatrice had no wish to meddle in her affairs, but perhaps she could offer a listening ear. "Are you well, Lucy?" She gave the girl a sympathetic smile in the mirror.

Lucy bit her lip and nodded. "Yes, my lady." But her hands shook all the more, and the comb fell from her hands. Covering her face, she dropped to her knees and sobbed almost hysterically. "Oh, my lady, I've done a terrible thing."

An awful foreboding crowded out Beatrice's joy. She leaned forward and pulled Lucy into an awkward, kneeling embrace and patted her back. "There now, it cannot be so terrible." Sending up a silent prayer for wisdom, she gently pushed the girl away so she could see her face. "Tell me what you have done."

Her face awash with tears, Lucy gulped and hiccuped, trembling all the while. "I—I hid Lady Greystone's necklace so everybody would think the brats stole it."

Beatrice could hardly grasp her words. So her forebodings had not been baseless. "Why?" She guessed the girl's motives, but must hear them.

"B-because I didn't want to be a nursemaid to street trash." Lucy swiped at her tears. "If they'd been his lordship's children, it wouldn't have been so bad. But they were filthy little climbing-boys." Beatrice offered her a handkerchief, and she blew her nose with great force. "Besides—" indignation crept into her tone "—you can see how good I am at coiffing your hair. That's the position I want...to be a lady's maid."

Praying again for wisdom, Beatrice sensed that she should not address that particular matter, at least not now. Perhaps she had made a mistake in promoting this girl to a much-prized senior servant position, something many women of the servant class worked for years to attain. "And where did you put the necklace?" A shiver of dread went through her. Lord Greystone's staff had searched every inch of the town house's four stories.

Lucy began to wail again, this time so fiercely that her babbled answer was unintelligible.

"Stop it, Lucy." Beatrice gave her a firm shake. "Nothing can be solved through hysterics." When the girl quieted somewhat, she asked again, "Where did you hide it?"

"I-in the nursery in a little hole in the wall behind the bed." She gulped back another sob.

"Well, then, we will simply go over and inform Lord Greystone so he can restore it to the viscountess." Just as she was about to thank the Lord for the answered prayer, Lucy burst out with another flood of tears.

"But it's gone!"

"What?"

"I went to get it this morning so I could put it out someplace for someone to find, but it wasn't there." She slumped back to sit on the floor and stared off vacantly. "Now they'll hang me for sure."

Beatrice shuddered. Indeed they just might do that.

"Oh, Greystone, I hardly know what to think." Mrs. Parton stood on one side of Lucy while Lady Beatrice stood on the other, each holding an arm lest the girl fall to the floor. "We trusted her, and she has betrayed us all."

Greystone felt sick to his stomach. He was glad these two good ladies had sent for him instead of taking Lucy to his house. Now he had time to devise a way to soften the blows he must deal to both Mother and Crawford.

"Lucy, are you certain the necklace is gone?"

Whimpering out some sort of answer, she nodded.

"Shh. You must control yourself, Lucy." Lady Beatrice patted the girl's shoulder, an overly kind gesture, considering the circumstances. But he would not fault her, for it exhibited her compassionate nature, one of the many reasons he had come to regard her so highly. He expelled a long sigh and paced across the drawing-room carpet, rubbing the back of his neck as he considered his next step. A vague suspicion crept into his mind. "Are you telling us everything?"

Lucy's eyes widened. After a moment she shook her head. "No, milord. I did wrong, but I had help. That is, until—"

The pieces began to fall into place. "The new footman,

Warren." He made it a statement rather than a question. "You arranged for him to be hired, did you not?"

Her tears increased, but at least she did not become hysterical again. "Yes, milord."

Again the ladies tried to quiet her, but he grunted with disgust.

"I learned this morning that Warren left last night. He gave no notice, just disappeared." Greystone wanted to drop into a chair and sort it all out, but he would get more from Lucy if he stood over her. "Now it makes sense. I have no doubt he has sold the necklace and is on his way to America or some other foreign land."

As he suspected, this conjecture brought on a painful wail. He moved in for the kill. "Did he promise to take you with him? Is that why you stole the viscountess's necklace?"

Now she looked horrified. "No, milord. I never meant to steal it. I never meant to leave, and I had no idea he meant to." Her face dissolved into misery. "I was ever so proud to work with my grandfather in your house. I've wanted to ever since I was old enough to understand what it was all about."

Greystone dismissed her words with a harsh laugh. "I doubt you ever understood what it was all about. Now consider what this will do to your beloved grandfather, my faithful butler who has given my family nothing but exemplary service for over forty years."

She merely nodded.

"But what about Kit and Ben?" Lady Beatrice asked Lucy. "What happened to them?"

She bit her lip and trembled anew. "Warren gave them laudanum to keep them quiet, then carried them out to their old master."

Greystone's heart sank. That explained the shoes still

lined up beside the bed. But how would he ever find the lads and bring them home?

"Mrs. Parton, would you be kind enough to keep Lucy here until I can sort this all out and speak with Mother and Crawford?"

"I would be pleased to help in any way," Mrs. Parton said.

"And I, as well." Lady Beatrice's affectionate gaze encouraged him, and it was all he could do not to kiss her smooth ivory cheek.

"It may take some time."

"Take all the time you need." Mrs. Parton left Lucy's side to give him a maternal embrace. "Greystone, do be sure to call me over before you speak to your mother. She will need my support in this."

He returned the hug. "I thank you, dear lady, and I will accept your offer." Again towering over Lucy, he gave her a stern look. "If you dare to leave this house, you will never be able to come back, nor will you ever find a decent way to support yourself."

Despite the circumstances, her shamefaced expression did her credit. "Yes, milord."

He took his leave of the ladies, but made no haste to return home. In all his years since his elevation to the peerage, he had never faced anything like this, for Mother had made every difficult decision for the family. But he would be the one to decide Lucy's future, and only God could give him wisdom in the matter. Yet finding Kit and Ben seemed more urgent. And in the midst of it all he must make time to visit Melton and try to befriend him.

By the time he reached his front door, he had decided that Lucy could wait. The longer he delayed making a judgment, the more she would feel the gravity of her actions.

But which of the other situations should he deal with first—a matter of the heart or a matter of charity?

Chapter Twenty

Greystone had never entered a more disgusting abode. Melton's apartment in the slums of Seven Dials hardly had the look of an earl's residence. Beyond the musty stench of the place, everything from carpet to furniture to cheap artwork was shabby, even the mousy little man-of-all-work posing as a butler in oversized livery.

The servant went in search of his master, leaving Greystone to wait in what some might call a drawing room, a dusty, smoky space unfit for entertaining people of his rank. An unmarried peer with no London house should settle for no less than the Albany Gentleman's Apartments, but Melton probably did not have sufficient funds to live in that exclusive residence. Or perhaps he was rejected. What a horror for Lady Beatrice if Melton had insisted that she share this place and serve as his hostess. The man should be flogged for his selfish, wastrel ways.

No, he chided himself, this was not the way to begin. He had come to humble himself to Melton, not criticize him for wasting a considerable fortune in three short years. And it seemed Melton was pleased to see him humbled, for he made no haste to put in an appearance.

Greystone chose not to sit on the dust-covered furniture,

but rather stood and stared out the window onto the narrow street below. Noisy tradesmen of every sort hawked their wares, as did several women whom he had been forced to pointedly ignore on his way here. Was this the sort of street where Kit and Ben had been taken? Or did their old master inhabit an even darker hole in the depths of London's slums?

He prayed that Jeremy Slate would soon bring him the information he needed to reclaim his little charges. The Bow Street Runner had accepted his assignment with all eagerness, certain he could find the boys *and* the necklace. But he'd advised Greystone not to set foot in those darker neighborhoods without escort and weapons, for desperation often led the poor to commit evil deeds, even against a peer of the realm. All the more reason for Parliament to provide an equitable pension to soldiers returning from the war, lest they likewise turn to crime in order to survive.

"Well, well, well." Melton sauntered into the room in his dressing gown, with his curly blond hair uncombed and several days' growth of brownish stubble marking him as the self-indulgent shirker that he was. "If it isn't the exalted and well-favored Lord Greystone." He flung himself down on an overstuffed settee, sending up a cloud of dust, and ordered his servant to bring him a brandy. "Anything for you, Greystone?"

"I thank you, but, no." *No, but I would like to wring your neck, you foolish young jackanapes.* Greystone again rebuked himself and prayed for the grace to do what he must. "But I would like to give you something—my apologies over the incident at my birthday ball."

Melton's jaw dropped, and a hint of innocent surprise filled his expression. Instantly Greystone could sense his own insincerity, though he doubted Melton realized it through his hungover haze. "Actually, I would ask something of you. Your forgiveness, if you would be so gracious as to grant it."

Melton still stared at him, but a wily grin took over his features.

"I realize this comes as a surprise." Greystone hurried on, lest his own mood change in reaction to such deplorable conduct. *Lord, this is so difficult.* "And therefore I do not expect an immediate reply. If you wish some penance on my part, I am more than willing to perform it." Where had that thought come from? It was a far too dangerous offer to make to this sort of person. But he could not retract his words.

Melton threw back his head and laughed, a high, giddy sound affected no doubt by the drink his servant had brought. "Oh, Greystone, Greystone, do you take me for a fool? I know exactly why you're here. You want my pretty little sister." He tossed down another gulp of brandy. "Do you really think I haven't noticed you at the theatre, watching her like a besotted schoolboy?" He emitted an unpleasant laugh. "And of course you may have her."

"I—" *I want to smash your nose for speaking so carelessly of Lady Beatrice.*

"For a price."

Greystone breathed out a hot sigh, feeling for a moment very much like a fire-breathing dragon. Would that he could direct his angry flames at this unworthy drunkard. But that would not save the man. It would only destroy Lady Beatrice's fond hopes for her brother's rehabilitation. With considerable difficulty, Greystone dismissed his anger. For now, he would play along with Melton. "And that price is?"

"Hmm." Melton tapped his chin thoughtfully. "What would you say to eighty thousand? I'm sure you have that available in your wallet." He chuckled drunkenly, evilly.

Greystone grasped his composure as if it were a lifeline. *Lord, is it ever acceptable to strike another man? To knock some good sense into him, of course.* "Eighty thousand, you say? Is that what you owe Rumbold?" That amount was likely three fourths of Melton's annual income.

"No." Melton's face fell into a petulant pout. "At least, not all of it. I have one or two other creditors who keep harassing me." He took another drink. "Blasted beasts. Common gutter trash, thinking they have the right to demand an earl's attention to such a petty matter as gambling debts."

Greystone moved back to the window and stared out at the "common gutter trash," most of them hardworking people who simply wanted to earn their daily bread. At odds with the setting, a well-dressed gentleman in a tall hat strutted along the street until blocked by a cart of freshly caught mussels and herring. While he scolded the fishmonger, an emaciated lad no bigger than Kit stole up behind him and snatched his wallet from his jacket pocket, then disappeared into the crowd. The outraged gentleman gave chase, and Greystone was tempted to dash down and help him. But he had another matter to finish first. Yet he could not ignore the irony. Melton was trying to pick his pocket. But unlike the lad who stole to feed his empty belly, the earl planned to feed his insatiable hunger for wicked living. And even if Greystone possessed eighty thousand in discretionary funds to give him, it would only further his descent into degeneracy.

"Well?"

To Greystone's surprise the desperation in Melton's tone moved him. Perhaps he truly was like the emaciated little thief, starving for something to nourish not his body, but his soul. Of course. Why had he not thought of it before? Melton needed Christ, not money, to solve his problems.

But how did one introduce the subject? If Greystone's brother Richard were here, he could employ the persuasive pastoral skills that had set Greystone on the right road all those years ago. Only one thought came to mind, and he plunged in before he could overthink it.

"You are correct in assuming I love Lady Beatrice and would be honored to have her for my wife." Having said it, he knew it to be true, but his joy over that realization would have to be delayed. Instead, he injected a tone into his words that was at once soothing and devoid of accusation. "However, if we are to be brothers—" The thought did not sit well, but it would soon be the necessary evil accompanying his greatest happiness. "We should come to some accord."

Melton sat up, all eagerness. "Yes. Exactly. I would not wish to be related to a miser." He waved a hand carelessly in the air. "And of course I would not wish for my dear sister to be married to one." Clearly that "dear sister" was an afterthought. "So you will give me the eighty thousand?" Desperate hope seemed to sober him, for his intense gaze seemed clear and focused.

This was not the direction Greystone wanted for this conversation. He must hasten to clear up the matter. "What I have in mind is actually a payment plan for you to abide by, with a worthy mentor to help you keep your gambling under control so your losses are no longer so devastating. In a word, you would be accountable to—"

"Payment plan?" Melton's expression went through a succession of changes: shock, horror, disgust and finally arrogance. "Accountable?" His voice rose in pitch and volume. "I am the fourth Earl of Melton. I am accountable to no one."

And there will be no fifth Earl of Melton if you do not mend your ways. But once again, Greystone refrained from rebuking him. "I fully understand your sense of privilege, Melton, but perhaps you might consider that with your title comes responsibility, as well."

Melton snorted. "My tenants are well taken care of. What more do they need than to work my farmland and send me the profits." He downed another drink. "Why should I have to defer my enjoyment of life? Eat, drink and be merry, I always say."

Aha, the perfect opening. "Yes, that scripture is often quoted in defense of merry times. But perhaps you recall that when our Lord related the story, he added that God spoke to the wealthy man, saying, *'Thou fool, this night thy soul shall be required of thee.'*" There was much more to the biblical story, but perhaps facing his own mortality would cause Melton sufficient alarm.

"Ugh! Have you become a preacher amongst us, Greystone? A Wilberforce?" He uttered an oath. "Why, you will never have any fun."

Greystone counted to ten before responding. "And you regard being eighty thousand pounds in debt as fun?" Again he withheld all accusation from his voice.

"Oh, enough of that." Melton stood, wobbled a bit, then sat back down. "I will not grant you permission to marry Beatrice. In fact I have promised her to another suitor whose generosity is not dependent upon payment plans and accountability." His lips curled in disgust as he said those last words.

A chill went down Greystone's spine, and this time he could barely contain his anger. He guessed that suitor to be Rumbold, for the man had worked long and hard seeking a wife who would elevate him to aristocratic circles. "If you recall, Melton, Lady Beatrice is of age. She and I have an agreement. I came to you only as a courtesy."

He could feel the strain on his face, and his fists clenched seemingly of their own will.

Melton stood and made an attempt at mirroring Greystone's rage, but his swagger lacked any semblance of a threat. "We shall see about that. When I tell her about my friend, she will see the light." His gaze shifted toward the door. Then he put wobbling fists at his waist. "Are you still here? Really, sir, we have nothing more to say to one other."

Greystone spun away and stalked out the door. For if he had waited even one more second, his only response would have been to thrash Melton until he begged for mercy.

Melton flopped down onto the settee, sending up a flurry of dust that made him sneeze. He waved away the haze and swigged down another drink. Cheap brandy. Vile stuff. Nothing at all like the rich amber brew Rumbold had taught him to enjoy, along with a few other pleasures worthy of an earl. But then, if Father had done his duty by him, Melton never would have had to depend upon Rumbold to teach him anything. Drat the man for his lack of care, his lack of instruction. He'd left so many lessons untaught, so much influence not yet established.

Influence. What a laugh. In spite of what he'd told Beebe, he hadn't the slightest whit of influence in Parliament. After three years most of his peers turned away at the sight of him. All except that Winston fellow, the somber baron with an untarnished reputation. Who wanted that sort of bore for a friend? A gentleman had to have fun, just as he'd told Greystone, another bore. It was all too annoying.

But guilt quickly replaced his annoyance. He should have seized the opportunity to have either peer for a friend, even if he refused to be accountable to Greystone. Yet the idea of settling his debts with Rumbold and getting out of his stranglehold sounded appealing. All he needed was a little more time. Once his tenants sent their rents, he could make his first payment.

He shuddered. Had Rumbold listened to the conversation through those thin walls? He spied on everything Melton did these days, he and Miss Carlton, that paramour of his who lived in the next apartment. Pathetic girl. Did she really think Rumbold would marry her when he could have an earl's sister?

But that thought brought a sick sensation to Melton's stomach. Given a choice between the two men, he would far rather have stuffy Greystone for a brother than an illegitimate social climber.

"Having a rest, are we?" Rumbold ambled into the room from the outer corridor, with Miss Carlton on his heels. "Should you not be up and about, ready to go and speak with Lord Blakemore about that matter we discussed?"

"Oh, bother." Melton huffed out a sigh. "Must I?"

"But of course you must." Rumbold sat beside him, his tone smooth, his eyes threatening. "Why must I continue to remind you of how important it is to present my case for legitimacy?"

"I shan't go. I have a headache." Melton flung a hand over his forehead for emphasis.

Rumbold grabbed his arm and came near to twisting it. "You will do as I say."

"Ow. Let go of me. I am an earl. How dare you?"

"Oh, I dare, *Lord* Melton. Now we must talk about your little visit with Greystone. Did you know he was coming?"

The threat in his tone caused a flurry of nerves inside Melton's belly. "Of course not. But I do think I handled him very nicely."

Rumbold's laugh was not pleasant. "Is that what you

think, eh? You fool. The man thinks he can marry Lady Beatrice without your permission. You know we cannot let that happen."

So Rumbold *had* eavesdropped and heard every word.

"Yes, yes, I know." Melton was tiring of this conversation. He took another drink and shuddered. As hot as the day was, he felt a chill. "You want to marry my sister, though I cannot think it possible, old boy." If she chose this man, she would straightaway lose Melton's good opinion.

"Marry her?" Miss Carlton screeched. She always screeched. "You promised to marry me, Rummy."

"Shut up." In two shakes Rumbold stood and walked across the room to slap the girl to the floor. "You keep your mouth shut."

Without answering, she curled into a ball, whimpering.

Melton looked away. Pathetic creature. But now Rumbold stood over him, and he felt a bit pathetic himself.

"You will arrange for me to meet Lady Beatrice as soon as possible." Rumbold's eyes held an evil glint. "If you refuse, I shall ruin you."

How had this man come to have such power over him? But in truth, he did. Like a fool, Melton had gambled all of his father's wealth away, and now he held only one card to trump this man: the ace of hearts. But would Beebe care enough to save him?

Mrs. Parton insisted that Lucy must occupy herself with charitable work until Lord Greystone decided what to do with her. With Beatrice's help, she instructed the girl in how to make aprons for the St. Ann's orphans. But as Lucy attempted to sew careful stitches, her hands shook, and she kept sticking herself with the needle. At last she stopped and stared toward the window of the small back parlor while drops of blood stained the pristine white linen.

Praying that she was considering how to mend her ways, Beatrice did not try to converse with her.

Mrs. Parton's house was never noisy, but today it was particularly quiet. Even servants tiptoed about as if they knew something was out of order. One or two cast surreptitious glances at Lucy, the maid who seemed privileged to keep company with their employer and her companion. But no one breeched decorum by daring to ask about it.

"Mrs. Parton." Palmer stood in the parlor door, confusion filling his usually stoic face. "Lord Greystone's Crawford is here to see you."

The lady nodded grimly. Beatrice set aside her sewing. Lucy renewed her tears.

"Send him in, Palmer." Mrs. Parton moved to the settee and took her place on the other side of Lucy.

Crawford entered, his bearing stiff and mechanical. "Begging your pardon, Mrs. Parton."

"One moment, Crawford." She waved her butler in. "Palmer, you must go out and close the door. Make certain no one eavesdrops on our conversation, even you."

Palmer lifted his chin, offended. "Of course, madam."

Once he closed the door, she waved Crawford to a chair across from the settee, dismissing his objection to sitting in her presence. "Do you have a message for us from Lord Greystone?"

His pale face even whiter around the edges, the old servant seemed to wilt a little. "Yes, madam. I am to take the girl back to Greystone Hall and keep her in confinement."

At his reference to her as "the girl," Lucy whimpered. "Grandfather, I—"

"Hush, girl." His eyes blazed briefly before his facade fell back into place. "We are not to say anything to Lady Greystone for now, so if I may ask your indulgence?"

"Of course." Mrs. Parton sighed, a sad sound that broke

Beatrice's heart. This usually merry lady was as devastated by Lucy's crime as Beatrice. "We will not speak of it."

He stood and whipped his hand in the air to order Lucy to follow.

"Wait, please." Beatrice could not let them go this way. "Crawford, do you know what Lord Greystone plans to do?"

He winced slightly. "His lordship has retained the services of a Bow Street Runner. I expect him to send her to the magistrate for judgment."

Beatrice shuddered. If Lord Greystone brought charges against Lucy, as he well had the right to do, the only future she could see for the girl was prison or transportation to Australia. Although she could not bring herself to pray for utter forgiveness without punishment, she could pray that the viscount would be merciful and not seek to have the girl hanged for her crime.

Chapter Twenty-One

Blinding rage filled Greystone as he flipped a coin to the boy tending his horse and leaped into the saddle. As much as he wanted to whip the gelding into a mind-clearing gallop, such an exercise would endanger the people crowding the streets. They were not at fault for his anger any more than they were at fault for their own wretched lives.

Why had he ever thought Melton would see reason and reform his evil ways? He was not Richard. He had no gift for converting sinners. He was Lord Greystone, the viscount, for goodness sake, with an entirely different set of responsibilities. Richard gave sermons in order to persuade people to godliness. Greystone gave orders and expected obedience.

Reaching a less populated avenue, he urged his horse to a trot, while a haunting suspicion crept into his mind. Did everyone in Melton's family harbor his evil tendencies? Greystone had known Lady Beatrice for only a short time. Like a smitten schoolboy, he had fallen wildly in love with her outward beauty and graciousness. But were there hidden faults beneath that exquisite face, that flawless deportment? He had been in London long enough to see numerous aristocratic gentlemen assume that a lady's outward appearance revealed the heart within. Once married they were tragically disappointed when their wives' true natures revealed selfishness and excess. But how did a gentleman discover a lady's worthiness before he became irrevocably tied to her? Even Mrs. Parton's endorsement could not be trusted, for she always thought the best of everyone.

He knew he was being unfair. Lady Beatrice was not her brother. She had even endeavored to avoid Melton. But even if she was perfect in every way, she was still the man's sister. Mother's admonitions aside, Greystone had seen for himself how bad associations could hinder good works. That was why he had endeavored so strenuously not to surrender his heart to the lady. Now if he married her, Melton would use it to his advantage and wedge himself into every worthwhile project Greystone supported. As an earl his superior rank alone should grant him favor with certain powerful people, despite his debts being beyond reason. After all, the Prince Regent was terribly in debt and laughed the whole thing off as inconsequential.

One thing Greystone knew: God had called him to good works, especially in regard to unfortunate boys like Kit and Ben. But the Almighty had not spoken as forcefully to him about Lady Beatrice. Perhaps his heart had been shouting so loud that his mind could not hear the Lord. How would he ever know? Perhaps he should visit Richard, if he was still in town, and seek his advice.

Arriving at his town house, he could not keep his eyes from aiming at the residence next door, even as he hoped Lady Beatrice would not see him from one of the many windows. If he went to her now and told her about his visit to Melton, he would not be able to hide his rage and indignation. She would defend her brother. They would argue. All would come to an end. No, it was best for him to ponder the matter for a while, seek Richard's advice and try to pray over the noise of his emotions.

In any event he still must deal with Lucy and figure out how to rescue two tiny lads. Greystone hoped Crawford had been able to fetch Lucy quietly without arousing Mother's suspicions. He prayed Jeremy Slate had discovered where Kit and Ben had been taken. And perhaps he would learn where Warren had sold the necklace, if indeed he had. The man would be mad to keep it in his possession for long.

He hoped, prayed—but enough of that. With one last glance toward Mrs. Parton's house, he strode up the steps into his own.

Beatrice turned away from her window, swallowing her disappointment. She had wanted to peek out from behind the curtain and wave to Lord Greystone, but after deciding it would not be proper, had remained hidden. Moreover he looked none too pleased as he surrendered his horse to the waiting groom. If all had gone well with Melly, surely he would have come here first. This did not bode well for their friendship. If he was angry with Melly, did Greystone think she would not support him? That she would choose her brother over the gentleman who had won her heart, as indeed he had? Now she could not even tell Mrs. Parton about their agreement, which had caused her such joy only yesterday and now burned in her heart like a coal in the hearth.

But perhaps this was best. Lord Greystone had many responsibilities, not the least of which was dealing with Lucy and finding the lost boys. She would wait patiently for his explanation.

But an inner voice protested that he should have come to see her. After their heartfelt conversation, it seemed somehow inauspicious for their future that Lord Greystone would not seek her help in sorting out whatever had happened with Melly, just as he had trusted her in the matter of Lucy.

In the entryway Greystone tossed his riding gloves on a side table before the footman could reach for them. He strode toward the staircase, determined to avoid Mother in the event that she was in the drawing room.

"My lord," the footman called after him.

Greystone spun around, ready to shut the man up. But once again, this person was not at fault for his difficulties. "Yes, Robert."

The man's posture was impeccable, something Greystone had never noticed before.

"Lord Winston awaits you in the drawing room, milord."

"Winston. What the deuce does he want?" He cringed at his own words. Mother never approved of what she called *veiled swearing.* "Never mind. I will see him." He started toward the closed double doors of the drawing room, then paused. "Where is the viscountess?"

"Out, milord." At Greystone's questioning expression, he added, "With Mr. Grenville."

"One of my brothers?"

"No, sir. The older Mr. Grenville."

Curious. Mother had been out with Uncle Grenville three of the past nine days. But he would have to address that issue later. He strode across the wide entryway, his heels clacking on the finely polished marble tiles as a sense of foreboding lurched into his belly. What could Winston possibly want?

The baron stood in front of the hearth studying the

painting above it, a massive work of art that only slightly enhanced the beauty of Greystone Hall.

"An exquisite painting." Winston did not turn to face Greystone. "A charming country manor house."

"Hmm. Come to admire the artwork, I see." Greystone had a twinge of guilt over his rudeness, but he could not help himself. "Shall I give you the tour?"

Now the baron turned and gave him a sardonic grin. "And then perhaps I can return the favor and give you a tour of my home in Grosvenor Square."

"Of course." *Easy, Greystone. Keep a civil tongue.*

"My lord." Robert stood in the doorway. "Shall I bring tea?"

Crawford would have done so without asking.

"Yes, of course." Greystone eyed his guest. "You will take tea, will you not?"

"Of course."

The baron's grin was beginning to annoy him. Might as well get this over, whatever *this* was. "To what do I owe the pleasure of your visit?"

"You may not think it a pleasure when you hear me." Winston frowned and shook his head. "That was a bad beginning. Forgive me."

"Of course." Unlike Melton, Greystone would readily grant forgiveness to his guest. "Proceed."

"Very well. I will be blunt. I am not unlike any other peer of our age, and the Season has come for me to choose a wife." He coughed softly into his hand, no doubt to give himself time to think. "I flatter myself that I am not without the attributes necessary to attract a young lady with her own distinctions."

Greystone wanted to send the baron packing so he could get on with his urgent matters, but Winston was, after all, a decent gentleman, if a bit priggish. Pompous, actually.

"How may I assist you in this, sir? Ah, never mind. I know exactly where to send you. Lady Grandly has two fine daughters with considerable dowries—"

Winston shrugged. "That is but a small consideration, one I would be willing to entirely dispense with for the right lady of good social rank." As if unaware of his actions, he looked in the direction of Mrs. Parton's house. Or so it seemed to Greystone. "Look here, Greystone, I will be blunt. Have you offered for Lady Beatrice?"

Greystone had to admire his candor. More could get done in this world if people would simply speak their minds. At odds with that thought, he himself could not so much as answer the baron honestly. No, he had not offered for Lady Beatrice. Yes, he did love her. But after today's interview with Melton, could he bring himself to marry the earl's sister and be forever tied to him? That question hung over him, one minute a ray of sunshine, the next Damocles' sword. But he could hardly refuse to answer the baron. And he certainly would not step aside for the gentleman. Not yet.

A reprieve came in the form of Robert bringing the tea tray. "Begging your pardon, my lord, but the Bow Street Runner has returned."

Greystone's heart lurched. "Send him in, Robert. Will you excuse me, Winston?"

"A Bow Street Runner?" Winston's eyebrows arched, and his smirk disappeared, replaced by interest. "Having an adventure, Greystone?"

Before he could answer, Jeremy Slate strode into the room, his ruddy face beaming with promise. "Good afternoon, Lord Greystone." He spied Winston and stopped. "My lord?"

Greystone studied Winston briefly. If nothing else, the baron was discreet, and it was possible he could offer some advice regarding this situation. "He's all right, Slate." The remark earned him an appreciative nod from Winston. "What did you learn?"

"Well, sir, I have it on good authority that the lads are with their old master, all right, but he ain't where he used to be, and he ain't a sweep no more."

A cold anger now gripped Greystone. The chimney sweep had not been his usual man, which meant someone had let the scoundrel into his house, undoubtedly to search for valuables to steal. Warren the footman, of course. But how had that one passed Crawford's careful examination? Even with Lucy's recommendation, the old butler should have seen what kind of man he was. "Where is this former sweep?"

"In a tavern down by the river that caters to his sort. He's buying drinks for everybody who comes in, saying he's got two boys for sale and bragging about how he put one over on a lord." Slate tapped the side of his nose in a knowing gesture, and his dark eyes gleamed. "What he don't know is that Warren Snead's been caught by my colleague and carted off to the magistrate."

"So they were in collusion." Greystone felt sick at the thought of him selling the boys for who knew what sort of labor. Nonetheless he began to hope they could be rescued. "And the viscountess's necklace?"

"That's how we got 'im in the first place. Snead sold it to an honest man, who knew something wasn't right. He bought it with a hundred pounds of his own money, then brung it to the magistrate." One of Slate's eyebrows went up, the other went down, and he dipped his chin. "If you get my meaning, my lord."

"A hundred pounds? Why, it's worth ten thousand." The revelation was so astounding, Greystone could hardly maintain his dignity. "Of course I shall repay him and add a handsome reward."

Slate smiled his approval, and in this significant moment, Greystone took no offense at his insolence. "And where is the necklace?"

Grinning broadly, Slate reached into his pocket and drew out a small cloth-covered bundle. He unfolded the black material to reveal the ruby necklace in all its glory. "'Tis all in one piece, as best I can tell, my lord."

Overwhelming relief flooded Greystone. He gently took the jewels in hand as if they might break, studying them carefully. "Yes, completely undamaged. Indeed the man will receive a handsome reward."

"You know, Greystone," Winston said. "We should go straightaway to the tavern and nab the other scoundrel."

"We?" Greystone stared at the baron. He had only a vague idea of what was going on, yet he appeared as eager to join them as a hound before the hunt.

"I don't know, my lord." Slate scratched his chin. "'Tis not a place for quality to venture, if you get my meaning." He repeated his favorite catchphrase. "Maybe I should fetch another Runner or two."

"I appreciate your concern, but I am going." The boys would be frightened enough without having strangers grab them from their kidnapper. Greystone tilted his head toward Winston, wordlessly asking Slate's counsel.

"Well, my lord, if you insist." He clicked his tongue. "Three's better than two." He seemed about to nudge Greystone, then wisely changed his mind.

Greystone again studied the baron. He possessed a sturdy frame and, if Greystone's memory served him, had boxed at Oxford, both of which would recommend him for the task. In the absence of his two brothers, perhaps this fellow would make the perfect accomplice. "Very well. Let us make haste."

"One thing, my lord." Slate pointed to Greystone's blue jacket. "You'd best put on some plainer clothes, and black like this gentleman's, so you won't stand out as the night draws on."

"Easily done." He had noticed the baron's preference for dark clothing. Perhaps with that blond hair, which made him appear younger than his five and twenty years, he hoped to present a more mature, even severe appearance. Perhaps that accounted for his pomposity, as well.

Eager to change, Greystone hastened upstairs to his bedchamber and, with Gilly's help, hid the necklace deep within a bureau. Mother would require an explanation, but that would have to wait until later.

In addition to his advice about clothing, Slate said they must pack weapons, so he located pistols, knives and swords in the old armory room. Within the hour they stood at the front door prepared to leave, when Crawford approached and took Greystone aside.

"My lord, I have some apprehension about keeping my granddaughter—" he choked on the word, something he never did "—about keeping Lucy confined in the nursery any longer. It has already ignited gossip among the staff, and I fear it will soon reach Lady Greystone's ears."

Anxious to be on his way, Greystone nevertheless summoned patience to deal with this faithful old servant. And of course Mother must not learn of Lucy's crime until he decided what to do with her. Indeed she must be judged. His possession of the necklace did not diminish the girl's part in the affair. "What do you propose?"

Pain ripped across the usually stoic facade, and Greystone experienced a wave of pity for the man. "My lord, could you see fit—" He coughed away emotion. "I realize the girl deserves no mercy, but if you could grant a measure of grace…"

"Tell me what you are thinking."

"If I could accompany her to Greystone Lodge, there to place her in guarded service as a scullery maid, she would have no access to anything valuable. A few years of that drudgery would perhaps be sufficient to reform her." Again he coughed. "More than transportation." He straightened to his full five feet nine inches. "And if you will have me, I will be pleased to serve as a footman under Johnson."

Greystone regarded the man, who was clearly struggling. He had hired his own granddaughter, believing her to be of good character. Yet her head had been turned by a clever boy who wanted only to use her. Greystone had considered transportation to Australia a more lenient punishment than simply casting her out without references, for that would undoubtedly lead to a sordid life. But this solution trumped them all. Of course this meant Crawford would be demoted to footman to serve under the Greystone Lodge butler. Truly, his devotion to his granddaughter was costing him dearly.

"A good plan, Crawford." Greystone clapped him on the shoulder and received a gasp of surprise for the gesture. He started to turn away, his anxiety about the climbing-boys beginning to consume him.

"My lord." Crawford's pained expression conveyed his regret over delaying his master. "May we do this post-haste? The gossip?"

Greystone would have laughed had the situation not been so serious, for the Almighty certainly had a way of bringing together important matters. "When I return with Kit and Ben, have Lucy prepared for the journey. You and

I will take the coach and deliver them to Greystone Lodge ourselves. Convey my orders to Gilly. He must go, as well."

Crawford's eyes reddened. "I thank you, my lord." He bowed away, clearing his throat as he went.

Greystone returned to his companions. "Shall we go?"

Within minutes they had mounted three of Greystone's best horses for the ride across town. He found himself beyond eager to see the boys again, for he felt the urgent need to reassure them that they had not been abandoned, that he would keep his promise to see to their futures. And to add a tangible note to his pledge, he had tucked their new shoes into the satchel that hung from his saddle. They might be required to run.

But as evening drew on and they traveled deeper into the London slums, Greystone sensed this mission would involve more than a struggle against one vile kidnapper. They were descending into a world of darkness and evil such as he had never before witnessed, and he prayed God's mercy upon them all.

Chapter Twenty-Two

"Melly!" Beatrice hurried into Mrs. Parton's drawing room, hoping against hope that her employer would not be told of his visit before she could persuade him to leave. "What are you doing here?" A movement in the corner of her eye drew her attention to another man—a gentleman, if his clothes were any indication.

"Beebe, darling." Melly walked toward her none too steadily. "Is that any way to greet your only brother and his friend?"

A sick feeling came over her. This was not a gentleman at all, but Mr. Rumbold, against whom Mrs. Parton had so emphatically warned her. "Who let you in? Not Palmer. He has strict orders to keep you and this person—"

"Hush!" Melly's pasty complexion reddened. "I forbid you to insult my friend." After a scolding look from his companion, he drew himself up and tugged at the hem of his blue jacket as if to regain his dignity. Unfortunately that endeavor would require much more. "Besides," he leaned close and murmured urgently, "you agreed to meet him." Again he straightened. "Lady Beatrice, may I present my good friend, Frank Rumbold?" He chuckled, an odd little sound so unlike him. "Rumbold, this is my sister, Lady Beatrice Gregory."

She did not offer her hand, but nonetheless the man stepped over and took it, raising it to his lips in a familiar way rather than bowing over it as a gentleman would. When she tried to pull back, he held tight and smiled in that same familiar way that made her stomach turn.

"Lady Beatrice, I have longed for this day. When I saw you across the room at Lord Greystone's ball, I was utterly smitten with your beauty. And now, so close to you—" he kissed her hand again, holding his lips against her knuckles for entirely too long "—I see that my eyes did not fail me. You are the most ravishing creature I have ever met."

Beatrice yanked her hand away. "How dare you?" She spun around toward the door, but Melly grabbed her arm, emitting that horrid, nervous laugh again.

"Now, Beebe—"

She pried off his hand and thrust it away from her. Strangely, he seemed to have very little strength to stop her. "I demand that you leave this instant."

"Why?" He blinked innocently, as if he had no idea why she was angry. "I have merely come to make a good match for you, dear sister, just as I promised."

"Yes, Lady Beatrice." Mr. Rumbold moved close to her, far too close for even a brother to approach a lady. "We shall make an excellent match. You have the social credentials, and I have the wealth. We will take London by storm. That is, after they get over the shock." He laughed, an evil sound that sickened her clear into her bones.

She stepped away, praying he would not follow. Perhaps this required a different tactic. "But you are too late, Melly." She would not honor this man by addressing him directly. "I have an understanding with someone else."

She would not speak her beloved's name to these two. But how she wished he would come calling this very moment.

"Oh, we know all about Greystone." Melly snorted. "Came to me today all high and mighty to ask for your hand." He winked at Mr. Rumbold. "Unfortunately he didn't have the bride price." Both men guffawed as though he had just made a clever witticism. "It didn't take much to send him packing."

"Indeed not." Mr. Rumbold continued to chuckle. "I was in another room listening the whole time, and all the man did was whine. Said you weren't worth the trouble. That he'd find a wife who actually possessed a dowry."

Lord Greystone never would have said such a thing, but she would not respond to them. Nor would she excuse herself. Praying they would not follow, she strode toward the door—right into Mrs. Parton.

"Well, I must say." The lady's face resembled a threatening storm. "The very idea." She glanced over her shoulder. "Palmer, escort these *gentlemen* out."

The burly butler and two equally burly footmen stepped into the drawing room, their faces properly blank, their postures properly threatening.

"If you please, milord." Palmer gave Melly a slight bow and aimed one white-gloved hand out toward the door.

"Beebe, please." Melly's face crumpled into the pout that had always swayed her to his will. And then there was that strange, almost frightened look in his eyes. Did he fear his friend?

But she would have none of it. Instead, she settled her gaze upon Mrs. Parton's much-loved countenance.

"Never mind, Melton." Mr. Rumbold's grating voice rasped across Beatrice's soul, for she sensed a hint of growing desperation in the vile man. "You'll find another way to settle your debts. Even if I have to take it out of your hide."

Beatrice gasped and tried to turn, but Mrs. Parton held her fast. "He would not dare to lift a hand against a peer of the realm."

"No," Beatrice whispered. "But he could force Melly to raise the rents on his tenants or sell off valuable heirlooms or some other dastardly thing."

From the sounds of footsteps moving behind her, she knew they were leaving. Once the door closed behind them, she heaved out a deep sigh and resigned herself to the comfort of her good friend's arms.

A yellow-brown fog blanketed the docks and lay over the river like a shroud, while water lapped against the unstable old wharf, causing it to sway in the strong current. Greystone's knees felt as wobbly as the boards beneath him, and he lifted a silent prayer for strength and courage. Other than the usual gentleman's fisticuffs, swordplay and wrestling with his brothers, he had never faced any real danger, had never been tried in the fire of warfare as his brother Edmond had when he was a soldier. Strangely, Winston seemed unconcerned, almost cavalier about their surroundings. But perhaps it was mere bravado, a mask in keeping with his usual arrogance. In one way, his attitude gave Greystone confidence, in another way, concern. Bravado not undergirded with real courage would not save Kit and Ben.

Both he and Winston had placed themselves under Slate's command, trusting the man to know his business, and had been warned not to flaunt their rank. Thus he resisted the urge to retrieve his scented handkerchief to deflect the miasma of death and disease permeating the place.

At a shabby stable—a shed, actually—they had found a reliable lad to keep their horses out of sight until needed. Now with capes around their shoulders and black slouch hats low over their faces, they crept along the outside of a tavern where the sounds of drunken laughter, threatening quarrels and discordant music wafted out into the night air.

A person could barely see ten feet ahead, so they stuck close to one another. Then, with a wave of his hand, Slate silently ordered Greystone and Winston to wait by the tavern's outside wall. He changed his posture and staggered through the fog toward the dimly lit entryway. One would never know he was an upstanding officer of the law.

While they waited, they could not ignore the sounds coming through the open windows of the tavern's upper floor some eight feet above them. Greystone ground his teeth. The depravity of this place sickened him, and from Winston's snort of disgust, he could sense his comrade shared his sentiments. That spoke well of the baron. Perhaps there was more to the gentleman than pomposity and swagger.

Slate slithered back toward them through the fog, his posture straightening as he came. The man was nothing short of brilliant, as good an actor as Elliston. "My lord," he whispered. "There's some dozen-odd villains in there. I don't advise marching in without more men on our side."

"What?" Winston huffed softly, and an odd bit of merriment colored his tone. "Why, that is a mere four drunks apiece." He elbowed Greystone. "I'm up for it if you are." He grasped the hilt of the sword hanging at his side.

"Uh, sir?" Slate's face was unreadable under his hat brim, but Greystone caught his meaning.

"No sense in getting banged up until we are certain the boys are here." He hated sounding like a coward, especially in front of his rival. Though he could not imagine why he still thought of Winston as a rival.

"Hmm. You may have something there. I have a younger sister to provide for. Guess I should take care." Winston shrugged. "What's next, then?"

Slate stared up at the window above them. "You hear that, my lord?"

"Not that I wish to, but one could hardly miss it."

"No, sir. Not that. I would never…" Slate cleared his throat. "It's the other sound. Like a child coughing."

Instantly alert, Greystone strained his ears. "Yes, yes. I hear it. Kit!" He stepped back and studied the wall. "I am going up. Boost me through that window." He removed his hat and beckoned for them to give him a leg up.

"Begging your pardon, my lord." Slate stayed him with his hand. "I've a bit of experience with this. I'll go."

Greystone gave his offer only the briefest consideration. "The boys know me. I shall go." It was an order, and Slate bowed to it.

Greystone also set aside his cloak and gun, but kept the sheathed knife at his side. Then the other two men formed a step with their joined hands and launched him through the window. Barreling over the casement, he landed with a thump in a narrow corridor, and for the briefest moment, the entire establishment went silent. Then riotous laughter burst forth from below, and the evil merriment continued.

Light from below filtered up the staircase to reveal some six or seven doors. Greystone listened for Kit's voice to no avail. Then…another cough and a whimper. He moved down the corridor toward it.

"Shut yer face, you wretched brat." A woman's voice. Probably an older woman, from the croaking sound of it.

"Leave 'im be!" Kit cried. A smack, another whimper.

Greystone burst through the door just in time to seize a barbed stick the slattern raised.

"What—"

None too gently Greystone covered her mouth from behind and pulled her against him, fighting off nausea from the odors of sweat and ale. "Not another word," he hissed.

"Gov'ner." Both boys seemed to understand that they must speak softly. They leaped off a narrow filthy bed and grabbed his legs, clearly not understanding that he needed to keep his balance. The whole group came near to falling in a heap. All the while the stout woman tried to scream beneath his gloved hand and struggled to free herself.

"Kit. Ben. Stop." He managed to huff out the words.

They backed off, good lads, freeing him to take out his handkerchief and cram it into the woman's mouth, then pull out his knife. Too bad he had not thought to bring a rope, but perhaps a stern warning would sufficiently bind her. "If you make a sound." He whispered with as much of a growl as he could manage while his emotions threatened to strangle him. He could never use the weapon on her, but he must not betray that sentiment. He punctuated his words with a fierce scowl that likely would have made Elliston proud.

Success! In the dim candlelight he read raw fear in the woman's face as she stared at the knife. From the dark bruises on her face he guessed she had seen her own share of beatings. No doubt she would receive another one for letting the boys escape. But he could do nothing for her, at least not now. "We are going to leave, and you will not make a sound." He sweetened the order with a gold florin—entirely too much, of course, but the first coin he found in his waistcoat pocket—and was gratified to see tears and a small nod in response.

She pulled the handkerchief from her mouth. "Well,

ain't you a pretty one, milord?" She fingered the mono-
gram, then held the cloth out to him. "Fer the coin and
yer good looks, I won't say nothin'." Her ale-laden breath
forced him back a step.

"You keep it." He could not resist a derisive snort.
"And if anyone wants to know what that *G* stands for, it
is Greystone, the lord whom your master bragged about
besting."

He resisted the urge to embrace the boys and instead
herded them down the corridor toward the window.

"'Ere now, what's this?" The erstwhile chimney sweep
staggered up the stairs and lumbered toward Greystone.
"Them's my property. What'ya think yer doin'?"

"Out the window, boys," Greystone ordered as he
slammed his fist into the drunken miscreant's jaw, knock-
ing him to the floor. Even though his knuckles stung from
the blow, the urge to beat the man to a pulp was palpable.
But he must not take the time. "Jump down to the gentlemen below. You can trust them."

"Help! Thief!" The man scrambled toward the staircase.

Greystone started after him, but the woman stepped
from the room and tripped the crook. He barreled down
the staircase head over heels.

"That's a bonus, milord. No need to pay extra." The
woman cackled. "Been wantin' to do that fer twenty
years." She waved a hand toward the window. "Best be
off now."

Unable to stop himself, Greystone blew her a kiss, then
jumped to the ground. His feet hit harder than he'd expected, and pain shot up his legs. He grunted in disgust
at his weakness. He should be in better shape, but who
expected a peer to face this sort of danger?

"That's them what stole my property." The sweep

limped out of the tavern with half a dozen thugs behind him. "Get 'im. Get all of 'um."

Greystone shook off his discomfort and snatched up Kit. Slate pulled out two pistols, while Winston unsheathed his sword, a double-bladed rapier.

"Take the boys," Winston said. "I shall manage this lot."

"Sir, it's my duty to deal with this sort," Slate said.

Winston smirked. "My good man, this is a mere trifle. Be gone." He gave a careless wave of his free hand. Turning to the mob, he aimed the rapier first at one, then another. "Who will be the first to die this night?"

"Come, Slate." Greystone prayed the baron would not be injured, but these criminals would not likely kill a peer. A Runner was another matter.

"Aye, sir." Slate grabbed Ben, and the two men dashed up the pitch-black alley toward the stables where their horses awaited.

Within five minutes Winston sauntered into the run-down shed and sheathed his rapier. "Cowards, the lot of them. Not one would take me on."

Greystone shook his head. This gentleman was not all pomp and bluster, after all.

In a short time the small troop had paid the lad who had kept their horses, reclaimed the beasts and now hastened through the fog back toward Greystone Hall. Even in the hazy darkness he could see the boys trading looks as Kit sat in front of him and Ben clung to Slate. His arrogance firmly in place, Winston had rejected the opportunity to carry one of the lads. The baron had no idea what he was missing.

"Coo, Ben," Kit called out, once they had left the docks far behind. "He brung our shoes, just like I told you he would."

With some difficulty Greystone squelched the swell of emotions engendered by that declaration of trust. No, the baron had no idea what he was missing.

Chapter Twenty-Three

"If that is what you call an adventure, you lead a life that is entirely too sheltered." Still on horseback, Winston offered Greystone one of his characteristic smirks.

Greystone laughed. The escapade had taken less than four hours, and they arrived at Greystone Hall before first light. He felt too pleased and far too exhilarated over getting the boys safely home to let the baron's arrogance annoy him, even if he spoke the truth about a sheltered life. Perhaps all that would change now. Here in front of Greystone Hall, with a sleeping Kit in his arms and Slate beside him holding Ben, he felt a new sense of empowerment, a feeling that he could accomplish great things. Even his bloody, stinging knuckles seemed like a badge of honor instead of something he would have to explain to Mother.

"Will you come in for some refreshment, Winston?" He forced the invitation out, lest he be accused of ingratitude.

To his relief the baron shook his head. "But if I may borrow your horse? I sent my carriage away thinking to get some exercise by walking home, but I hardly expected to be going back at three in the morning."

"Of course. Return it at your convenience." Perhaps he should amend that. He would not like for Winston to spend any more time in this neighborhood than necessary, lest he feel the urge to call upon Lady Beatrice in Greystone's absence. "Of course I mean you should have your groom see to it."

"Of course." Winston did not seem eager to leave. "What will you do with them?" He nodded toward Kit with a sneer, as if the lads were stray mongrels.

"I am taking them to my boys' school in Shrewsbury." Not that it was any of his business. "So if you will excuse me?"

"Hmm. Going now?" Even in the darkness Greystone could see a glint in his eyes.

"Yes. I want them safely away from London." A chill went through him. The trip should take just over a week, plenty of time for Winston to insinuate himself into Mrs. Parton's good graces and perhaps even Lady Beatrice's. Greystone had known her for such a short time and had no idea whether or not she was at all fickle. "I should not like for their former master to know where they are, however." Foolish of him to have answered the baron's question.

Winston grunted. "Have no fear. I am not one to gossip." He turned the horse and disappeared into the darkness.

One day soon Greystone would have to show his gratitude for that admirable discretion. Winston was pompous, but he had been a bold and fearless companion during their small adventure. But now to the matter at hand. The instant he tapped on the front door, Robert opened it.

"Good morning, my lord." The man gave him a flawless bow, just the proper degree for an upper servant. "Lady Greystone returned home a few minutes after midnight and retired straightaway." The very news a good butler would offer. Then he tilted his head toward Crawford, Lucy and Gilly, who stood beside several pieces of baggage. "Your bags are packed, sir, and the coach is hitched and ready in the mews to be brought around upon your order."

"Yes, send for it." Greystone looked the man up and down. He could not recall how long he had served the family, but he had never been known to blunder in any of his duties. "Robert, what is your last name?"

He cleared his throat. "Roberts, my lord."

Greystone could hardly stifle a laugh. "Robert Roberts?"

He shrugged ever so slightly. "Who can answer for one's parents, my lord?"

"Yes. Who, indeed?" Greystone certainly would not try. "Well, Roberts, I should like for you to serve as my butler while I am gone. When I return, we can discuss the matter fully."

"Yes, my lord." He gave another bow, a little too low this time, perhaps to hide the smile spreading across his face.

But Greystone also noticed that Crawford's usually stoic expression had faltered. After more than forty years in his position, he must be devastated to have it snatched away over something not his fault. "Crawford, we will lay Kit and Ben on the settees in the drawing room. You and Lucy are to watch over them while I write a letter to Mother about our trip." And one to Lady Beatrice, of course. "Roberts, you are not to discuss any of this with the staff. If anyone comes to call, say I am away on business. Nothing else."

"Of course, my lord."

In his study Greystone penned a brief note to Mother citing unexpected business at the estate as an excuse for his sudden departure. He added that Crawford's and Lucy's assistance were required in the matter. He also instructed her that Roberts would have charge of the household staff. Then he spent considerably more time on the missive to Lady Beatrice, explaining that the boys were safe and he would return in about ten days. Not for a moment did he truly think her fickle, despite his earlier concern. But this letter would ward off any uncertainties she might have about his devotion to her. He was about to seal it when another thought occurred to him, and he added a postscript. He would return in time for Lady Drayton's ball and requested the first and third dances *and* the dance before the supper. That would ensure she would be his dinner partner. It would also effectively announce to Society that they had an understanding.

Mother's letter was placed on the silver tray in the front entryway. For the letter to his lady love, he decided to enlist Jeremy Slate, another discreet and supremely dependable man. It would not do for anyone to read of his sentiments toward Lady Beatrice.

"Are you free to deliver this letter to the lady next door in a few hours?"

"I'd be pleased to do it, my lord, if it can wait until after I seize the sweep and carry him to the magistrate. We mustn't give him time to get away." He gave Greystone a worried frown. "Will that suit you, sir?"

Greystone would prefer for him to be awaiting Lady Beatrice, letter in hand, when she arose in the morning, but he dare not trust another messenger. "Perhaps in the early afternoon?"

"Yes, my lord, you can count on me."

"Indeed I can." He offered the man a gold florin, noting to himself that he deserved it far more than the wretched woman who had so cruelly watched over the boys.

But Slate held up a hand in refusal. "No, thank you, my lord. Just doing my duty."

"I understand what you are saying, and I appreciate your integrity in regard to your job. But being my messenger is not a part of your police duties." Again he held out the coin.

Slate hesitated, then shook his head. "No, thank you, sir." Pride borne of self-respect shone in his eyes.

Greystone returned the coin to his waistcoat pocket. "You are a good man, Mr. Slate."

"Thank you, sir. Your good opinion is reward enough." He cleared his throat. "And in the matter of the merchant who secured her ladyship's necklace?"

"Ah, yes. You have my thanks for reminding me." He returned to his office and took a hundred and fifty pounds from the safe, delivering the sum into Jeremy Slate's trustworthy hands.

With all these matters attended to, at last Greystone and his little band could be on their way. Just as first light dawned, the coach rumbled out of the city on the road to Shrewsbury, with a small sleeping boy nestled on either side of Greystone, and Gilly and two very unhappy servants across from him.

Beatrice idly stirred her morning coffee while Mrs. Parton thumbed through her mail and the usual invitations delivered first thing that morning. When the lady set it all aside and returned to her breakfast, Beatrice suppressed the disappointment rioting within her. Obviously Lord Greystone had not sent her a message. Perhaps his duties to Parliament would not permit him to visit until later this afternoon. She tried not to think about his angry countenance upon his return from visiting Melly yesterday. But she would have no peace until she knew everything, whether good or bad.

"Goodness." Mrs. Parton savored the last bite of her

pastry. "My new cook truly is exceptional." She waved for the footman to remove her plate. "Now, my dear, what shall we do today? I am eager for some sort of adventure."

"I am at your disposal, madam." Beatrice hoped she would stay home, but that was unlikely since last night's lingering fog had dissipated with the morning sun.

"Of course you are, my dear. But I should like to give you the opportunity to state your preferences."

"You are too kind." Indeed she was, as evidenced by this morning's delivery from Giselle. New gowns, shoes, hats, gloves, everything a young lady who was *out* could wish for. Except that she was not *out*. "But I truly have no preference." *Other than to stay in.*

"Ah." Mrs. Parton's face took on that wily look that suggested she had a plan. "Then we shall visit Lady Blakemore for her *at home*. I have not seen my good friend since her midnight supper, and we must discuss presenting you at Queen Charlotte's upcoming Drawing Room."

Beatrice's heart leaped. "Truly, Mrs. Parton? Did I receive an invitation?" Now she would be able to hold her head up in Society, and Lord Greystone would never have to explain why his bride had not been invited to meet the queen. She truly would be *out*.

"But of course. Did you not know I would secure an invitation for you in time?" Her merry smile was accompanied by a chuckle. "And I have no doubt that an Almack's voucher will arrive soon after."

Beatrice kept her smile in place, but she felt no added excitement. After all, Almack's was the place for young ladies to go when searching for a husband. Beatrice had found hers. Or so she hoped. Lord Greystone had not officially proposed. But he would. She was sure of it.

Unless in some way her brother had irrevocably destroyed any chance for her happiness.

* * *

His head aching, Melton trudged up the steps to his apartment, anxious for some time alone to sort things out—serious things, such as the way his life had plummeted to such desperate depths. He needed a drink to stop the pounding pain. Drat Lord Blakemore for turning down his request for an interview. Even appealing in his father's name had brought no success. Where was the earl's loyalty to the previous Lord Melton?

He reached the top of the staircase and entered his apartment. And froze. There on his settee sat Rumbold, his head in his hands, his jacket flung carelessly to the floor. How unusual for such a well-dressed gentleman. But, then, he wasn't truly a gentleman, simply a man masquerading as such amongst his betters. What gentleman would try to blackmail a friend to force the repayment of silly little gambling debts? He shoved away the thought that sixty thousand could not exactly be called little, not to mention the twenty thousand he owed other creditors.

"What are you doing here?" With an elegant town house of his own, why did this man continue to come here and harass him? Why was he not next door with his pathetic little mistress?

"Melton." The man jumped up and rushed across the small room to grab him by the upper arms. "You've got to help me."

"What?" Rumbold had never before appealed to him, only given orders. Melton tried to shake him off, to no avail. "What are you talking about? Where's Sims?" The little man who served as his butler, cook and valet often bore the brunt of Rumbold's anger.

"H-he went out." Rumbold's eyes were wild, his hair all askew. And bright red splotches covered his usually pristine white shirt and cravat. "Listen to me." He shook him. "I've got a...a problem."

The icy fingers of premonition sluiced through Melton's veins, and sobering clarity flooded his head. "What sort of problem?" He twisted out of Rumbold's grip, suddenly despising everything about this man.

"I...she...the woman was driving me mad. She burned—" Rumbold dropped into a chair. "No. I must not say that. But I never meant to...to—" He stared toward the closed door.

Now Melton understood, and a door of another sort closed within him. No matter what this man did to him, he would never wield any influence over him again. He made his way to the apartment next door, with Rumbold at his shoulder. To his horror and yet not his surprise, poor wretched Miss Carlton lay on the floor in a pool of blood, battered so badly that he had no doubt she was dead. Had Melton not killed his share of game, the sight might have made him sick. But this was a human being. A low-class paramour, but a human nonetheless.

That could be Beatrice.

Who had said that? Melton looked around, and a violent shiver swept over him. Was it God? Was it conscience? Whatever being had voiced the thought, it was true beyond all doubt. If he had, in effect, sold her to Rumbold, this could be his beloved sister lying bloody and dead. Beebe, who had never done anything but good for him. Now nausea threatened him, and he had difficulty not throwing up.

"You see." Rumbold fluttered his hand in front of his own blood-spattered clothing. "She grabbed my new suit, threatened to go to Lady Beatrice, demanded that I marry her."

His headache now completely gone, Melton straightened to his full height, shocked into lucidity. "So you killed her."

"No. No. It wasn't like that." Rumbold stared at the body wide-eyed, as if seeing it for the first time. "She did it. She forced me to—"

"I am going for a constable."

Melton made it to the corridor before Rumbold seized him and flung him back into his own apartment, then shoved him to the floor. Grabbing a cane from the umbrella stand, he raised it to strike. In that instant Melton realized this indignity was no less than he deserved. He held up his arms to ward off the expected blow.

"You madman, will you murder an earl? They will hang you."

No blow came.

"You're right. Yes, that's it." Rumbold slammed the apartment door, then grabbed Melton's arm and dragged him to his feet. "You killed her. That madwoman invited you into her den of sin and then attacked you. You were forced to kill her in self-defense."

"What?" Melton shook him off. "You are the one who's mad." He tried to back away but bumped into the wall.

"No, no. Don't you see?" Second by second, his former self-confidence returned. "A peer can do anything and never be punished. The matter is all swept away like yesterday's garbage. No one in Society will ever need to know it happened." Odd how enticingly evil his voice sounded, like the serpent in the Garden of Eden. The same voice he had always used to tempt Melton to foolish actions—the next hand of cards would surely be the winning one; the next drink would surely soothe away his pain. "After all I have done for you, you will do that for me."

Dear God, please help me. I beg You. Shaking with a marrow-deep terror, Melton tried to swallow but could not. This man wanted him to take the blame for the murder. How far would he go to try to force him?

"You owe me!" Rumbold roared, snatching up the cane again. "I will cancel all your debts if you do this."

As heavily as those debts had weighed upon his soul, Melton would not be a party to murder. While he could not reclaim his long-lost dignity—not shaking as he now was—he could show courage if the man had the gall to murder him, too.

"I am going for the constable," he repeated, wincing as he spoke and knowing his own death was imminent.

The front door burst open, and Sims dashed in, a dark-uniformed man close behind him.

"That's 'im, m'lord. That's 'im what killed the poor girl."

The other man looked from Rumbold to Melton and back again. "Gentlemen, I am Jeremy Slate of the Bow Street Runners. I understand there's been a bit of difficulty here. Would you care to explain?"

Rumbold stepped forward and slammed his cane down upon the Runner's head. The golden-orbed knob cracked against his skull with a sickening thud, and the man crumpled to the floor. Before Rumbold could strike again, Melton and Sims tackled him. Twisting out of their grasp, he dashed from the apartment.

"Shall I give chase, milord?" Barely five feet tall, Sims became Melton's new hero for that bit of courage.

"No." Still shaking violently, he exhaled a sigh of relief to see Rumbold gone. "No. But make haste to find a surgeon. This man needs help."

The servant obeyed, and Melton pulled the Runner up

on the settee and cushioned his bloody head with a dusty pillow.

Then he knelt beside him and, for the first time since his father's funeral, prayed.

Chapter Twenty-Four

"I cannot imagine what is keeping Frances busy these days." Lady Blakemore watched while her companion served tea, overseeing her like a mother hen, although the young woman appeared to Beatrice as skilled as anyone at the art. "I refer, Miss Hart, to the viscountess, Lady Greystone. We were friends at school and have always called each other by our first names. You understand that this is not done except among family and the closest of friends."

"Yes, my lady." The companion handed a steaming teacup to Mrs. Parton.

"Why, I have no idea what Frances is up to these days. She is rarely home and does not come calling on us." Mrs. Parton received her tea with a smile. "I thank you, my dear. Now Grace, you must tell me. What has Blakemore decided in regard to the soldiers' pension?"

While the older ladies discussed politics, Beatrice offered the companion a smile and received a shy one in response. Seated beside her on the settee, Catherine Hart was a dark-haired beauty whom she longed to know better. Other than the pleasantries shared in Lord Blakemore's box at the Drury Lane Theatre, they had not enjoyed any private conversation. Yet Miss Hart's subdued demeanor made her a preferred candidate for friendship, unlike Lady Grandly's daughters, whose excessive interest in fashion and gossip were not to Beatrice's liking.

"Tell us, Lady Beatrice, how does Melton plan to vote?" Lady Blakemore asked. "Surely he has some opinions on the matter."

Startled from her thoughts, Beatrice felt heat creeping up to her face. Mama had always taught her that a lady must pay strict attention to conversations over tea, for failure to listen was an insult to her hostess. Not only that, but how could one give an intelligent response if one had no idea what had been said?

"Why, um, my brother and I have not discussed it." Whatever *it* was. Nor had they spoken of anything significant in three years, other than his attempt to ruin her life. "I fear his political leanings are a mystery to me." She took a bite of her currant tart to avoid saying more.

The older ladies offered sympathetic nods, and Beatrice could not help but wonder whether Mrs. Parton had told the countess about yesterday's terrible scene with Melly and that horrid Mr. Rumbold.

"Ah. Well." Lady Blakemore took a sip of tea, always a helpful thing to do when one wanted to change the subject. She sent Mrs. Parton a knowing smile. "But let me return to my original question regarding Frances. All I can say is that she seems to have abdicated her position as matchmaker for Greystone. We are almost four months into the Season, yet she has not found him a bride." Her perfectly formed brown eyebrows arched with aristocratic hauteur at odds with her smirk. "Did you not have a wager of some sort with her in that regard?"

"Why, Grace, you know I do not believe in wagering," Mrs. Parton said in a singsong voice. "'Twas merely a harmless competition. And I will add that I happen to have someone in mind who would suit the viscount very well." She blinked innocently in Beatrice's direction.

Had Mrs. Parton eavesdropped on her conversation with Lord Greystone? Would Mama's old friends make their secret understanding a matter of gossip? Beatrice struggled not to choke on her tart.

Miss Hart stared at her in alarm. "Shall I pat your back, Lady Beatrice?"

Shaking her head, she washed down the offending sweet with a gulp of tea. But it seemed that the older ladies were not yet finished with her.

"Why, Julia," Lady Blakemore said, "to whom do you refer?"

Both of them turned knowing smiles in Beatrice's direction.

Her face burning, she stared at them wide-eyed, trying to think of some way to deflect their interest. Had she and Mrs. Parton not come here to discuss her upcoming introduction to Her Majesty? But she had much to learn about clever repartee among the *ton,* so denial seemed the only safe response. "Surely you do not refer to me." She tried a laugh. It sounded much like a mouse's squeak. Somehow she must protect both herself and Lord Greystone from their speculation. "I—I..."

"Yes, you, my dear," Mrs. Parton said. "Why do you think I invited you to London? Did you truly think it was to be my companion?" She glanced briefly at Miss Hart. "A worthy occupation, to be sure, but not what I had in mind for an earl's daughter."

"No, no, child." Lady Blakemore leaned toward her. "You and Greystone are perfectly suited to one another, and you have two allies in Mrs. Parton and myself who intend to see you wed before the Season ends."

Swallowing the tears that threatened to undo her, Beatrice set down her teacup with trembling hands. "I fear my brother has made that unlikely."

"But you cannot mean he will try to force you to marry that horrid...*person* who dared to come to my house yesterday without so much as an invitation." Mrs. Parton looked for a moment like the fierce Queen Boadicea, who long ago had defended Britain against the Romans. "I shall not permit it."

"Nor I," Lady Blakemore added just as sternly. "And you may as well know that Lord Blakemore is in agreement with us. In fact, I regret to say this, but he has refused to see Melton. After three years of being rebuffed while trying to help the young man, my ever-patient husband has completely lost his patience."

"I understand." Beatrice's heart ached to think her brother had sunk so low that his would-be mentor had abandoned all hope for him. Yet she could not blame Lord Blakemore. Her brother had willingly chosen to follow the advice of an evil man. She would not make that same mistake, but would rely upon the wisdom of these good ladies for guidance, beginning with telling them right now everything that had transpired between Lord Greystone and her.

"He may stay here as long as necessary." Melton fished in his pocket for a coin to pay the surgeon who had tended Mr. Slate. "You must come again tomorrow and see how he is faring."

"Very well, my lord." The elderly surgeon eyed the sixpence, obviously disappointed by its value. Still, he tucked it in his waistcoat pocket.

Shame burned in Melton's chest. How often had he carelessly spent hundreds, perhaps thousands of pounds for a single evening's entertainment? Yet now he had only pennies to pay a surgeon to save a good man's life. The only honor he could bestow upon Slate was to surrender his own bed to him. "What care does he need?"

"I fear there is little we can do, my lord, except let him rest." He packed away the needle and silk thread he had used to stitch up the gash on Slate's head, then closed his leather satchel. "I do believe he will recover, but someone should watch over him at all times. If he awakes, send for me and give him water and broth, nothing stronger. And of course Bow Street must be alerted."

"Yes, my man has already gone there." Melton hoped Sims would return soon so they could get another man or two on Rumbold's trail. Of course someone needed to carry off poor Miss Carlton's body. And the landlord must be notified. Faithful Sims would have to see to those details.

The surgeon departed, leaving Melton to his thoughts.

How had he fallen so low? This shabby abode, in the same building where Miss Carlton had plied her trade in the very next apartment, was no fitting place for an earl to visit, much less to live. Father would say he never expected anything good from him. Mother would die all over again. He could not even think of letting dear, innocent Beatrice know of such evil.

He had found little relief in his prayers over the Runner. All he had felt was shame, shame and more shame. What had that priggish Greystone said? A peer should assume some responsibility? Something like that. As much as the idea had galled him, he knew it to be true. Father had carefully managed his estates. Had increased his own father's fortune. But he died without passing along his skills to his heir.

Three years ago, as the new earl, Melton had decided he needed a time of…what did the scriptures call it? Riotous living? Yet just like the Prodigal Son in Christ's parable, here he was in a pigsty with nothing to eat and only debt to show for his tenure as a peer. And of course, a dead body to deal with. How could he have strayed so far from the boy who had eagerly looked forward to confirmation at twelve, racing with Beebe to memorize their catechism? Where had that boy gone?

He dropped down into a chair beside the wounded Runner and rested his head in his hands. How he longed to run home to his father and beg forgiveness. Too late for that. Too late for everything.

Suddenly thirsty for something to take away the dull ache throbbing in his head and chest, he went in search of brandy, the cheap stuff that was all he could afford. On the sideboard in the drawing room he poured the amber liquid into a smudged glass and tossed it down his throat. And promptly lost it all into the coal bin beside the hearth. His throat and belly on fire, he slumped down upon the settee. Had he really been drinking that vile concoction all this time? Thank God it had not killed him.

Yes. Thank God he was still alive. Thank God he had not convinced Beatrice to marry Rumbold. Thank God the surgeon was optimistic about the Runner's recovery.

Once again he tried to pray, but could only repeat by rote, "Our Father, Who art in heaven…" *Father* in heaven. He surrendered himself utterly to that thought, and a sweet peace started to grow near his heart, spreading out through his entire being.

Never in his life had he felt so lifted up, so infused with hope and joy. Surely God had heard him. Perhaps it was not too late to run home to Him, after all.

Chapter Twenty-Five

"Once you have been introduced to the queen, you will be the talk of London." Mrs. Parton studied Beatrice's new gown, specially ordered for Queen Charlotte's Drawing Room. "Turn around, my dear."

Beatrice obeyed, sneaking a peek at the horrid white creation in the tall mirror in her bedchamber as she turned. Queen Charlotte insisted that young ladies presented to her must wear these gowns fashioned after the styles of the last century, yet still having a hint of a more modern shape. With a hoop above the waist and a skirt that billowed out all around, it made the wearer resemble a great white bell. And then there was that silly extension of material in the back that looked more like a tail than a train. At least the single fluffy white ostrich feather in her coiffure was pretty enough. Of course it added another eighteen inches to her height, something she must take into account when walking through doorways.

She had a sudden horrendous thought of Lord Greystone seeing her in this odd clothing. Would he attend the Drawing Room? But she really must cease all this thinking about a gentleman who clearly had no thought for her. She had not seen him in a week, nor had she received a message from him and could not but assume that Melton had indeed destroyed her chances for happiness with the viscount. No, she must turn her attention to the days ahead and the honor of meeting Queen Charlotte.

The Drawing Room would take place tomorrow, and excitement filled the town house on her behalf. The entire staff had expressed their pleasure over her new position in the household, although not one of them had ever understood how the daughter of an earl could be a mere companion.

"What do you think of the gown, my dear?" Mrs. Parton studied it up and down, her frown advertising her own opinion.

"Well, um, in truth, I cannot say it is beautiful."

"Nor can I. But it is what it is, and all the girls will be wearing them. But never mind. When it is broadcast that I am your sponsor, everyone will forget the dress and your brother and beg to meet you." She tapped her chin thoughtfully. "I still have not decided whether to give a ball to formally bring you *out* after you meet Her Majesty. I do not mind the expense, but perhaps Lady Drayton's ball would be an even better setting. As a marchioness, she has a guest list that includes only the cream of the *ton*." She winked, a scandalous gesture that Beatrice found endearing. "Plenty of excellent young peers to make Greystone jealous."

Beatrice's heart skipped. "Do you think he will attend?"

"La, my dear, I have no idea." Mrs. Parton's merry face sobered. "No one has seen him, and Frances has not often been at home for these many days. The new butler refuses to answer any questions, and even bribes cannot garner any news from the staff."

"Bribes? Why, Mrs. Parton!"

"Tut-tut. Our new cook simply took a friendship cake

over to get acquainted with their cook. 'Tis done all the time. Still, not one word about his lordship."

Beatrice laughed even as her heart sank with disappointment over Lord Greystone's silence.

"Now, do you remember everything you are supposed to do at the Drawing Room?"

"Yes, madam. Wait for your name and then mine to be called. Walk to Her Majesty and kneel. Wait for her to kiss my forehead. If she does not—" A true horror for any girl! "—simply stand up and back away." Just thinking about it made her anxious. What if she tripped on the gown's silly train? What if Melton's reputation had reached Buckingham Palace? That might do great harm to Mrs. Parton for sponsoring her.

At a knock on the door, Mrs. Parton's Poole answered.

"My lady," a footman said, "Palmer asked me to tell you that Lord Winston has come to call upon you and Lady Beatrice."

Now her heart skipped for another reason. She did not dislike the baron, but she also could not in all good conscience encourage him. Oh, how was one to sort out this business of courting?

"Do you wish to see him?" Mrs. Parton's face was unreadable.

"I have no objection." None that was reasonable.

"Then you must hurry and change. I shall go down and entertain him." She started toward the door, then turned back. "Poole, fetch the green for her." She gave Beatrice another wink. "We shall see what my kinsman has to say for himself."

Why Mrs. Parton insisted upon the dull green gown, Beatrice could only guess. She had said more than once that it did not flatter her. Still, she had resolved to accept the lady's advice in all things, so she quickly donned the dress and made her way down to the drawing room just as tea was served.

Lord Winston rose from his chair and strode toward her. "Lady Beatrice, you are a vision. You should always wear green."

Behind him, Mrs. Parton rolled her eyes.

Catching a laugh before it escaped, Beatrice dipped a curtsey. "I thank you, Lord Winston." Was she supposed to compliment his appearance in return? Another quick glance at Mrs. Parton told her no. "How kind of you to call."

They took tea and chatted about the weather. About his estate in Surrey. About the end of the war with France. About the responsibilities of Parliament. All the while Beatrice tried to think of some way to ask whether he had seen Lord Greystone in the House of Lords. But as the gentleman's attention to her increased, she realized how rude it would be to ask about his supposed rival.

"I assume your neighbor has told you all about our little adventure." He stared at her with such intensity that she could not breathe.

"Why, no." Mrs. Parton saved her from having to answer. "We have not seen Lord Greystone these past ten or so days."

"Ah, yes. Of course." He coughed softly, but it sounded suspiciously like he was covering a laugh. "He and I found his stolen little chimney sweeps at a tavern on the Thames. He resolved to take them straightaway to some sort of school in Shrewsbury. Did he leave no message for you in that regard?" He seemed to address Mrs. Parton, but his gaze was still fixed upon Beatrice.

Again, she could not breathe. What was he saying in those long, brooding looks?

"Why, I hardly think Lord Greystone owes us an accounting for his actions." Mrs. Parton couched her rebuke in her usual merry tone. "Though I am pleased to hear that he rescued Kit and Ben. What jolly little lads. His staff at the school will turn them into fine men who will be a credit to England."

As happiness for the boys vied with disappointment in her thoughts and emotions, Beatrice's eyes stung, but she refused to let tears form.

Lord Winston must have noticed her high emotions, however, for his countenance fell, then grew blank. "Just so. Quite commendable."

Yes, quite commendable for the viscount to take care of the little boys to whom he had become attached. But what of his attachment to her? Could he have not left a message, no matter how cryptic, to let her know where he was going? As nothing else could have done, his silence spoke loudly of what had happened when he had gone to see Melly. As she had feared, her brother's evil ways had destroyed her chance for happiness. Yet the injustice of it stung even more. After claiming to care for her, Lord Greystone had proved himself to be as inconstant as shifting sand, just like Papa.

As the coach rumbled over the rough road through the Shropshire countryside, Greystone calculated his chances for arriving in London in time for the Marchioness of Drayton's ball. He must not miss that event, for it was his first opportunity to show the world that he and Lady Beatrice had an understanding. Or more precisely, he must dance with her at least three or four times, which would effectively warn off interlopers such as Winston and show every member of the *ton* that the lady belonged to him. Once they were engaged—the sooner, the better—the matter would be settled.

The journey back would take at least three days, depending upon circumstances. If the weather remained dry and fresh horses were available at every inn along the way, he might reach Greystone Hall just in time to change clothes and travel across the city to Drayton's mansion. He would have simply ridden back to London had he not needed Gilly to arrive with him. Without his valet, he would not be able to make himself sufficiently presentable for such an important ball. How foolish of him not to leave a curricle at his country estate, for that would have been a much faster mode of transportation for the two of them.

He had been gone much longer than planned. But at every turn some problem had arisen to delay him. Two days had been lost when an axle had broken halfway to Shropshire. Fortunately a worthy wheelwright had been found in a village not far from the breakdown. Then at his school for boys Kit and Ben had hung upon him, terrified over being abandoned in a strange place. He had been required to stay there an extra day. Only when Miss Nelson and Mr. Bacon had introduced the lads to some well-behaved boys their own age had they agreed that the school would be a fine place to grow up. Of course Greystone had had to promise to visit soon to secure their pledge not to run away from their new home.

But the worst situations had occurred at Greystone Lodge, where both the butler and the housekeeper had misunderstood Crawford being there, and Crawford had taken offense with their being offended. Even the old scullery maid had been put out with having Lucy as her new assistant, as though it called into question her many years of service at the post. It had been no easy task for Greystone to smoothe all the ruffled feathers. How had Mother managed all these years?

One thing should bring the old dear great happiness,

however. Although Mother was fond of their aged vicar, Mr. Partridge, the elderly gentleman had requested his pension so that he could retire and marry Mrs. Billings, the village schoolteacher. Now perhaps Greystone could convince Richard to accept the Greystone living. He would be even more pleased than Mother to have his brother shepherding the congregation in his home parish. But that matter too had delayed his return to London, for he had felt a compelling desire to attend services at his home church. The effort had proved rewarding. Not even in the grandest London cathedrals could he find the quiet, comforting godliness of the people of Greystone Village.

In that peaceful setting he'd settled several concerns with the Lord, not the least of which was the one dearest to his heart: proposing to Lady Beatrice. How glad he was that he had sent her a message about his sudden absence. If anything, he wished he had reaffirmed his love to her in the missive, for over these many days, that love had continued to grow. Of one thing he was certain: she was not at fault for her brother's profligate ways, nor was she in any way like him.

Should he propose at the ball? Should he do it in Mrs. Parton's elegant drawing room? Should he ask the older lady's permission? It vexed him sorely that there was no proper person to ask for her hand. The more he thought about it, the more his anger at Melton welled up inside him. How could a peer misuse his sister so cruelly, trying to marry her off to a scoundrel like Rumbold? Greystone fisted his right hand, longing to give the young earl a much-deserved thrashing. Like the facer he had planted on the master sweep's grimy face, a solid strike or two would surely knock some sense into Melton's drunken brain. Yet a long-forgotten memory of a similar situation crept into his thoughts, and he swiped a hand down the length of his face, as if that would erase the picture.

"A bit anxious, are we, milord?" Gilly rubbed his eyes, waking from his peaceful rest.

Greystone chuckled softly. "You know me well, my friend." Friend, indeed. Who but his valet had been with him since childhood? "Perhaps you can help me sort something out. Do you recall a decidedly unpleasant encounter I had with a youth from the village? I must have been twelve years old, perhaps thirteen." Nagging guilt swept into his chest, as it always did with this memory.

"Indeed I do, milord." Gilly chuckled. "Quite the hero you were that day."

"What?" Greystone stiffened. "Hero? I was a monster."

Gilly gaped. "Not at all, sir. You stopped an older boy from beating a wee one and taught him a lesson he never forgot."

For a moment Greystone stared out the window at the passing scenery. "Are we speaking of the same incident? I thoroughly bloodied an innocent's face and broke his nose. He dared not fight back because I was his lord."

"Innocent? Not at all, milord." Indignation covered Gilly's countenance. "Even if he couldn't fight back, he got what he deserved. He was a bully, and the little one he was hitting wasn't strong enough to protect himself. You showed William what it felt like to be on the receiving end. And it did him good, milord." He chuckled. "He enlisted in the army and has made a fine soldier these many years."

"Well." Greystone huffed out his astonishment. "That is a surprise of the first order. All this time I have felt like a bully, a monster, like my fath—" He swallowed hard. Gilly was the only person in the world who knew what he had suffered at his father's hands, for he had washed the blood from Greystone's back and nursed his wounds.

"Gracious, no, milord." Compassion and affection filled Gilly's face. "Just as you did for the little climbing-boys, you've always protected the less fortunate." He grunted. "You'll never be like your father. You just don't have it in you to be that wicked." A cough escaped him. "Not meaning to speak evil of the dead, milord, but that's just how it is. If I'd known you harbored such concerns, I'd have told you long ago." He looked away, and his jaw worked.

"Did you have more to say?"

Gilly gave him a sad smile. "Milord, don't you know you saved Lady Greystone's life, too?"

Greystone could only stare at him.

"'Tis true. You stepped between her ladyship and the late Lord Greystone as he was beating her with a cane, and received the blows yourself." Gilly gazed off and shook his head, as if seeing the scene again. "It was then her ladyship took you boys and fled to Mr. and Mrs. Parton, for she feared her husband would murder you all."

A cane? Greystone remembered a whip, but then, he'd been quite small, barely older than Kit, so perhaps his memory was faulty. "And you helped us get there safely."

Tears reddened the old man's eyes. "I did what I could, milord. But, oh, what a brave little lad you were."

"Mother was the brave one." He had been too harsh in thinking she should get over the past. "What lady could endure such treatment and survive to raise her sons so well?"

"Indeed, milord."

Gilly's revelations stunned Greystone. This man had been more than a valet, more than a friend. He had been his lifelong protector and guide. Like a shepherd he had gently led him along the right path, always appealing to his better instincts. Without his realizing it, Gilly had been a father to him, despite the disparity between their stations.

Healing peace settled into Greystone like warm soup

on a cold day. He could not entirely dispense with caution over his temper, but he could dispense with the fear that he would be like his father. Hope for a bright future with Lady Beatrice swept away all his former concerns, and he anticipated Lady Drayton's ball all the more.

Chapter Twenty-Six

"Milord, a woman to see you." Sims hesitated outside of Melton's bedchamber, wariness in his eyes. "'Tis the wife of that Slate fellow, sir, and I fear she may be wanting more money."

Melton finished tying his cravat, a skill he had yet to master. He sighed as he studied his poor appearance in the mirror. Nothing could be done for it, of course. He simply must go out as he was: rumpled, tattered and a bit stained. But after many days of sober thinking and much prayer, he had resolved that his first step in regaining his self-respect was to go to Beatrice and beg her forgiveness. If Mrs. Parton refused him admittance, he would simply sit on the lady's doorstep until they tripped over him on their way out.

But first he must deal with Slate's wife. Over a week ago the poor wretch had fetched her still-unconscious husband home with the help of two other Runners. Melton had emptied his pockets and his small stash of money into the woman's hands so Slate could continue to receive visits from the surgeon. Perhaps she came now to say the good man had died without ever waking up. At the thought a sick feeling threatened to overwhelm Melton, and he longed to drown it with a drink. But he quickly dismissed the impulse. From now on he would be made of sterner stuff.

"Tell her I will see her shortly." He would wait at least fifteen minutes for effect, just in case she had nefarious intentions. Rumbold had taught him that was the best way to unnerve beggars, creditors and blackmailers—perhaps even put them off entirely.

Rumbold! How could he still be heeding that murderer's advice? Two Bow Street Runners had pursued the man and pulled him from a ship in Southampton about to set sail for Italy. When they reported the incident to Melton, they took pride in the fact that Rumbold had been treated none too gently for his conduct toward their fellow officer of the law, not to mention his murder of a harmless lady of the street. After a hasty trial in Old Bailey, he now sat in Newgate Prison awaiting hanging. Melton shuddered to think he had ever wished to emulate such an evil man as Rumbold.

Lord, may I never again consider his wicked advice nor follow his wicked ways.

With that prayer in mind he made haste to see poor Mrs. Slate. He found the woman standing in the drawing room.

"Mrs. Slate, please be seated." He waved a hand toward the settee, which Sims had attempted to improve in recent days. The Runner's bloodstains had blended into the faded floral pattern, but it still was a shameful piece of furniture for an earl's residence.

The woman, who appeared near to thirty years old, stared at it askance. "No thank you, milord." Her slight grimace suggested that its deplorable condition kept her from sitting rather than a reticence to sit in an earl's presence.

Now that he looked at it with a clear eye, he wondered how he ever could have sat there himself. He returned his attention to his guest and saw no anxiety in her expression. Perhaps she had good news.

"Is your husband well?"

Her slender face lit up in a smile. "He's awake, milord, and soon to be up and about." Her brown eyes dimmed only a little. "He don't remember what happened to him, but he feels a bit anxious about something he was supposed to do." She shrugged. "The surgeon says he'll remember soon enough if he's supposed to."

"Ah, very good." And a huge relief to Melton. One less thing on his conscience. "Now, how may I help you?" He gave her an encouraging smile, hoping she would not ask too much. At odds with that thought, he longed to give her a small fortune, as if that would make up for the evil done to her husband. Perhaps when he received his rents—

"Nothing, milord, but I may be able to do something for you." She pulled a sealed vellum page from her reticule. "This here was in my Jeremy's pocket, and we don't know what to do with it. He don't remember what it's about, and none of the Runners know nothing. Was it something you gave him?"

Melton accepted the sealed letter and turned it over. The address, written with a flourish, said only *Lady Beatrice Gregory.* Beebe! Who would be writing to her, and why had Slate had it in his possession? It seemed odd that none of the Runners knew about it.

"No, it is not mine, but as Lady Beatrice is my sister, I will take care of it." He fished in his pocket for a coin, but found none. He cleared his throat. "Sims, by any chance—"

The man winced. "It'll be either supper for you tonight or a tuppence for her today."

Mrs. Slate blinked her eyes, then chuckled as if it were

a fine joke. "I don't need yer coin, milord. I just wanted to do the right thing."

"That is very noble of you, madam. Sims, give her the tuppence."

After the woman departed, Melton overcame his reluctance to sit on the ruined settee and settled in to study the letter. In former times he would have opened it without a hint of guilt. Now he could only reason that God had placed in his hands the very tool for gaining admittance into Mrs. Parton's home.

Beatrice could not help but feel a wave of pride over her perfect performance before Her Majesty. As much as she stood in awe of the regal queen, as much as her legs threatened to buckle beneath her, she had managed to walk and kneel and rise and back away with a grace that would do any royal personage proud. The queen's approving kiss on her forehead would remain with Beatrice all her days, as would her devotion and admiration for the king's consort. Pale and slender in her old-fashioned silver gown with wide panniers and flared sleeves, the queen had nonetheless presented an elegant picture of imposing majesty wearing a king's ransom in glittering jewels. And yet this German princess also exuded a genuine kindness that had won every English heart for the past fifty-odd years. Observing the serenity in her eyes, Beatrice could not help but wonder if she herself could have such peace if one day her own husband went mad like poor old King George.

That is, if she ever had a husband. Lord Greystone, the gentleman who owned her heart, had not attended the Drawing Room, so he was probably still in Shropshire. Polite but distant, Lord Winston had attended the event and had briefly congratulated her on her honor. Not that she felt any serious attachment to the baron, but his previous attentions had been flattering. And now in the open landau wheeling away from Buckingham Palace, her ostrich feather headdress fluttering in the breeze, Beatrice refused to be dismayed by her lack of prospects. From now on she could hold her head up with unabashed pride as a true member of London Society. Never mind that she still possessed no fortune or dowry.

The next afternoon, perhaps hoping to put that pride into proper perspective, Mrs. Parton insisted that they must visit St. Ann's Orphan Asylum. There among the sweet girls seeking to find their own places in the world, Beatrice was reminded of all her blessings. Most were destined for work as housemaids, a situation to which she would never be reduced. Even those who showed talent for other occupations, such as cooking, sewing or hairdressing, were not ensured an easy future.

After finishing their usual duties as audience and encouragers for the girls, Beatrice and Mrs. Parton bade them all farewell and made their way to the awaiting carriage. But Beatrice felt her heart lingering with the orphans.

"You seem reluctant to leave." Mrs. Parton gave her an understanding smile as she tugged at her gloves.

"I am." Beatrice hesitated, knowing she had no right to ask her mentor for yet another expenditure on her behalf. While Mrs. Parton had never hinted that any form of repayment was necessary, Beatrice felt the weight of the debt on her soul. No, she could not ask another favor, not after Lucy's betrayal. "But we will return, will we not?"

"Oh, indeed we shall." Mrs. Parton accepted the footman's hand to climb into the phaeton, then took up the reins from the tiger while he handed Beatrice up. "What would you say if I told you I have arranged for young Sally to become Poole's student?"

Beatrice's heart skipped. "I would say, madam, that you are the most generous lady I have ever known." She laughed. "I would also say that you have a singular talent for being able to read my mind."

Sally arrived the next day, a picture of shy eagerness and a study in wonder over her good fortune. Poole took her in hand, and within two days, Beatrice was treated to a new and flattering coiffure just in time for Lady Drayton's ball.

"Do you like the way I've done the curls, my lady?" Sally stood back to study her work with a critical eye.

"Indeed I do. You have done a very fine job." Beatrice saw in the dressing-table mirror that her compliment brought a blush to the girl's cheeks. How different her demeanor was from Lucy's brashness. Once her training was completed, she would surely have a secure future as a lady's maid, perhaps Beatrice's.

A knock sounded upon the door, and Poole, who had hovered over Sally's work, answered. When she returned, she carried a letter in an unfamiliar hand and passed it to Beatrice.

"For you, my lady." Poole instinctively picked at a spot or two of Beatrice's coiffure. "Lord Melton is requesting an audience with you."

The address on the folded and sealed vellum page was not in Melly's handwriting, nor anyone else's whom she could recognize. No doubt it was from that Rumbold person. She tossed it aside. It would make good kindling for a morning fire, should the summer turn cold.

"Does Mrs. Parton know, Poole?"

"Yes, my lady. She said to tell you it is your decision whether or not to see his lordship."

Beatrice heaved out a great, unlady-like sigh. An interview with her brother would only ruin her mood for Lady Drayton's ball. It would be sufficiently difficult for her without Lord Greystone in attendance. She had long ago forgiven Melly for squandering her dowry, but she would give him no further opportunity to do her injury.

"No, I will not see him." Even as she said the words, her heart wrenched. But how could he expect her to receive him and his despicable friend after their last visit? How did they even dare to come here? Did they expect to impose themselves upon Mrs. Parton, assuming they could tag along on her invitation to the marchioness's ball? After all, it was one of the grandest of the Season, and everyone coveted an invitation. She could just imagine Lady Drayton's horror at seeing Mr. Rumbold in her ballroom. All of the decent attendees would scatter like geese running from a fox. And Beatrice's standing in Society would be forever tainted.

Before her mind could conjure up any more bad scenes, she inhaled deeply. "Now, Sally, my gown."

Chapter Twenty-Seven

"My lord, Lady Greystone has already left for the marchioness's ball." Roberts seemed to have taken well to his new role as butler. His posture, his grammar, even his inflections replicated Crawford's flawless form. And although he could not have known Greystone was about to arrive, he stood completely unruffled at the front door to greet him when the coach stopped in front of the town house. An added indication of his suitability for the position was his instinctive understanding of what Greystone would like to know upon returning home.

"Ah. Very good." He hurried up the front staircase, motioning for Gilly and the butler to follow him. "I must hurry and get ready to go, as well. Did the viscountess take the landau?"

"No, my lord." Roberts kept up with his pace without losing his breath, something Crawford had not been able to do in recent years. "Mr. and Mrs. Grenville came in a barouche to accompany her, along with Mr. James Grenville."

At the top of the staircase Greystone stopped so suddenly his two servants almost collided with him. "My uncle Grenville?"

"Yes, my lord." The perfect butler, Roberts recovered from the near mishap without so much as lifting an eyebrow *or* tumbling down the stairs.

"Well, well, well." As they proceeded up the corridor, Greystone could not help but feel a slight unease about his perfectly proper mother's activities of late. It was commendable that she wanted to spend time with Edmond and Anna, and they with her. But exactly where did Uncle Grenville fit into all of this? Before the night was over he would insist upon an explanation from her.

"What can you tell me about, uh, Mrs. Parton these days?" Asking about Lady Beatrice's comings and goings would hardly be appropriate.

"Lord Melton visited some days ago, accompanied by his friend. Lord Winston called once or twice." He coughed into a gloved hand. "The lady has employed an exceptional new cook, a Frenchman, if I am not mistaken." Obviously the man had tasted some of this new cook's creations, for a jolly smirk crossed his face. It quickly disappeared.

That brief lapse did not disturb Greystone. He had never been one to think his servants should behave like wooden soldiers. But then perhaps his kindness to Lucy had fostered a lack of discipline in her.

Nor was he concerned about Melton and Rumbold visiting. Mrs. Parton no doubt made quick work of whatever scheme they had presented to her.

What did disturb him was the idea of Winston visiting Lady Beatrice. He had suspected that adventurer would try to step in, knowing Greystone would be gone. At least his letter should have ensured her patience in awaiting his return. Perhaps he should have declared his deepest love and devotion in the missive. No, that was a responsibility and a pleasure one reserved for a private conversation.

"I thank you, Roberts. That will be all." He hurried to

his bedchamber and began the process of washing and putting on his new evening clothes. He had missed the last fitting, but Gilly quickly applied needle and thread to shorten the jacket's sleeves to keep them from crowding the ruffled, white lace cuffs.

Roberts returned to the bedchamber some twenty minutes later, and his expression was decidedly disapproving. "My lord, Lord Melton awaits you in the front drawing room."

"Melton?" Greystone snorted out his disgust. "What does he want? Tell him I am going out and have no time to receive him."

"Yes, my lord." The butler walked toward the door.

"Wait." Curiosity seized him. He had certainly prayed for Melton at every turn, but with little hope for his rehabilitation. Perhaps this was an answer to those prayers. "Is that Rumbold fellow with him?"

"No, my lord. He is alone. And rather disheveled, if I may say so, sir."

Gilly snipped the last threads of his alterations and assisted Greystone with donning the blue satin jacket. Without his valet, he would no doubt look a bit disheveled himself. Something must have happened to bring Melton here. All Greystone could do was pray it was something good. Melton could not prevent him from marrying Lady Beatrice, but if he could have a decent relationship with the man who would be his brother-in-law, so much the better.

"Tell him I will be right down."

Roberts's face became a granite wall. "Yes, my lord."

Greystone hoped his new butler's instant stoicism did not portend a bad interview with the earl.

The Marquess of Drayton's mansion lay on a broad green property about a half mile from Greystone Hall. Standing apart from other St. James's Square residences, it had the air of a royal residence, though was not quite as grand as Buckingham Palace. As Mrs. Parton's landau rolled up the drive amidst dozens of other conveyances, Beatrice looked from side to side to enjoy the estate's impressive grounds. With sufficient daylight to showcase the immaculately kept lawns and flower gardens, the landscape was a tribute to wealth but not excess. The closer they came to the house, the more her anticipation grew. By the time they reached the front portico, she felt a giddy, girlish excitement over seeing Lady Drayton again and meeting the marquess.

Beneath the front portico, green-liveried footmen and black-uniformed maids hurried about, making certain every guest received proper attention. Once guests crossed the threshold into the broad entryway, wraps and cloaks were surrendered, slippers brushed and coiffures straightened, so each visitor could make an entrance befitting his or her station in life.

"Humph." Mrs. Parton adjusted her turban, checking the angle of her albino peacock feathers in a mirror beside the front door. "I am quite put out with Lord Greystone. He should be here to escort us into the ball."

"But, why?" Beatrice would not admit to her mentor that she longed for the viscount's company, as well. "In spite of your conjecture, we have no claim upon him."

"Humph," the lady repeated. "I do hope that changes soon." She linked an arm in Beatrice's, and they ascended the elegant staircases to the second-floor ballroom.

At the door the butler bowed to them, took their calling cards and announced in a rich baritone, "Lady Beatrice Gregory. Mrs. Julia Parton."

All around them the fragrances of countless perfumes mingled in the air, giving Beatrice a heady sense of having arrived. This was just the sort of event Mama had often spoken of. Although she would have liked to have been presented at her own coming-out ball, this was more than sufficient, considering her current circumstances. Despite Lord Greystone's absence, despite Melly's attempt to way-lay her, she resolved to enjoy the evening to its fullest.

The June daylight lasted until after nine of the clock, but finally it faded into a hazy purple darkness. In the vast ballroom hundreds of candles blazed in crystal chande-liers, with several servants carefully attending to the drip-ping wax lest it fall on the guests while they danced. As Beatrice entered arm in arm with Mrs. Parton, music met her ears, and she located the source: musicians on a dais at the end of the ballroom. As if they had a mind of their own, her feet ached to move in time with the merry tune.

"Over here, my dear." Mrs. Parton ushered her toward a group of brocade chairs set off from the dancing area by a row of large potted plants. "Shall we sit?"

"Yes, madam." Beatrice felt a pinch of disappointment. Once they had settled into the green chairs, she found the courage to ask, "Will I be introduced?"

"Oh, yes, indeed. The marchioness will present you and several other young ladies to the room." She gave her a knowing smile. "But of course you must not speak to anyone until they are presented to you. You are, after all, the daughter of an earl."

Beatrice smiled her appreciation, even as sorrow pushed aside her happy mood. Yes, she was the daughter of an earl, but she was also the sister of his heir. To think of Melly being forever shut out of this grand company al-most broke her heart.

"What do you want, Melton?" Greystone stood in the doorway of the drawing room, refusing to cross the space to greet the earl.

"Greystone." The man's clothes were as rumpled as Roberts had reported, but his hair was combed, and he appeared clean-shaven. As he strode over, hand extended, the usual stench of cheap brandy did not accompany him.

Greystone stared at the presented hand and crossed his arms. "As I said, what do you want?"

He withdrew the appendage and shrugged. "I do not blame you for…see here, old man, I came to apologize… to ask forgiveness for the unforgivable." His words were uttered in a tone that could only be described as humble, almost beseeching.

A strange chill at odds with the warm evening swept down Greystone's back. Was this an answered prayer or some sort of trick? Something Melton had learned from Rumbold in order to get into Greystone's good graces and renew his plea for the eighty thousand?

"Go on." Greystone sauntered toward a nearby grouping of chairs and waved to one. "Sit."

Although Melton ranked above him in precedence, he had the courtesy to honor his unwilling host's order.

Greystone dropped into a chair opposite the one Melton had taken. "Talk."

He coughed out a laugh, clearly embarrassed. "I have been a fool. No excuses. No explanations. Please forgive me for dismissing you so rudely from my home, when was it? Over two weeks ago." Another ironic laugh. "My *home,* rotten hole that it is."

All this self-abasement rang true, but Greystone still found himself unable to put any faith in his words. "Very well. You are forgiven." He put a note of finality in his response, not wanting to invite the inevitable plea for funds.

Melton exhaled a long sigh shaded with yet another laugh, this one resounding with relief. "I understand you just returned from Shropshire, so perhaps you have not heard…?" He tilted his head in question.

Greystone said nothing, but curiosity burned within him.

"Very well. Here is the whole story, which I bring to *you* only because my sister—"

"You will keep Lady Beatrice's name out of this conversation."

"Yes, of course." He scrubbed a hand over the back of his neck. "A double shame," he muttered, "that another gentleman must defend her honor." One more explosive sigh. "Very well, then. The long and the short of it is this. My creditor—I will not call him friend—lies in Newgate Prison where he awaits hanging for the murder of his mistress."

Greystone's jaw dropped, and his tongue could not form words.

"'Twas a speedy trial. Seems there were few to defend him, and many will be glad to see him gone. Of course all of his possessions are forfeit to the Crown. Of the eighty thousand I owed my creditors, his note was for sixty thousand. His mistress burned it, hoping to stop his marriage to—" He grunted. "So he murdered her."

"God have mercy." Greystone could hardly take in these developments.

Melton breathed out a heartbreaking sigh. "Like the devil, Rumbold took hold of my soul. To free myself, I became willing to sell him that which is most precious to me, my sister." He winced. "In spite of what you may think, I hold her in highest regard."

Greystone swallowed the rage this admission engendered. "But why come to me with this tale?" As much as he was glad to know what had happened, he could not easily accept Melton's claim of caring for Lady Beatrice.

"Because God has granted me a grace I do not deserve, and I am prepared to accept your offer to hold me accountable for my finances and m-my excessive consumption of brandy. And wine. And many other such beverages." There was a boyish quality to his half grin that reminded Greystone of little Kit, except that Kit had never been this pathetic. "If I place myself at your disposal, will you help me find the right path?"

"I?" Greystone felt another chill sweep over him. "Why do you ask *me?*" When he had spoken to Melton of accountability, he had planned to suggest the ever-patient Lord Blakemore.

Melton's childishly wily expression held no cunning. "Because if you are going to be my brother, I know you would prefer to make certain that I bring no further scandal upon the family."

Greystone suddenly had the feeling that he had walked right into a trap as clever as any that Rumbold had set for his victims.

Chapter Twenty-Eight

Still reeling from Melton's revelations, Greystone arrived at last at Lord Drayton's ball. The marquess welcomed him personally, a singular honor but one Greystone could do without at this particular moment. While Drayton pressed him for support on a measure regarding the American war, something close to Greystone's heart because his brother had come near to dying in the conflict, his attention nonetheless strayed to the vast ballroom.

He must find Lady Beatrice. In his letter he had requested several dances, but with his late arrival he could not expect her to decline other invitations amidst all of this merriment. At least he was in time to claim the supper dance. Surveying the room, he did not see her among the dancers. But just as he spied Mrs. Parton's unmistakable red hair beneath a feather-plumed orange turban, Mother swept into his line of vision *waltzing* with Uncle Grenville.

He could only gape. She looked at least ten years younger than her nine and forty years. And very, very happy. Never once in his own eight and twenty years had he seen such radiance on her still-beautiful face. This entire scene astonished him. Had she not recently expressed disapproval of this intimate dance form? Yet here she was waltzing blissfully with a gentleman she could never marry. Greystone's heart wrenched for both of them.

Beside him Drayton chuckled. "Ah, yes. Lady Greystone is enjoying herself as she has not since she was first presented to Society some thirty years ago." He clapped Greystone on the shoulder. "No doubt you would like to dispense with politics for the evening, so go along. Find some young lady to stand up with for the next dance. It is the last one before supper is served."

"I thank you, my lord." Thus released, he made his way around the ballroom toward Mrs. Parton, who stood talking with Edmond and Anna.

And there beside them was the lady of his dreams, a vision of loveliness in a frothy pink gown, her golden hair curled becomingly around her flawless oval face. His pulse began to race, and his heart hammered in his chest. As best he could without being rude, he pushed his way through the crowd. Then he spied Winston approaching the ladies from the other direction, and he increased his pace, murmuring apologies to those he bumped into as he went.

They reached Lady Beatrice at the same moment, and both bowed.

"Lady Beatrice." Greystone breathed out her beloved name. "May I have this dance?"

"Lady Beatrice." Winston's tone was at once icy and warm, a feat only a pompous prig could accomplish. "I have come to claim our promised dance."

"Why, I—" The lady looked from one to the other, bewilderment clouding her beautiful blue eyes.

His heart near to bursting, Greystone was certain he could hear Mrs. Parton tittering. Edmond's laugh was unmistakable. Not long ago he had snatched Anna away from Winston after a ball very much like this one.

Proper social form demanded that Greystone back

away, but for some reason he felt a stubborn inclination to flout convention just as Mother was doing.

"My dear lady," he said, "perhaps the good baron would permit me—" He stepped closer to her.

"Really, Greystone." Winston moved up shoulder to shoulder with him. "Give way, my good man. This dance is claimed."

"I think I will not." Greystone recalled the baron's swordsmanship against the ruffians on the Thames. A duel with him might present mortal danger. But even though Winston had every right to be offended, Greystone refused to give way. "Lady Beatrice, would you kindly explain to this gentleman the importance of *his* giving way, since I have a prior claim to this dance?"

Oddly, instead of offering a smile, she glared at him. "Indeed. And how is it that you have a prior claim?"

Winston snorted out a laugh. "Yes, Greystone, how did you accomplish that, since you just arrived?"

"But, my lady, I requested the supper dance in the letter I sent you."

"Letter? What letter?" Understanding dawned upon her lovely countenance. "*You* wrote that letter. Oh, my." She placed a white-gloved hand over her lips, then turned to the baron. "Lord Winston, Lord Greystone is correct. His invitation came first. Please forgive me."

Winston's face became as blank as that of the best of butlers. "Of course, my lady." He bowed away, then turned back and gave Edmond and Anna a brief nod. "I say, Greystone, do you have any more brothers, or may I proceed in my search for a wife without further interruptions from your family?"

With great difficulty Greystone did not so much as smirk in response, although he could hear Edmond coughing in the background and Anna's chiding tsk. "No, my lord, no more brothers. We are all claimed."

Claimed? Beatrice lost her breath for a moment. Lord Greystone had not proposed, nor had they sorted out all of their concerns regarding marriage or Melly or Lady Greystone's disapproval. Perhaps he had addressed those matters in the letter, which she prayed Sally had not thrown away.

"My lady, I believe this is my dance." Lord Greystone, exquisitely dressed in a blue satin jacket and tan breeches, held out his hand.

Beatrice glanced at Mrs. Parton, who nodded and smiled her approval.

"I thank you, sir." Beatrice placed her hand in his and permitted him to guide her toward the end of the line for the country dance.

As they walked, he leaned close to her ear. "Did you truly forget that I asked for this dance in my letter?" Couched in his amused tone was a hint of hurt feelings.

She shook her head. "I received your letter only today." At the shock on his face she hastened to add, "My brother delivered it just this afternoon. I thought it was from that horrid Mr. Rumbold, so I did not open it. How silly of me not to look at the seal."

"This afternoon? How odd. I sent it in the care of a Bow Street Runner the night before I left. A dependable man, or so I thought. Did Melton explain how he came to have it?"

"I refused to see him." She took her place in the ladies' line.

He took his place opposite her. "Ah, I see. And I do not fault you for it." A frown flitted across his noble brow. "My dear, do you have your heart set upon this dance?" He tilted his head toward a row of empty chairs. "We truly must talk."

The music began, and the first couple made their way down the line in a series of intricate steps. She knew the pattern well and would have loved to have shown him her skill. But then, if he considered himself "claimed" by her, she had no need to impress him with her dancing.

"Yes, we must." She once again took his offered hand, and they excused themselves from their fellow revelers to take refuge behind the lovely row of large potted plants she had previously found so annoying. Mrs. Parton, her ever-faithful sponsor, moved near enough to protect their reputations with her presence, but not within hearing distance.

Greystone gripped her hands and bent forward to touch his forehead to hers, as he had done over two weeks ago. Should anyone be watching, they might be scandalized, yet Mrs. Parton beamed her approval in their direction.

"My darling, I understand why you did not receive your brother." Lord Greystone brought her gloved hands up to his lips for a gentle kiss on each. "I almost refused him, as well. Fortunately the Almighty prompted me to see him. What I learned will astonish you even more than it did me."

Her beloved then unfolded a tale so enthralling that Beatrice was soon in tears. "Oh, Greystone, he has come to his senses at last." Would he mind that she used a more familiar address by leaving off "Lord"?

"My dearest Beatrice, before we parted company Melton gave me permission to ask the question closest to my heart. Will you marry me?" His omission of her courtesy title answered her concern. And now, with his blue eyes catching the nearby candlelight and reflecting the rich blue of his satin jacket, the intensity of his gaze made her knees weak. She was grateful to be sitting.

"I should tease you and play coy, but I cannot." Joy bubbled up inside her, and she laughed, perhaps a bit too loudly, if Mrs. Parton's widened eyes were any indication. "Yes, yes, my darling Greystone, I will marry you."

And there, hidden among the potted plants, he gave her a proper kiss to seal the matter. And she responded with great enthusiasm.

Chapter Twenty-Nine

"I am grateful to have the necklace locked in the family vault." Lady Greystone sat shoulder to shoulder with James Grenville on a settee in Greystone's drawing room. "But in the interval when I did not know what had become of it, I discovered that some things—" she placed a hand on the gentleman's forearm "—such as friendship, are more important than material possessions."

Beatrice could only feel honored to be included in this intimate gathering presided over by the matriarch of the family. The afternoon following the marchioness's ball, she and Mrs. Parton had been invited to the town house next door so Greystone could announce their engagement to his relatives. But the viscountess took charge of the conversation before he could even speak, announcing that she and her brother-in-law were spending a great deal of time together.

"But let us be very clear." Lady Greystone pulled her hand back, as if she had decided that touching her brother-in-law was improper. "We cannot marry, and we will not live in sin."

"And no law prohibits our being the best of friends." James Grenville, a white-haired older version of his three handsome nephews, took Lady Greystone's hand and gazed at her with a tenderness that bespoke the deepest respect and affection. This time she did not break the contact.

Mrs. Parton had informed Beatrice that the gentleman was a barrister of excellent reputation who had always lived above reproach. Yet Beatrice could see a note of sadness in both of them. She could not imagine being forbidden to marry the gentleman whom she loved so dearly.

"You could go to Scotland, Mother," quipped Edmond Grenville. "Scottish law does not prohibit a man from marrying his late brother's widow."

"Edmond!" Richard Grenville, the picture of a country vicar in his black suit and white collar, sat with his wife, Mary, and scowled at his younger brother. "The laws of the Church supersede man's laws and customs, and our faith forbids such a marriage."

"But I believe," huffed Edmond, "it was a political move that established—"

"Do you mind, Edmond?" Lady Greystone glared at her youngest son briefly, but quickly softened her expression. "I do thank you for thinking of our happiness, but we have accepted our situation as God's will."

"And we thank you and Anna for playing the part of chaperones for us these past weeks." James Grenville's blue eyes glinted with humor. "Imagine the gossip if two old friends like us were accused of impropriety."

The entire family laughed, easing the tension in the room.

"And Mother has at last found a companion who can please her," Edmond said, eliciting more chuckles around the room.

"You may be certain of that," Lady Greystone said. "Now, we have taken enough of everyone's attention.

Greystone is the one who summoned all of you here." She turned to her eldest son. "Greystone, you are in charge."

He stood by the hearth, a bemused expression on his dear face. Beatrice wondered if at last he had won the battle of wills with his parent, and all without a struggle.

"I thank you, Mother dear. I will endeavor to do you credit." He gave her a half bow. "I think my brothers and I all agree that we owe you a great deal for your selflessness in rearing us. When our father died you could have abandoned us to tutors and servants and lived for your own amusements, as many widows do. But you carefully directed every part of our lives so that we would be a credit to England."

A soft grumble came from Edmond's direction, but Anna chided him with a tsk. After her marriage made them sisters, Beatrice would have to ask her the cause of this brother's complaint.

"And in that light," Greystone continued to address his mother, "even though I requested your assistance in choosing a wife for me, I think it will come as no surprise to you that I have found a lady of flawless grace and reputation to be my viscountess." He strode across the Persian carpet to Beatrice's chair and took her hand. "Lady Beatrice has agreed to marry me."

Beatrice's heart leaped with joy and anticipation. Surely his mother would not object to their marriage, even though she doubted the news of Melly's repentance had reached Society's ears.

"Humph." Lady Greystone's indignation was clearly artificial. "'Tis hardly a new thing for a son of mine to choose his own bride."

Again the room resounded with laughter, even louder this time. Surely Beatrice would hear many interesting stories once she was wed.

"But I must say this," Lady Greystone continued. "I have no cause to be ashamed of any of your choices." She smiled at Beatrice. "I welcome you to the family, my dear."

Eyes stinging, Beatrice rose and hurried to the viscountess, bending to place a kiss on her cheek. "I thank you, Mother Greystone. I am honored."

"Will you plan her wedding, Mother?" Edmond, clearly the family tease, smirked and winked at his wife.

Another family joke Beatrice must investigate.

"She most certainly will not." Mrs. Parton had sat quietly to this point, her round face beaming with enjoyment over the antics in her friend's household. "I demand that privilege as my reward for finding Greystone's bride. Remember our competition, Frances?"

"Nonsense. I shall—" Lady Greystone began. James Grenville patted her hand, and she laughed softly. "I shall leave it to Greystone to decide."

Greystone sauntered over to kiss his mother's hand, then put an arm around Beatrice's waist. "My darling, you are very brave to join this family. Are you certain that you—"

"Hush." Ignoring their company, she put a finger on his well-sculpted lips. "If you can overlook the, um, complexities of my family, I certainly have no qualms about joining this merry band."

"Well said!" Edmond was the first to leave his chair and clap Greystone's back, and was soon joined by the others. "Congratulations!"

Once again Greystone had difficulty breathing, but this time his health was not in danger. Beatrice was without question the most beautiful, the most stunning bride he had ever seen.

Escorting his sister down the aisle of St. George's

Church, Melton looked every inch a proud earl of the realm, his sober black suit in keeping with his physical and mental condition these past three weeks while the banns were cried. Contrary to Greystone's fears, Melton's repentance was proving genuine, his rehabilitation progressing. He would report all his expenditures to Greystone and follow the financial plan he and Blakemore had devised. After Blakemore spoke to the newspapers, rumors of any connection Melton may have had to Rumbold had been quietly put to rest. Further, the murderer's hanging barely made a ripple of gossip amongst the aristocracy whose ranks he had so desperately attempted to breach. Had the man only realized that a life of honor would have won him many friends, no matter what his parentage, perhaps he would have succeeded in garnering the respect which he had tried to force from them.

But Greystone now focused on his bride, a vision of beauty floating toward him as he stood before the altar. Her pristine white gown was a high-waisted cloud of snowy silk and lace, her veil a gossamer shade that could not hide her wide smile. The closer she came, the more he forgot to breathe.

Until Edward thumped his arm. "It won't do for the groom to faint," he muttered. "If I made it through my wedding, you can do the same." He snorted out a muted laugh. *"Milord."*

Greystone sucked in his lips to keep from laughing, both at his brother's humorous taunt and his own joy over his imminent marriage. Gratitude and happiness emanated from Melton's eyes as he surrendered Beatrice to him. She moved to her place beside Greystone, sending a sweet smile to Anna on her other side. Then they all turned to face Richard.

"Dearly beloved," he intoned in his rich baritone, "we

are gathered together here in the sight of God, and in the face of this congregation, to join together this man and this woman in holy matrimony, which is an honorable estate…"

Beatrice and her new husband took their places of honor at the long table in Mrs. Parton's elegant ballroom. Her mentor had gone to great expense to arrange a lavish wedding breakfast, and Lady Greystone graciously surrendered her right to hostess the event. Among the guests were Lord and Lady Blakemore, Lord and Lady Grandly and their daughters, and Lord Winston. Greystone had developed a fondness for the latter after their adventure in rescuing Kit and Ben, and Beatrice could only be flattered that the young baron had considered her a worthy object of his interest. As she surveyed the two-hundred-odd aristocrats who had gathered to celebrate their nuptials and wish them well, she saw many a pretty young lady who would suit Lord Winston, should he deign to consider them.

On the opposite side of the table, Melly sat beside Miss Waddington, who seemed enchanted by his every word. Melly must have sensed Beatrice's gaze, for he turned her way. With practiced grace, he brushed his right hand over his ear and then rested it above his heart. The worried hope in his expression almost made her weep, so she quickly returned the gesture. Yes, they would forever listen to each other, would forever care. She lifted a quick prayer of thanks that God had redeemed her prodigal brother.

After a quick survey of the room, she turned her attention to Greystone, who was conversing with Lady Blakemore on his other side. Beatrice nudged him and received attention from them both.

"My darling Greystone." She still felt a thrill at being

privileged to address him so familiarly. "Should we not help Lord Winston in his search for a bride?"

He laughed, that wonderful carefree sound he emitted so often these days. "Why, I cannot think of any reason we should not. Lady Blakemore, what think you on the subject?"

"Oh, yes. Tell us what you think." Beatrice knew the countess had many connections, but one stood out. "What about your sweet companion, Miss Hart? Have they met?"

Lady Blakemore gave them a wry smile. "No, they have not met. I fear our good baron considers himself too far above a mere companion."

Greystone laughed again. "Ah, that is an affliction from which many a peer should strive to heal." He gazed at Beatrice with such devotion that her heart felt near to bursting. "As for me, I have stolen Mrs. Parton's companion and made her my own."

"And you are mine." In that moment, the whole room and everyone in it disappeared, and Beatrice saw only him. The love of her life. Her husband.

Her companion for the rest of her days.

* * * * *

Be sure to look for the next book in
Louise M. Gouge's
LADIES IN WAITING *miniseries,*
coming in 2013 from Love Inspired Historical.

Dear Reader,

Thank you for choosing *A Suitable Wife,* the second book in my LADIES IN WAITING series. I hope you've enjoyed this journey back to Regency England. I love to write stories about this unique and fascinating era, the setting for Jane Austen's timeless novels. One of the most appealing things about this time is that everyone knew exactly what was expected for someone in her/his station in life, and diligent people strove to play their roles well. But of course, this means it was also a time of much social injustice (great conflict for a novel!). Still, many godly reformers sought to make changes in social inequities. Not until 1864—fifty years after my story takes place—did Lord Shaftesbury succeed in eliminating the use of "climbing-boys" through the Act for the Regulation of Chimney Sweepers, which established a penalty of £10.00 for offenders. That was a hefty sum in those days.

When I learn such an interesting historical fact, I love to incorporate it into my stories. Getting the details right, however, is one of the tricky things about writing historical fiction. The social structures of the Regency era were quite strict and confining, so if you're a die-hard Regency fan and find an error, please let me know! And please know that I tried to get it right!

As with all of my stories, beyond the romance, I hope to inspire my readers always to seek God's guidance, no matter what trials may come their way.

I love to hear from readers, so if you have a comment, please contact me through my website:

http://blog.Louisemgouge.com.

Blessings,
Louise M. Gouge

Questions for Discussion

1. In the beginning of the story Lord Greystone has asked his mother to find him a wife suitable for someone of his social rank (not unusual in that time period). What circumstances change his mind about letting her make that decision? Would you like to have a matchmaker choose your spouse? Why or why not?

2. From the instant Greystone sees Lady Beatrice, he is smitten by her beauty and grace. Why does he turn away from her? Do you think he is justified in that response, considering the expectations of the era and his own charitable concerns? How do you think this reflects upon his character? What causes him to change his opinion over time?

3. When Beatrice sees Lord Greystone, she is immediately attracted to him, and that feeling only grows throughout the story. What attracts her to the viscount? Do you agree with her assessment? What qualities do you think make a man or woman attractive?

4. Beatrice finds great satisfaction in ministering to the orphan girls. In what ways does she identify with them? What do you foresee in her future ministries now that she will be a wealthy viscountess?

5. What sort of person is Lady Greystone? Why does she reject the idea of Beatrice becoming her titled son's wife? Considering the times, is she justified in her opinions?

6. Greystone does not hesitate to listen to God's direction when it comes to helping the little chimney sweeps. What draws him to their struggle? What does this say about his character? Do you think he fits the image of a "hero"? Why or why not? What is your definition of a hero?

7. What expectations did Lady Greystone have of her sons? Why were her expectations different for Greystone?

8. Both Greystone and Beatrice are Christians. Which one changes the most in the story? In what ways does each one mature and become stronger? In what ways do they stay the same?

9. The overarching theme of this story concerns young people choosing a mentor. In what ways is Lord Melton's chosen mentor very different from Beatrice's and Greystone's? Have you ever had a mentor? How did this person help you choose your path in life? Have you ever mentored someone else?

10. This was an age in which the aristocracy ruled and held all of the privileges. As much as we romanticize the era, would you like to travel back in time for a visit? At what level of society did your ancestors live?

REQUEST YOUR FREE BOOKS!

2 FREE INSPIRATIONAL NOVELS
PLUS 2
FREE
MYSTERY GIFTS

Love Inspired.
HISTORICAL
INSPIRATIONAL HISTORICAL ROMANCE

YES! Please send me 2 FREE Love Inspired® Historical novels and my 2 FREE mystery gifts (gifts are worth about $10). After receiving them, if I don't wish to receive any more books, I can return the shipping statement marked "cancel". If I don't cancel, I will receive 4 brand-new novels every month and be billed just $4.49 per book in the U.S. or $4.99 per book in Canada. That's a saving of at least 22% off the cover price. It's quite a bargain! Shipping and handling is just 50¢ per book in the U.S. and 75¢ per book in Canada.* I understand that accepting the 2 free books and gifts places me under no obligation to buy anything. I can always return a shipment and cancel at any time. Even if I never buy another book, the two free books and gifts are mine to keep forever.

102/302 IDN FEHF

Name	(PLEASE PRINT)	
Address		Apt. #
City	State/Prov.	Zip/Postal Code

Signature (if under 18, a parent or guardian must sign)

Mail to the **Reader Service:**
IN U.S.A.: P.O. Box 1867, Buffalo, NY 14240-1867
IN CANADA: P.O. Box 609, Fort Erie, Ontario L2A 5X3
Not valid for current subscribers to Love Inspired Historical books.

Want to try two free books from another series?
Call 1-800-873-8635 or visit www.ReaderService.com.

* Terms and prices subject to change without notice. Prices do not include applicable taxes. Sales tax applicable in N.Y. Canadian residents will be charged applicable taxes. Offer not valid in Quebec. This offer is limited to one order per household. All orders subject to credit approval. Credit or debit balances in a customer's account(s) may be offset by any other outstanding balance owed by or to the customer. Please allow 4 to 6 weeks for delivery. Offer available while quantities last.

Your Privacy—The Reader Service is committed to protecting your privacy. Our Privacy Policy is available online at www.ReaderService.com or upon request from the Reader Service.

We make a portion of our mailing list available to reputable third parties that offer products we believe may interest you. If you prefer that we not exchange your name with third parties, or if you wish to clarify or modify your communication preferences, please visit us at www.ReaderService.com/consumerschoice or write to us at Reader Service Preference Service, P.O. Box 9062, Buffalo, NY 14269. Include your complete name and address.

LIH11B

Brave police officers tackle crime with the help of their canine partners in TEXAS K-9 UNIT, *an exciting new series from Love Inspired® Suspense.*

Read on for a preview of the first book,
TRACKING JUSTICE by Shirlee McCoy.

Police detective Austin Black glanced at his dashboard clock as he raced up Oak Drive. Two in the morning. Not a good time to get a call about a missing child.

Then again, there was never a good time for that; never a good time to look in the worried eyes of a parent or to follow a scent trail and know that it might lead to a joyful reunion or a sorrowful goodbye.

If it led anywhere.

Sometimes trails went cold, scents were lost and the missing were never found. Austin wanted to bring them all home safe. Hopefully, this time, he would.

He pulled into the driveway of a small house.

Justice whined. A three-year-old bloodhound, he was trained in search and rescue and knew when it was time to work.

Austin jumped out of the vehicle when a woman darted out the front door. "You called about a missing child?"

"Yes. My son. I heard Brady call for me, and when I walked into his room, he was gone." She ran back up the porch stairs.

Austin jogged in after her. She waved from a doorway. "This is my son's room."

Austin followed her into the room. "How old is your son, Ms....?"

"Billows. Eva. He's seven."

"Did you argue?"

"We didn't argue about anything, Officer…"

"Detective Austin Black. I'm with Sagebrush Police Department's Special Operation K-9 Unit."

"You have a search dog with you?" Her face brightened. "I can give you something of his. A shirt or—"

"Hold on. I need to get a little more information first."

"How about you start out there?" She gestured to the window.

"Was it open when you came in the room?"

"Yes. It looks like someone carried Brady out the window. But I don't know how anyone could have gotten into his room when all the doors and windows were locked."

"You're sure?"

"Of course." She frowned. "I always double-check. I have ever since…"

"What?"

"Nothing that matters. I just need to find my son."

Hiding something?

"Everything matters when a child is missing, Eva."

*To see Justice the bloodhound in action, pick up
TRACKING JUSTICE by Shirlee McCoy.
Available January 2013 from Love Inspired® Suspense.*